About the Author

A semi-retired groundsman and gardener, with an interest in crime fiction, growing organic fruit and vegetables, World War Two, writing poetry, and reading.

To Chris
Hope you enjoy the read.

Ryan Fitzgerald.

The Poisoner

Ryan Fitzgerald

The Poisoner

Olympia Publishers
London

www.olympiapublishers.com
OLYMPIA PAPERBACK EDITION

A CIP catalogue record for this title is
available from the British Library.

ISBN: 978-1-84897-776-1

This is a work of fiction.
Names, characters, places and incidents originate from the writer's
imagination. Any resemblance to actual persons, living or dead, is
purely coincidental.

First Published in 2016

Olympia Publishers
60 Cannon Street
London
EC4N 6NP

Printed in Great Britain

Dedication

Alex and Anita Moss, for giving the kickstart I needed to write the book.

Chapter 1

Joshua Chavender had taken the afternoon walk along one of the coastal paths of Middleshire alone. This was, in part, his own fault, due to him making that prawn curry for his wife and daughters the previous evening. He didn't like curry, so he didn't have any, which spared him the trip to the hospital that his family undertook with a dose of food poisoning. They were being kept in as a precaution. He found a large rock and sat down at a particularly scenic spot, letting the weak winter afternoon sun warm his face while he watched the contrails of the jets weave their patterns in the clear blue skies. As he sat, Joshua Chavender, who was fifteen years older than his wife of thirty-three, marvelled at his good fortune of marrying Tiffany Mills, then, a twenty-year-old Detective Constable in the Metropolitan Police force. She was the only female on this particular case, and she was a real head turner. He was the Detective Inspector in charge, and had fallen head over heels in love with her from the first time they met. This was during the case of the centre fold murders. He had defended her against the enquiry that followed, when the force disciplined her for selling the nude photos of herself to a popular men's magazine.

It could be said that Joshua Chavender had a face that only a mother could love, but really it was only his fine Roman nose that made him standout from the crowd. It was this nose that gave him the nickname of 'Beaky' at school, and it had followed him into the force. He didn't mind the name, but it was not said to his face after he tore into a rather young Detective Constable and sent him back to the uniform branch.

As he sat, his phone rang, it was his wife calling to say that they all would be home the next day. They chatted for a while until he lost signal. He was happy that the call had come through. Little things like this made him smile, just as when both sets of twins were born with what he called 'normal' noses. He was very relieved that his wife and two sets of twin daughters, aged seven and nine, would soon be home, for he dearly loved his family. Although the move to the Middleshire County Constabulary as Detective Chief Inspector was a promotion, he knew that they had given up a lot of family and friends to come with him. He shivered, got up and slowly walking back to his car, noticed that, in the shade, the frost still lingered and the air now had a bite, making it feel as though he was swallowing daggers. The sky was no longer blue, but heavy with cloud. With each cold breath he inhaled; he let out a cloud of steam when he exhaled. He made a note to call the Chief Constable, and explained that he would be in to work the day after tomorrow, after his family were discharged from hospital. When he finally got back to his car it was getting dark, and after starting the engine he sat there, letting the inside warm up and defrost the outside. He picked up his phone and started to scroll through the numbers, looking for the Chief Constable's number. As he rang it, he thought what a great start as DCI of the MCC, not turning up for work on his first day, he would never live it down. The phone stopped ringing and went dead, he looked at the handset and saw a blank screen. He started to search the front of the car for the charger, but all he found was a bag of old toffees, far too many CDs, some wet wipes, and several used car park tickets, but no charger. Joshua then rummaged in the back where his children sat, but all he found was one pink sock, several empty sweet packets, plenty of sweet wrappers and a cuddly toy! But still no charger.

Joshua thought for a moment, he knew he was a least two hours from home, but only an hour or so away from Plympton - or was it Bryantsand-on-Sea? He knew one was a working port, whilst the other was a tourist destination, he tried to remember what the Chief Constable said about them at his interview.

It was a large conurbation of two small towns now merged into one almost seamless city, with territorial differences that bordered on fanaticism by the inhabitants of the respective town. The older, indeed more ancient of the two, being overpowered by its newer neighbour, and resenting it, but both could not survive without the other, and they were only united in that they resented the fact that the county town was Middlechester, and was smaller than them! They thought that they should have held the county library, law courts and police headquarters, and not be a subsidiary to Middlechester. As he drove, following the signs to Plympton, he could see in the distance the bright glow of the conurbation, destroying the blackness that surrounded the countryside around. No mistaking that here was a living vibrant city/town.

As he approached the outskirts, he looked for signs directing him to a police station. After driving for ten or so minutes, heading towards the town centre, he finally found a police station. He parked the car and walked the short distance. Joshua rang the bell and waited to be let in. Inside the Duty Sergeant looked at the CCTV display of the front door. He recognised the new DCI and thought he might have a bit of fun with him, or 'haze the new boy'. He waited awhile and pressed the buzzer that opened the door. Joshua Chavender walked in and made his way to the window, just in time to catch the Duty Sergeant disappear out the rear door, saying he would not be long. He took a seat and started to scan the various posters on the wall. The posters formed a rather thick layer, and he could see that instead of taking the older posters down they had just pinned the new ones over the top in a most haphazard way. The latest and largest by far which, according to his reckoning, was at least five years out of date, was one warning the public 'to be alert' and on the lookout for unattended bags. Whilst waiting his eyes searched the walls for something more interesting, but always came back to that poster, he remembered that one such poster was defaced by adding the line 'your country needs lerts!', or some such similar joke.

Whilst he was contemplating this, the duty sergeant popped his head round the door and said, "Won't keep you waiting long, sir," and disappeared again. Ten minutes later the same thing, only this time it was a Constable. Joshua Chavender had an inkling of what was happening and so bided his time. He accepted the prank now, but would they accept his when he would make sure that all those old posters would have to come down, be catalogued and stored somewhere, much to the Duty Sergeant's annoyance, and the newer ones put up straight and level with four drawing pins and only be one layer thick? Yes, he would send a memorandum to this station requesting that this should be done by the next time he visits. Yes, that would be nice, nothing too sinister, just a request to make sure it was done.

Finally, after a full half-hour of waiting, the Duty Sergeant reappeared, and asked if he could help. Joshua Chavender got up and produced his warrant card.

The Duty Sergeant said, "I thought it was you sir, but I was dealing with some urgent business. I hope I've not kept you waiting too long. Now, how can I help you?"

Chavender replied that he would like the Chief Constable's telephone number and the use of a phone so he could call him.

"Certainly sir, if you would care to come this way you can use the Inspector's office if you like? Perhaps a cup of tea?"

"Coffee would be preferred if that's okay. I only have good old-fashioned loose tea at home and I don't suppose you have that here, Sergeant…?"

"Err… Jenkins, sir."

"Okay, Sergeant Jenkins, I take my coffee white, no sugar please, and I'll use your phone if I may?"

After getting through to the Chief Constable, a retired army officer who thought he was still in the army, and found that being the Chief Constable was just as satisfying, answered.

"Hello, Featherstonehaugh here!"

It was actually pronounced Fanshawe, but the CC enjoyed seeing people's discomfort when faced with the spelling.

"Good evening, Chief Constable, sir, it's DCI Chavender. Sorry to disturb you sir, but my wife and family are in hospital, and I've been advised that they will come out tomorrow morning, so I was wondering if I could start the day after at Headquarters?"

"What's that you say Chavender?"

Joshua had to explain to him what had happened, that he had poisoned his family with his homemade prawn curry. Unfortunately, the Sergeant overheard and sniggered a little. *Great*, Joshua thought, *now the whole of the county constabulary will know that the new DCI tried to poison his family.*

"Ah… Um… Oh dear… Um… Right, Chavender, yes, yes, that will be fine. See you the day after then, 9am sharp. Great. Goodbye," and he hung up.

Chapter 2

Chavender finished his coffee, said goodnight to the Sergeant, and left the building. Just has he got to the door, he thought he could hear sniggering, but he let it slide. He was tired and wanted to get home. It took him a few hours to finally get there, and it was gone midnight when he finally put his key in the front door of his new house. He did very little in the choosing of the new 'Chavender Mansions' as he called it, it was mainly down to Tiffany and the girls, who'd spent several weeks looking on estate agent websites. He only did the weekend driving to check out the places. It did not take them long to pick this four bedroom place, with two bathrooms and a downstairs toilet, and a nice, large garden, mainly grass. He could see the logic in three toilets - why four bedrooms? Still here he - and it - was.

Josh went to the kitchen, where the faint smell of curry still lingered. It turned his stomach a little, so he walked straight back out again and into the front room, where he poured himself a large scotch, turned on the TV, sat in the large brown leather easy chair, and started to channel surf. After selecting a documentary on poisoning, which seemed interesting but which he could not get into, he switched over to catch the end of a Miss Marple. He probably only saw a few minutes, with the TV providing the only light in the room and the warmth from the central heating, tiredness soon had him fast asleep in the chair.

He awoke with a start just before 7am, feeling rather stiff and dry mouthed from a rather uncomfortable night's sleep in the chair, and the majority of scotch he had poured still not drunk.

TV news was blaring away at some new tragedy in India, and an earthquake or something somewhere else; his mind was not taking anything in yet, he was trying to get his bearings, or, as he liked to call it, 'body and soul' together. It normally took him only a few seconds, but this morning he stretched, stretched again, yawned, coughed, yawned, scratched, stretched once more, and finally got himself up, and, walking stiff-jointed, moved to the kitchen to make a nice cup of tea. Tea for him was a ritual - warm the pot, two spoons of loose tea, milk in first in his pint mug, let the tea brew in the pot for a while till it was nice and strong, then pour through a tea strainer, checking that the colour was just the right shade of orangey-brown. If not, swirling the pot, so the tea was strong enough to stand a spoon up in, as his Grandmother would say. Whilst the tea was brewing, he opened some windows, turned the extractor fan on and tried to remove the last faint aroma of that curry. He now wished he had done that last night. He then poured his tea, sat down at the table and took the first sip of that magical reviving brew, the cure for all sorrows. As he took his first gulp of the lovely liquid, he felt an invigorating refreshment, or empowering, course through his body. He could never quite work out which, but it certainly set him up for the day, whatever that might bring.

After his morning ablutions, and putting on a fresh suit, Josh went back to the front room, turned the TV off, poured the remains of last night's scotch back into the bottle, took everything to the kitchen and loaded the dishwasher. Just after 10am the house phone rang. He went into the hall and answered it.

"Hello, Chavender speaking."

"Hi Josh, why didn't you answer your mobile phone? We're ready to be picked up. We're fine… All okay now, although the girls will need to take the rest of the week off just to make sure. Can you phone the school please? By the way, have you got rid of the curry and smell?… Cleaned up yet? And…"

Josh interrupted her flow of questions, "Oh, hi Tiff, my mobile was flat and I forgot to put it on charge last night, yes I cleared away, I'm just loading the dishwasher now. I'll be with you within the hour. I phoned the Chief Constable and let him know that I will be in tomorrow... See you soon... Bye... Bye... Love you!"

By the time she replied he had already put the phone down and was heading out the door. In his haste to collect them, he completely forgot to do all those things he was supposed to have done. She heard the click of the phone as it went dead, just as she said "love you too".

Josh rushed out to his wife's Land Rover station wagon, and, just managing to miss the front bumper of his car and the gateposts, in fifty minutes was at the hospital collecting his brood from reception. His girls rushed him all at once, bundling into his arms like demented octopi and babbling about all the fun they had had in the children's ward, even though they had injections that hurt them, and how the nurses had lots of trouble in telling them apart and putting them in the wrong beds. In the end they had given them some old name plates to wear. He stood up, disentangled himself from his daughters and hugged and kissed his wife, whilst his daughters all talked at once, making an incoherent cacophony of noise, yet being able to understand what each other was saying, whilst to others it sounded like Swahili. He managed to quieten them and ushered them all out to the car. Once they had all settled in, he drove off while asking his wife where his phone charger was and why there was a pink sock in his car. She started to explain but he really didn't listen to her. He was a happy bunny again with his family close by, and was in a hurry to get them home.

Once home, he realised he had not done any of those things that Tiffany had asked him to do, so after letting the girls go to the front room to watch a DVD, he and his wife went to the kitchen, where he finally turned on the dishwasher, closed the windows, and made another pot of tea. From the front room came the sound of laughter as a particular funny point came in the film, he poured out the tea and sat down.

"Tiff, do you think you should get your mum down for the rest of the week or so, just to help out while we get settled in? Especially since I made that curry!" Josh already felt outnumbered five to one and he really did not mind, but his mother–in–law, who was only just coming round to the fact that he had managed to marry her daughter - and this was only after providing granddaughters - was another matter.

Tiffany mulled it over whilst drinking her tea, and knew what it meant for Josh to mention her mum. She called the girls in, and asked them what they thought - should Gran come and stay for a while? Whilst doing so, she gave them all the medicine as prescribed by the hospital, a semi-foul tasting pinkish syrup that smelt of tar but was really quite pleasant. Shouts of "Yeah, Gran's coming!" were heard amongst the slurping.

Tiffany smiled. "That would be nice, Josh, thanks. Did you phone the school?"

Josh looked a bit sheepish and replied, "Um… No… I sort of forgot… Sorry… Better do it now… Um."

And he got up to phone the school. Tiffany phoned her mum and arranged to pick her up from the station the next morning. The rest of the day passed in a happy blur for him, playing with his daughters, watching TV, feeding them almost burnt toast and beans, and finally putting them to bed at eight o'clock. He then spent a happy two hours sat in the big brown easy chair cuddling his wife whilst watching some historical drama on TV, getting the occasional elbow when he dropped off, and being sent to bed himself.

Morning came all too quick for him, but as the early light penetrated the curtains, he managed to stir himself and get up. A peek out of the curtains showed it had snowed last night. The girls and his wife were already up, the girls excited about the snow.

He bathed, shaved and dressed, drank his tea, kissed and hugged all goodbye, and left for work.

Chapter 3

It was still snowing as Chavender drove slowly along the country roads into Middlechester. The snow added emphasis to the patchwork nature of the fields, by making the hedgerows stand out in stark dark contrast to the white fields. He finally arrived at the County Police Headquarters, found a car parking space, and made his way into the building and to the front desk, here he showed the Duty Sergeant his warrant card, was allowed to pass through the door into the main building, and shown into the Duty Inspector's office.

The Duty Inspector stood up and introduced himself as John Carr. Shaking hands, Chavender introduced himself. Inspector Carr then showed him to Chief Constable Featherstonehaugh's office. In the Chief Constable's office, Chavender was introduced to deputy Chief Constable Jacob, Chief Inspectors Smith (County West), Morris (County East), Sword, for Plympton and, for Bryantsand-on-Sea, Chief Inspector Andersonn. Pleasantries over, they all sat down, and the Chief Constable thanked them for making the effort to meet the new Detective Chief Inspector for the county. He then launched into his pet subject, terms such as 'Boss' or 'Guv', for senior officers were to be frowned upon, whilst derogatory terms for the uniform branch such as 'wooden top' or 'plod' were to be positively discouraged. All ranks would be addressed by the correct title, and saluting, as taught by the police colleges, would be adhered to. This, he said, would make every police officer of the County Constabulary firstly have respect for himself, then pride in belonging and, finally, bring about some unit cohesion, especially between Plympton and Bryantsand-on-Sea, his two most troublesome sub-divisions.

Whilst at County Police Headquarters, he expected Chavender to wear a uniform, when he arrived, as well whenever he visited any one of the subdivisions. This, he said, would help the Inspectors, Sergeants and Constables feel respected. These were not fancy ideas put out by some nutty consultant or professor but his, learnt by experience, from his time in the Army. All ranks shown respect give respect, and, coupled with being treated fairly, unit cohesion was achieved. He thanked them all for coming, and then he turned to Chavender.

"I have assigned Inspector Carr to you for a few days, just to show you round the place. When you get to a subdivision, ask for a Sergeant. Oh, and when your uniform arrives, I expect all medal ribbons to be worn, is that clear?"

"Of course, sir," Chavender replied.

Chief Constable Featherstonehaugh then buzzed for Inspector Carr, and thanked Chavender again. A polite knock was heard at the door and after a "come in," in walked Inspector Carr. He saluted both and asked the new DCI to follow him.

Once outside, Carr said, "I'll show you to your office, sir, and we'll have a brief tour of the building, and then, if you wish, we could have a quick walk around town. I'll change so that we don't stick out so much, if that's okay with you?"

"Okay, that's fine, be nice to get out for a bit of air." replied Chavender, thinking how much warmer it would actually be in his office.

His office was very large and airy, with bright sun streaming in through the windows. It overlooked the industrial estate nearby and at the moment it was very antiseptic, no clutter or loose files on the desk, no pictures on the wall. Still, that would change when he brought his personal belongings in from home.

After a long tour around the building, taking in fire escapes, canteen, toilets and rest rooms, meeting a few of the staff and being introduced to the duty sergeants, they left for the 'quick walk' round the town.

To look at Middlechester it was, or appeared to be, quite old. It was only Victorian in age, but had grown rapidly after the First World War and again after the Second World War. Now it was undergoing another expansionist building programme, trying to keep ahead of its nearby rivals. Industrial estates and housing were putting pressure not only on the countryside, but on all the emergency services, hence the semi-restructure of the County Police force. A 'quick walk' done, thankfully the snow had almost cleared along the high street, through the parade of shops, past several old churches and finally ending up at the library and museum. Then through two industrial estates, a short walk across country where the snow was deeper, and they were back at headquarters within three hours. Chavender was pleased it was only a 'quick walk'.

Once back, Chavender and Carr headed straight for the canteen for a cup of hot coffee and some lunch to warm themselves. Joining the queue, Chavender saw what was on the menu - today's main meal was prawn curry! *Strange*, thought Carr, *it's Wednesday, we don't have curry on a Wednesday, that's a Friday dish.* Chavender saw the cook's nametag, Susan Jenkins. and laughed to himself, and just asked for some coffee. Once they were both seated, Carr remarked about the change in menu, and then tucked into his meal. Chavender got up and went to get another coffee, but, seeing that there was no queue, he asked her if she was arried to a Sergeant Jenkins of the Plympton Police Force. She nodded her head, he smiled and sat down. He then spoke to Carr, asking if he was free on Thursday morning so they could go to Plympton Police Station.

"Not a problem, sir. What time would you like to go? I'm on an early shift, so I will be here from 6am."

"Oh, about 0730hrs should be good enough. We will meet then, okay?"

After lunch, Chavender, finally thawing his feet out, spent a boring afternoon carrying out routine paperwork, so decided to wander round the building, just to make sure he could find his way back to his office. He got up and started down the corridor. Passing the CID room he thought he would pop his head in to see if anything was happening. He knocked, entered, and a hush fell on the room, he introduced himself and waited. A Detective Sergeant got up and spoke.

"Well, Guv… "

Chavender cut him short and told him that it should be sir, and sir only, from now on.

"And your name is?"

"It's Detective Sergeant Wootton, Sir, and these are Detective Constables, Owen, Connelly, and Grymes. Would you like some coffee, sir?"

"Yes please," Chavender replied with a smile and sat down. "Oh, I envy you lot, you can wear mufti but I've got to wear uniform every time I'm here - but that goes with the rank I suppose. Now," he asked, "what, if any, cases are you working on, anything interesting or juicy?"

The sergeant replied, "Not much sir - a couple of burglaries, a hit and run, and several car thefts for this week. Outstanding cases are plenty, but we're waiting for more information to come in before we can make a case stick."

Then it clicked in the Sergeant's mind where he had heard of Chavender before, some really big cases in London - the Rainy Day Cannibal Murder of Kentish Town, the Leg of Lamb Murder and the Centre Fold Murder case. The three DCs excused themselves and left the two alone. Wootton, thinking about the cases some more, asked Chavender how he had managed to solve such complicated cases? Chavender asked if the sergeant was busy tomorrow and if he could spare him some time around 11am in his office, when he would explain, he would be grateful.

That morning, after Josh had left for work, Tiffany had spent a frantic few hours getting the house tidy and the girls ready and out so they could meet Gran at the station. They just made it on time, which would have been good if the train was on time, but due to the wrong type of frost/snow on the line, they had to wait a further hour before it slowly slid into the station. The brakes screeching like a thousand banshees brought the train to a stop, as the station announcement, apologising for the delay, echoed and died away. Passengers disembarked. The opening and shutting of doors and the general hubbub of mixed noises added to the chaos, meaning that, for once, the girls' voices were drowned out. Tiffany embraced her Mum, and then Gran kissed each of her grandchildren in turn, being more pulled than led by the two youngest, whilst Tiffany and the eldest carried her bags past the ticket collector and into the car. Once all were settled, Tiffany headed for home.

On her way home, Gran looked at her grandchildren and smiled. Although she thought Josh was not a suitable catch for her daughter, she could not deny that he had furnished her with some beautiful grandchildren. Tiffany caught her mum looking and smiled, half-knowing what she was thinking.

She was just about to defend Josh, when unexpectedly her mum said, "How's Josh these days? Is he all right since he got this promotion and took you all away from me? It's just like him to think of himself and not his family."

Tiffany bristled slightly. "You know that's not the case, Mum; we all supported him on this move and he did discuss it at great length with us all - isn't that right, girls?"

They chimed back as one, "YES," and continued to chatter excitedly between themselves.

With that, they rolled up the drive and the girls got out to make a snowman, whilst Tiffany and her mum carried the luggage in and settled down for a cup of tea. After a while the hungry horde came in, all pink-faced and out of breath, and clamoured for something to eat and drink, on top of more medicine, and finally settled down to watch a DVD.

Josh, after an uneventful day, made his way home in the dark and after accidentally knocking down the girls' snowman and, groaning as he realised what he'd done, entered his house.

Chapter 4

Josh entered the kitchen, greeted his wife and said hello to his mother-in-law and, as he always did, called her 'Ma' just to annoy her, and started to make some tea. He left the kettle to boil and went to tell his children that he had killed their snowman, but it was all right, they could build a new one in the morning - just not in the middle of the drive! After hugs all round, he went back to the kitchen where Tiffany had poured them all a cup of tea.

Sitting down, he asked how her day had been, if the children were better, and asked how Gran was.

"Mustn't grumble," said Gran. "Just a few aches and pains that the cold brings on, a stiff leg here, dodgy back sometimes, and getting old I guess. But why did you have to move into the countryside and here to Middleshire? It's not the middle of anywhere apart from here, and here is not very nice, cold and bleak and that train journey, not once was I warm…"

Her voice trailed off as Tiffany looked at her mum and said, "Nonsense, Mum, you're tough as old boots and I already told you, we all agreed. Josh did not drag us down here; he was promoted and applied for the post, and this county is nice really - after all, we spent our honeymoon here, remember Josh?"

She looked at him coyly, but before he had a chance to answer, the girls came rolling in, in one large noisy mass, as if they were joined physically in some way and not as individual persons, joining them at the large kitchen table where they debated what they were to have for tea. In the end, good old fashioned bangers and mash with onion gravy won the day.

If ever a man could feel contented, and full, it was Joshua Chavender right now, after a double helping of bangers and mash, with lashings of onion gravy, surrounded by his four girls, his beautiful wife and, yes, even his mother-in-law, with a large mug of fresh tea in his hands, he sat in the front room watching the television. He felt life was pretty good and nothing was going to change his mood, not even the phone call from the tailors saying he could pick his uniform up tomorrow dampened his spirits. Soon after there was another phone call, this time from a Detective Inspector Daryl Pearce of the Plympton CID branch, saying they had a strange looking suicide and that, seeing as how he was down in the morning, would he call in and speak with him about it. Josh said of course he would, and told him he would be there at about 8.30 in the morning.

At half past seven the next day, Carr and Chavender set off to Plympton police station. After a journey lasting an hour through some snowy and frosty narrow country lanes, they emerged on the outskirts of Plympton, strangely enough at the same point that he came in to the town the other night. After arriving at the police station car park, they entered through the rear door of the building, and were met by DI Pearce and Sergeant Jenkins. Chavender looked at Jenkins and told him to thank his wife for the curry the other day. Carr, looking on slightly bemused, noticed a smile appear on the Sergeant's face as Jenkins thought, *no hard feelings there then*. Pearce led the way to the CID room and they sat down, while he briefed them both about what could only be called the strangest incident he had had the misfortune to investigate. About two weeks ago the couple, it was suggested, may have tried to unblock a sink with a do-it-yourself sink unblocker, a homemade concoction of bleach and ammonia, which gave off a rather toxic gas called Hydrazine, which they both inhaled at the time. It was possibly a mistake by either the wife or husband, the police were not sure, but they were waiting for the coroner's report. The couple had died yesterday evening in the intensive care unit at the county hospital, apparently in agony, they both suffered from badly damaged lungs, so much so that the hospital staff had had to ventilate them.

Now, DI Pearce informed them, as chemicals go they are both pretty much harmless, unless of course drunk, and if used correctly according to manufacturer's instructions, but DI Pearce had looked in the couple's house and could not find a bottle of ammonia, bleach, yes, and possibly the bottle that had been used. It may be too late to check if the bottle contained both, but his guess was that it did. If so, this could be murder, with the ammonia bottle being removed.

"It was Jenkins who spotted that only one bottle of bleach could be found and alerted me," said DI Pearce.

The four of them sat round drinking coffee. Thinking out loud, it was Chavender who spoke first.

"I suppose next of kin have been informed? What about the bottle - how much gas would it give off, and in what quantity do you have to mix them? If it's murder by gas, how come the perpetrator didn't gas himself? Perhaps you could get one of the DCs to check on those for you. Good work, Sergeant Jenkins, you too, Pearce. Best keep me informed. Perhaps if you give us the address, Inspector Carr, and I could have a quick look-see before heading back to HQ."

Having written down the address, he left the building and, entering the post code into the satnav, set off to find the place. It took some twenty minutes to get to the property and, parking up, they could see the Scenes of Crime officer just about to leave. Chavender showed his warrant card and asked a few questions, but all he got in reply was that it would take some time to garner all the facts. Leaving the officer to pack up, Chavender and Carr entered the house and, carefully moving on through to the kitchen, made a quick inspection of the place. Chavender's experienced eyes scanned the kitchen but nothing seemed out of the ordinary. It was a typical modern detached house, on a recently built estate with a smallish garden, nicely laid out and, he noted, the remains of a small vegetable plot on the sunny side, a few grow bags, a raised bed and some winter cabbage growing with some neatly trimmed shrubs around the edge covering a cheap fence, a shed in the corner and a small lawn probably no more than 30 by 20 ft, and that was it. The developer obviously crammed as many as he could get into the space allocated to him or laid down by Town Planning and/or greed. It was, it appeared to them, over looked, perhaps it would be best if they interviewed the neighbours to see if they could remember anything out of the ordinary. Chavender thought he would check later to see if that had been done, but for now it was time to go back to divisional HQ and meet with Wootton, Sergeant Detective, (using the army idiolectal way when naming something) whom he suspected knew about those cases he solved in London. He did not want naked pictures of his wife stuck all over the place!

On the way back, they stopped and collected the brand new uniform. In its clear suit protector bag, and making little impression on Joshua Chavender, was the George Cross medal ribbon sewn to his jacket. He hung it up from the back passenger handle, and they continued into town. By now the snow was melting partly due to the weak winter sun, and the going was easier on the roads since the gritting lorries had been out all morning. At HQ he took his uniform out of the car, slung it over his shoulders, thanked Inspector Carr for his time, arranged a time to meet the next day so they could go to Bryantsand-on–sea and asked if he could arrange a time with the DI there so he could meet with him. He would be free all day so anytime would be fine by him.

Chavender then went to his office, carrying his suit and a Gladstone bag, which he'd retrieved from his car. It was a few minutes to 11 when DS Wootton knocked at the door.

"Enter," Chavender said, and in walked Wootton.

He saluted and was invited to sit down whilst Chavender continued to place the contents of his bag. There were several pictures of his wife and children, one big picture in a glass frame of her in her wedding dress, which he placed on the right hand side of his desk, so that it appeared as though she was looking at him, whilst on the wall he placed several framed pictures taken at the investiture outside Buckingham Palace of him, his parents, another two of Tiffany holding the newborn twins, and one picture of the investiture when the Queen presented him with his medal, and his citation and medal and two commendations from the then Metropolitan Police Commissioner.

The uniform he hung on the coat stand along with his hat, then he turned his attention to his guest.

"Ah, Sergeant Wootton. Well now, you asked about cases I was involved with in London. You do know that the female detective constable, who was the centre fold model for that popular men's magazine became my wife, don't you? I do not want it spread about, so I am asking you to respect her and my wish not to broadcast that fact please."

Although said in a matter-of-fact way, there was no disguising the implications if Chavender's wishes were not adhered to.

"Oh, no, sir," said Sergeant Wootton quickly, and, just as quickly changing his mind about the stock of pictures that he'd accumulated and what he was going to do with them. "That was not what I had in mind, sir. What it was… Well, I'd just like to know how you managed to think of solving those cases, sir? It seemed an almost impossible leap of the imagination from those clues."

"Oh that's easy," said Chavender. "It was using lateral thinking and that old Sherlock Holmes mantra - 'if you eliminate the impossible, whatever is left, no matter how improbable, is the most likely or logical explanation to the question or truth.' Try this for size - two people died yesterday of gas poisoning by mixing bleach and ammonia. DI Pearce is investigating the case.

At the moment, we're not sure if its suicide, a mistake or murder. The only clue that may be or not is an empty bleach bottle, which may or may not have contained both chemicals. If so, how come the person who mixed them is not dead, and more importantly, what is - or was - the motive behind it?"

Wootton replied, "Um yes, I see the point about the mantra, or you could use the Miss Marple one - 'that the murderer is always someone known, or a close relative to the victim, or is in some way in-extricable tied to the murderer'. DI Pearce is a good man, I have worked with him on several local cases. If he suspects foul play, then you can be sure it is. I'll think on about this case and look back over some of our old open cases to see if I can spot something that may help."

They continued discussing the London cases for a while, about how things led on in some formal or logical way best described as *Post Hoc, Ergo Propter Hoc.*

Wootton looked a bit puzzled until Chavender said, "After, therefore, because of it! Or some such translation of it."

Wootton then answered, "Oh, I see; a bit like every reaction has an equal and opposite reaction - is that it? The consequences are of the action that starts the ball rolling, so to speak?"

"Yes, that's about the size of it," Chavender replied.

"Thanks for your time, sir, it was interesting."

"Not a problem," said Chavender as the young detective sergeant got up, saluted, and left the room.

Ah well, can't be put off any longer, thought Chavender, and decided to try on his uniform. He locked the door and changed. Once changed he put his clothes in the bag, put his hat on and, seeing the time, he decided to go home. Walking through the building, he felt quite conspicuous in the uniform with the George Cross medal ribbon on his left breast, but he had to admit, it certainly made him walk differently. As he approached the exit, the Chief Constable spotted him. Chavender stopped and they exchanged salutes, and the Chief Constable complimented him on the medal and left him to exit the building without further ado. Once he got in his car he drove home wondering what the girls would make of him in his rather stiff, but smart uniform.

Chapter 5

Josh made it home fairly quickly that afternoon. The roads were clear, traffic was light, and the snow had virtually vanished; only in the deep shaded pockets was there a trace of the white stuff. He was hoping that that would be it for this winter and, with February fast coming to a close, and March knocking on the door, and the evenings began to lengthen a little, it would give him some time after work to sort a few things out in the garden. Pulling onto his drive, he saw his wife's car was not there, but on opening his front door he could hear his children playing snakes and ladders, but their version of it. Roll the dice, climb the stairs, slide down the banister, four goes to see who could get the highest, winner takes all - sweets, that is!

This was the tamer version that he had taught them, much to the annoyance of Tiffany. Josh and his brother played a similar game but it was to scale/climb up the stairs on the outside of the banister, flip round the half way point and go on up the next half flight. Once at the top of all the flights of stairs, they would then slide down them on their bellies all the way to the bottom, and either a tray or towel was used to help smooth the decent. The one landing and the turn in the stair halfway down the flight posed a problem, but generally if you didn't crash into the door you could just crawl round and on down. Many a time it ended with one of them in a heap at the bottom of the stairs, and the other one laughing his socks off.

When his cry of "Hallo" reverberated round the downstairs, the children stopped playing and rushed to greet their daddy, giving lots of praise to how smart he looked in his uniform and wanting to inspect his medal ribbon. From the kitchen his mother-in-law shouted, "In here!", and after hugs all round, and answering their questions about what the medal ribbon stood for, the children carried on with the game and he entered the kitchen.

"Hello Ma, how's the day been? Tiff gone shopping has she?"

"Well, look at you, don't you look a dandy!" his mother-in-law exclaimed, spotting his new uniform. "Are you changing first, or how about some tea?" Ma replied. "It's been hectic, the girls are a barrel of fun, always on the go. I don't know how you two keep up with them. We're having toad in the hole for tea tonight. Tiffany has just gone to get some shopping."

"I'll change once Tiff has seen me in it if she's not going to be long," Josh said.

Within minutes, a fresh cup of tea was poured and at that moment Tiffany walked in, smiled at him and leant forward for a kiss while whispering in his ear how much she liked a man in uniform.

"You look great," she said as she stepped back, and the look between them said it all.

"You must have heard the kettle boil, girl," said Josh, slightly embarrassed at the innuendo in front of his mother-in-law. "Let me help you. Did we really need all this stuff?"

He helped carry the shopping in and empty the bags' contents on to the kitchen table, ready to be put away. One item caught his eye; it was a bottle of bleach. He picked it up and read the label carefully, but nothing sprang to mind apart from the warnings of dire trouble if swallowed, prolonged contact with the skin or a splash in the eyes, all required medical attention. He undid the top and took a small whiff; the fumes immediately made his nose run and eyes water. He could see how powerful the effect would be if mixed with something other than water that produced a gas. Both women looked at him quizzically and waited for an explanation, but he just put the top back on, placed the bottle well out of reach of nosy young girls, and continued to drink his tea.

"What was that in aid of, Josh?" asked Tiffany.

"Oh, nothing really," said Josh. "Just having a little look. We had a strange poisoning case involving bleach, and after reading that label, I don't want the children to get their hands on it. You know how dangerous it is, that's why I put it way up on the top shelf."

"Huh, dangerous stuff," Ma said. "That's tame compared to what I had to go through. You should have been around in the war, young man. Us children had to dodge shrapnel, falling bullets, bits of aircraft, and all sorts of dangerous stuff in the streets, gas and water mains blown up, buildings burning all day - and do you know the worst of it? Those bloody air raids, nearly every night they were, spent many a night down the tubes we did, did not trust those Anderson shelters, they took up too much garden space. Each night whole families would head for the tubes and do you know what, those naffing toffs, holding their noses as though we smelt of the plague or had fleas or something, picking their way to the exit for a night out on the town. The government tried to stop us - it was you damn police that blocked the entrance to the underground - but they were from the same stock as us, so they let us through. If they didn't, we would have marched over their dead bodies. Many folks could not stand it and killed themselves with rat poison or a gas of some form or something similar. I would've thought it would have been easier to stand outside whilst a raid was on, but you couldn't guarantee that the Jerries would hit you, couldn't hit a barn door at fifty paces they couldn't. The bombs just dropped where they liked I'm sure, not really what you call aimed! Do you know what we did? On any spare ground that we found, we grew vegetables on it, like on the allotments that we were supposed to have had, and no one nicked from them - see it was for the good of the community."

Ma had said most of this without hardly drawing breath! Josh half-listened and smiled at Tiffany. He got up and playfully smacked his wife's bottom and went to see the girls, leaving both Tiff and her mother to make the dinner. He went and changed out of his smart but still quite stiff uniform, breathing a sigh of relief as he put his casual clothes on, then joined the girls for a game of snakes and ladders until tea was ready.

The next day at work, he spent the morning with the Chief Constable discussing current caseloads and any unsolved crimes that could be taken off the list before Featherstonehaugh spoke about Chavender's George Cross. He also mentioned how pleased he was to have him working here in Middleshire, and perhaps he could do an article for the next police newspaper or speak to the local press about how he won the medal. Chavender said he would look forward to doing it, but really shunned such displays of self-aggrandisement. He then mentioned the strange case DI Pearce was investigating, but admitted they could do no more until either the coroner's or forensic reports came back. Chavender went to find Inspector Carr, and they left headquarters in a marked police car this time, driven by Carr.

They drove into Bryantsand-on-Sea, and here the town was much the same as it neighbour, but definitely more 'touristy'. A large central garden, signs to the beaches and a very large modern central shopping centre, with outlying shops of all kinds. Carr told him that the terminal train station dropped the holidaymakers a short walk from hotels and beach attractions. On the way, Chavender asked if they could stop at the shopping centre to have a look in the supermarkets, he just needed to check something out. Parking the car, both men in uniform walked the short distance to the shopping centre, where they met some constables and a sergeant, and they introduced themselves. After a short while, and some polite small talk, they continued walking whilst the sergeant and two constables dealt with call to arrest a shoplifter. The shopping centre was busy, and as they walked through they drew stares from the public. When they went into the supermarket, even more attention was gained as one of the managers approached them and asked if he could help.

Chavender said, "Could you show me where the household cleaners are?" - looking at the name tag - "Mr Stilton, please."

"Oh no, not Mr; Stilton is my first name... Yes, of course, this way please, err... I'm sorry, I don't know what rank you are?"

"Oh I'm a Detective Chief Inspector," said Chavender, "and this is Inspector Carr."

He deliberately did not mention his name as they followed the manager to household cleaners.

"Perhaps you would be good enough to point out were you keep the neat ammonia?" Chavender asked.

"Oh, we don't stock that here, maybe a garden centre or aquatics place, they may have it but we don't. Sorry if I can't help you, but I'm sure if you try those places you will find it."

"Ah well, thanks for your time, goodbye," and they walked out.

Carr asked if Chavender was pursuing enquiries for DI Pearce, he nodded, and went back to the car and on to Bryantsand-on-sea police station.

At the police station both Chavender and Carr walked in the front door. The duty sergeant hurried to let them in and phoned through to Chief Inspector Andersonn, who came down, saluted, and then tentatively shook hands with them both and ushered them into his office. They chatted for a while before Carr excused himself, the two men left, and talked for some time discussing the merits of a) saluting and b) staffing levels, together with other such mundane matters, until Chavender asked if he could meet with the DI, if he was available.

Andersonn took Chavender to the room allocated to DI Small, but they saw he was out.

"Oh, that's a shame; best go and find Carr I suppose. Well, thanks for your time, Chief Inspector."

"That's okay, Detective Chief Inspector, but perhaps when no one's about we can be less formal and call each other by our Christian names? Mine's John and yours, I understand, is Joshua - or do you like Josh better?"

"Josh will be fine, err… John," and he departed to find Carr.

They left, and Chavender asked if he minded calling by his house on the way back.

Once at home, Josh invited Carr in for a cup of tea whilst he had to do something. In the kitchen he introduced his wife, children and mother-in-law, whilst he took the bottle of bleach out of the cupboard and checked the label once more. Again he read the warnings about the danger of mixing with other products, but it did not list those products it just stated the dangerous nature of the contents and, right at the bottom, 'may cause or release Chlorine gas'. He then remembered reading in a book some years ago about tank tactics and that the poison gas (chlorine) was used for the first time at the Second Battle of Ypres in April 1915 by the Germans. He put the bottle away higher up this time, which did not go unnoticed by Tiffany, then sat down and chatted with Carr over tea. After half an hour or so, they had to leave. Carr thanked Tiffany for the tea as they left.

On the drive back to headquarters, they chatted generally and Carr, nervously, said, "Hope you don't mind me saying so Sir, but how did you manage to land such a beauty as your wife, and I don't mean any disrespect… Well… What with your nose… Sorry sir, but she is a real stunner, you must have batted over your averages to get her sir! Again, I mean no disrespect sir, but I could walk behind your wife for miles and not feel a thing when I finally walked into that lamppost!"

Chavender knew what the young inspector meant, so he did not feel too upset, but began to tell him that it took six months of asking before she agreed to go out with him, and then when she did, they were assigned to the same case, so they thought it best not to see each other whilst working together, just in case tensions arose. After the case was over they resumed the romance and finally he wore her down and they married. They both had not looked back since, and were happy with the way things were, four daughters in two sets of twins. He left out the bit about the nude photos in the men's magazine, as he felt no need to disclose that little bit of information. After they'd talked, Josh was surprised with himself, he didn't often open up like that about his personal life.

Back at HQ, Chavender thanked Carr and went to his office. On the desk was a note from the Chief Constable saying he had arranged for him to speak to the local press on Friday at 10am, he would be in attendance as well, and hoped that he wouldn't mind. In fact, Chavender felt annoyed, but in reality it would be best to get it over with sooner than later. He sat at his desk and wrote out several notes and made a few phone calls requesting that all Divisional DIs were to meet with him next Wednesday. He went to the CID room and bumped into DS Carruthers, and asked him if he could collate the number of deaths reported over the last few months. Before he left he decided to pop into the canteen for a coffee.

Chapter 6

In the canteen Mrs Jenkins greeted Chavender with a smile and a hello, before asking what he wanted. The canteen was quiet so she told him to take a seat and she would bring it over. She brought over two cups of coffee and sat down opposite him. He looked at her, and before he had a chance to wonder why.

She said, "Your girls go back to school Monday, don't they? My girls are in the same class, they told me yesterday that the twins hadn't been in because they were sick or something."

She'd wondered if it had anything to do with curry, seeing as though her Bert had asked if she could make some.

"Yes," he replied "unfortunately I made a prawn curry and they got sick from it, I didn't realise the prawns weren't as fresh as I thought, and they had to be taken into hospital for observation. I wasn't affected because I don't like curry."

They drank their coffee whilst chatting about girls' school uniforms and school in general. It made a pleasant change for a while for Josh, it took his mind off the poisoning which was a good thing really, although it was never far from his mind.

Suddenly he wondered, perhaps industrial bleach was stronger or had different contents. He stopped Mrs Jenkins in full flow and asked her if they had any bleach, or where it was stored.

"Yes we have some," she replied. "Why? We keep it in the store cupboard in the kitchen."

"Can I have a look please?" said Josh, and she led the way to the back of the kitchen, opened a cupboard and took out a five litre bottle of bleach.

Josh read the label, but this had the same warnings.

Then he asked, "What about ammonia, do you have any of that?"

She replied, "We don't have none of that stuff here, sorry but I can't help you there - strange! That's what my Bert asked me the other day. Anyways, got to go now, looks like the lunch time rush is starting. Nice to have chatted with you, Mr Chavender."

He noticed that she did not call him 'sir' but seeing that she was not a constable, she didn't have to.

When he got back to his office, he rang DI Pearce. "Ah Pearce, have you had a look in the shed at that couple's place who were gassed yet? No? Then send someone round to see if there's any ammonia in the shed. Anything from forensics yet or the coroner? No? Pity, until we get them we're just wallowing in the mud, yes… Yes, please call me back when you do get them. Did you get my message about the meeting next week? Yes, the other CID chaps will also be at the meeting, just in case, as you suspect, something sinister happened… Good, yes, thank you, bye for now." He put the phone down and started to jot some notes for the interview for the paper; once done he got up and left to go home.

At home the usual hubbub of noise greeted his arrival as each girl rushed up the passageway and then tried for, and successfully, got a hug and kiss each in her own turn. He asked if they knew any girls called Jenkins. The two oldest ones said together, "Yes Carol and Anne Jenkins," and went on to explain they were in the same classes and they had just asked Mummy if they could sleep over Saturday night, seeing that they were feeling so much better. He didn't doubt that, and knew that it was Tiffany being overprotective of them by keeping them from school the rest of the week, which was why he asked her to invite her mum down, that spiel she gave the other day about the Jerry air raids had had the desired effect on Tiff. Tiff's mum was tough as old boots and would probably live till she was a hundred years old, just out pure bloody pigheadedness! He went into the kitchen, kissed his wife, said hello to Ma, and saw that tonight's tea was something and bangers.

When Ma came to stay it seemed they would overdose on bangers till she went home. Ma's staple food was bangers and something, most probably with mash, but on the odd occasions just for a change, bubble and squeak, either with onion gravy or as she called it 'Liquor', as in 'pie and mash'. He had tried her on pasta once, but was met with the sort of face that sometimes only a five year old could pull when they had to eat something they did not like, and Ma was nearly seventy years old, so he and Tiffany decided just to go with it until she headed home, it was only for a week usually anyways.

They chatted for a while and Josh went and got the bleach bottle down again. It was bothering him that something so easily obtainable could be so deadly. It was probably kept in every house in the country, and more than likely in that cupboard under the sink with all the water pipes and other cleaning chemicals. Well, not in this house! He went to that cupboard and opened the door, looked at and read the contents of each bottle, and put the dangerous ones well out of the way.

Tiffany looked surprised but Ma said, "Huh! They're tame they are, not dangerous at all not like in my day, Jeyes fluid, ammonia, creosote and that coal tar burner we used when we had bronchitis and colds, a lot of that about then. Medicines I suppose cured that, but nowadays everyone keeps that tame stuff in there, otherwise why would they sell them in supermarkets?"

Tiffany said to her mother, "If Josh wants to move them he has good reason to," and with that, slipped the tray of bangers into the oven.

"Josh, the girls have asked if they could have a sleepover this Saturday, it's the Jenkins girls. I said it's ok, hope you don't mind? Their dad is a sergeant at Plympton nick," she added.

"That'll be fine," said Josh. "We can't stop the girls from making friends, much as I want to - especially boyfriends!"

With that passing remark he left the kitchen and went to talk to his daughters about not playing with or drinking anything from hard to open bottles that are placed on the higher shelves in the kitchen cupboards.

The following day Chavender met the press. He and Chief Constable Featherstonehaugh sat in his office and after a few photos were taken, one of him wearing the medal, shaking hands and so on, he gave them the story of how he won the George Cross. He was a young Metropolitan police constable off duty, in his first year, after passing out at Hendon, he was on leave in Doncaster doing some research into his family tree.

Whilst out shopping in the high street, he left a shop next to a bank and happened onto an armed robbery. Two of the robbers were already in the car running the engine, shouting for the third to hurry up, when the third came out he started shooting at members of the public, two were killed, and several wounded. The bank robber, hesitated to put a fresh clip in. Chavender who had been nearby, saw his chance and rushed at him, even though he had finished reloading his pistol. He took three bullet wounds, two to his right shoulder and one in the right lung, which collapsed, but his momentum carried him forward into the robber and they both fell down. The robber, taken by surprise, was knocked out when he hit his head on the floor. Chavender, laying on top of him, pushed the gun away from the robber to a nearby member of the public, before he finally passed out. The others, seeing this, fled the scene in their car, whilst a bystander picked up the gun and kept it away from the robber, who coming too was beginning to feel around for his weapon, but by this time pandemonium had broken out, some people were screaming and running away, while others were rushing to help those shot.

The bank alarm was wailing, combined with the noise of the panic-stricken screams of those wounded and the sirens from the armed response vehicles, police patrol cars and ambulances all vying for attention from the traffic as they rushed to the scene. Then an air of order and calm settled on the high street as the emergency services started the grim task of securing the scene, looking for bullets and holes, covering the dead and keeping curious onlookers away. As if by magic, national and international news crews arrived just as quickly as the local police. They encamped in the road round the corner sending out reporters to talk to anyone who was there. They filmed Chavender and the other wounded as they were put into the waiting ambulances to be rushed to hospital, but he was the most critical casualty out of them all. All told, seven were hit and two were killed. It made live news around Britain that day for several hours, whilst the Chief Constable of Yorkshire, in a statement to the press, 'warned members of the public not to tackle the two armed robbers at large, and that they were looking for an old Mark Five Cortina in cream with a black vinyl roof. Anyone seeing the car should call the number on the screen.'

After an operation to reinflate his lung and patch his wounds, Chavender was wheeled to recovery where, after two days, the Yorkshire Chief Constable met him to congratulate him for his bravery. The robbers were caught three days later on the confession of the fellow Chavender had downed, and he was hailed in the local press as a hero for saving many lives that day, in what they said would surely have been a bloodbath, or as one local paper put it, 'Massacre in the high street.'

The national tabloids had a field-day, knocking and praising the police in the same article, but Chavender said he felt that he was only doing his duty as a policeman, and it only emerged later once he had recovered, that he had been nominated for the George Cross, much to his surprise, he was subsequently awarded the medal. The paper went on to ask him about some of the famous cases he helped solve in London. Here he neatly sidestepped one case, but went on at length about the Cannibal

Case. After a few hours the press were thanked and they left. Chief Constable Featherstonehaugh thanked Chavender and he left as well.

Chapter 7

Just after the CC had left, DI Pearce called Chavender, "Hello sir, we've got the reports, do you want to hear them?"

Chavender replied, "No, not at the moment... I don't suppose you could bring them over could you? ... You can? That's grand, thanks, see you shortly, bye."

Chavender went to the canteen and waited for DI Pearce to arrive. Whilst waiting he spoke with Sue, asking about her daughters and the sleepover and about how excited his girls were.

Sue replied, "My Bert he loves his little girls you know, he hates to see them grow up, but then that's what kids do, they grow up all too soon nowadays!"

Chavender felt relieved when he heard that another father of girls felt the same way as he did. He took his coffee and sat down, drinking it slowly, and looked out the window. The sky was a steely grey and looked threatening, rain or snow? *Rain I hope*, he thought, and tried to not think or prejudge what was in the reports. Pearce found him in the canteen. After getting himself a coffee, he sat down next to Chavender, his face glum as he handed over the reports and Chavender read the forensic one first.

The report stated that they could not ascertain if both chemicals were present in the same bottle, several fingerprints, many too smeared to get a true reading, probably would not stand up in court due to the nature of how many times the bottle had been handled in the past, by person or persons unknown. All they could agree on was that mixing two chemicals in a solution of about fifty/fifty would create enough dangerous gas to kill, this gas would either be Chlorine or Hydrazine, both deadly. The house contained no extra fingerprints that were not the unfortunate couples, so that would rule out foul play. It went on that although a thorough forensic search was done, it may have been too late to get any viable information from the kitchen. The Coroner's report was just as vague, in it he stated two possible verdicts with the first one being the most likely, which was based on the evidence of the autopsy. These were 'Accident or Misadventure', whereby the cause of death was accidental poisoning by gas after mixing two cleaning chemicals, which burnt the inside of the lungs severely by destroying the alveoli and the capillaries where oxygen is absorbed into the blood. It also damaged the pleura, thus making breathing virtually impossible without ventilation in the later stages. It burnt other soft tissue of the body in the chest cavity before both died of suffocation or asphyxia in a most painful way.

The other verdict was 'Narrative', whereby he stated that couple having trouble unblocking the sink decided to use a homemade sink unblocking agent by mixing two dangerous chemicals, which gave off Hydrazine gas which eventually killed them. The report stated it could not say whether any intent of foul play could be proven. This verdict was taken as a whole from the police, forensic and investigation reports into the circumstances surrounding the deaths and backed up by the findings of the autopsy report, the bodies would therefore be released to the relatives for burial.

Chavender sat silently for a while, after reading the reports and passing them back to Pearce, said, "I guess we can close this case now, it seems accidental, but somehow… I've read many labels since and it quite clearly warns you not to mix with any other cleaning fluids."

Pearce replied, "Yes, but how many people read the instructions? I certainly don't and I bet my wife doesn't either! Could just have been an oversight. Anyways, thanks for your time sir; anything else needed of me before I shut the case down? No? Well, goodbye sir," and Pearce left Chavender to his musings.

After a few minutes, Josh finished his coffee, got up, said goodbye to Mrs Jenkins and left.

He went back to his office and started to make some notes about the investigative branch of the MCC meeting next week, noting in his diary that he had a top brass meeting Monday morning, and had arranged to meet with Chief Inspectors Morris of MCC East, Smith of MCC West on Tuesday morning and Sword and Andersonn that same afternoon. For his meeting on Wednesday he decided to expand the invite to all detectives, already the week looked like it had gone and all he had done was to arrange meetings!

At least the weekend was ahead, he had planned nothing, knowing that leaving the days alone, just going with the flow, they would fill themselves. Josh closed his diary and left to go home. As he passed the front desk, he handed the notes to the duty sergeant and asked him if he could make sure that they were received by all CID men. He thanked him for doing that, and left to get in his car. On his drive home the clouds were threatening again, looking quite multicoloured even though they were in monochrome, blacks, greys and dirty whites, with an almost boiling rolling appearance as the blacker the cloud turned it tumbled and rolled over the silvery-grey off-white ones, almost giving the appearance of being eaten, it was a thunderstorm in the making.

Josh just made it home before the heavens opened up, in what could only be described as a downpour of biblical proportions, stair rods, cats and dogs were tame compared to this, virtually solid sheets of water, not drops, as if the heavens decided to dump all the water in one go. The lightning storm, trapped by the hills, swirled, flashed and crashed its way up the valley for a full three hours, bringing localised flooding and chaos to some. Buildings and trees were struck countywide as the storm raged. Josh spotted a leak in the conservatory roof, they had sat in the kitchen, which opened on to the conservatory, when they all were startled by a bolt of lightning which struck nearby and had illuminated the darkened skies for a split second, and flinching when the large thunderclap that followed echoed round and round shook the house. Strange, he thought, they were more afraid of the thunder, which was harmless, than of the lightening which could kill. By eight o'clock it was a spent force and was moving slowly up country and they sat down to 'something' and bangers for tea again.

Although the storms ebbed and flowed during the night, they were not woken by it. Needless to say, the two oldest girls were excited by the sleep over and spent most of the day preparing for it. His two youngest daughters helped him mop up the flood in the conservatory and move the wicker furniture out into the garden, to try and dry it out. Before he knew it the Jenkins had arrived. He was pleased to see that it was only Mrs Jenkins who brought Carol and Anne, and it saved an awkward meeting with Mr Jenkins. The relief must have shown on his face because 'Ma' rounded on him.

"What's up? Just because her husband is a sergeant and you're a DCI doesn't mean you smell different you know, blooming snob that's what you are, traitor to your roots. Those Civil War Levellers didn't do a good enough job, we should have done what them Frenchies did and lop the heads off the toffs, too right we should have had a proper revolution not a half-baked one, you know just like them commies did in Russia, but I don't hold with killing royalty, not like what them reds done to the Romanovs - related to our royal family they were."

He knew 'Ma' was a lifelong socialist and member of the SWP, but she was also a staunch royalist, which he could never work out. Just like his working class, ex-coal miner, civil servant messenger of a father who voted Tory all his life but hardly had two pennies to rub together right up until the day he died, poverty was his bedfellow and hunger was his companion, yet unbelievably he stayed a staunch Tory supporter, even voting for the first woman Prime Minister!

Mrs Jenkins came to his rescue. "It's not that, love," she said. "He had to work today, it's the local football derby between the two towns, a lot will ride on this for the next year, trouble is he supports the 'Mints' which is Plympton's local team, but it's being played away, at the Cannon Row Ground just outside Bryantsand-on-sea, but I support them, the 'Dodgers' you see, well whilst he's on duty he has to remain neutral and won't get as much pleasure if they win... Oh! By the way, nice article in the paper about your husband this morning," she said to Tiffany in passing.

Josh helped get duvets, pillows and cuddly toys out of her car and a couple of bags. All the girls helped cart the stuff up to the older twins' bedroom and it was thrown in a heap on the floor. The girls went out to play whilst Tiffany, Sue, Ma and Josh had a cup of tea, discussed bedtime arrangements (which they all knew wouldn't be adhered to) and when she would call back for them on Sunday.

Mrs Jenkins then left, and Josh felt even more outnumbered by females as he got up and went into the front room to watch some TV. The sleepover for the girls was a success. They stayed up till past eleven o'clock, had pizza and fizz for supper, and slept soundly until 10am on Sunday. The girls, still dressed in their onesies, had for breakfast the remains of cold pizza and fizz, left over from the night before, eventually coming down stairs about midday, still in onesies. He had looked in to say goodnight to them about 10.30 last night but the girls screamed at him to get out! Mr Jenkins arrived at about 2pm to collect his girls, still in onesies. They thanked Tiffany for allowing the sleep over, and he got them in his car, left Saturday's paper and drove away. Tiffany, with Ma reading over her shoulder, read the front page article about Josh, under the headline 'Hero New Crime Boss takes over all Criminal Investigations in the County'. It went on to explain what, how and why he had won his George Cross, and how pleased the citizens must feel about having such a top man in charge at police headquarters. After they finished with it, Josh quickly skimmed through the paper, not really noticing anything in particular, he didn't usually bother to read about births, deaths and marriages, and letters complaining about the Council merger and what it will mean for people on the housing, allotments and special needs supportive housing waiting lists - his thoughts on those were generally, *what will be will be*. When he finished with it, he noticed Ma pick the paper up and put it in her handbag, he was not sure but he thought a faint hint of a smile light up her face.

Chapter 8

At the Monday meeting with the Chief Constable, who congratulated him on the newspaper story, Chavender gave Featherstonehaugh an outline idea of what he proposed to do with CID officers. He explained he would be meeting with the other Chief Inspectors on Tuesday, and all the Investigators on Wednesday. The Chief Constable agreed it would be a fine idea. Chavender was thanked for his input and dismissed.

Chavender went back to his office and put some more ideas down on paper about how he proposed to work his department. Several hours later, paperwork boredom set in and he just had to stop. He called Plympton police station and asked to speak to Sergeant Jenkins.

"Jenkins speaking, hello sir, what can I do for you?"

Chavender replied, "I just want to thank you about Sunday that's all, the girls really got on well with each other and enjoyed the sleepover."

"Yes they did," replied Jenkins. "But if they continue to have this friendship it may prove awkward - when we meet socially, I mean, sir."

"Yes, I'd thought of that," Josh started to say.

Jenkins interrupted him by saying, "Look, sir, I think it's best if we keep to rank for a while, until the girls really know if they are going to be best friends or what. Once they bridge that gap we can sort something out with ours. I know my wife likes your wife, sir, and to be honest we don't need to be friends, it's the wives and children that are doing that for us, so I think the status quo should remain between us, okay sir?"

"Well yes, I see that, Sergeant." Feeling relieved, Chavender had thought of the same thing but could not quite express it that way without it sounding just a bit snobbish. "But I may get flak from my mother-in-law over that. She has already ripped into me once about it when you picked your girls up, saying I was 'offhand' to you and being a 'snob'. My apologies if it seemed that way, it wasn't meant as such. Anyway, apart from that, I want you to attend the CID meeting Wednesday okay? I will be asking a sergeant from Bryantsand to come as well, I want the beat constables to know what is happening. Anyway, thanks again Sergeant, see you Wednesday, goodbye."

Chavender then went to the canteen, spoke to Sue, asking her to thank her daughters from him for being so good, got a coffee and sat down to drink it. Afterwards he went home, where he was greeted by Tiffany who told him, with a smile on her face, it was casserole for tea. After his initial excitement at eating something different, she then laughed softly, the laugh that had helped to attract her to him in the first place, and admitted it was sausage casserole. He raised his eyebrows, heaved a sigh and tucked into it, after all his mother-in-law being there was his idea in the first place! After tea, Ma told Tiffany she was going home in the morning, seeing as how the grandchildren were doing fine. She would not stop any longer and didn't want to outstay her welcome. Looking at Josh he knew she had heard his sigh as he tucked into his tea. Could she be dropped off at the station after the school run? That night the girls helped to pack Gran's things ready for the off.

The meetings with Chief Inspectors Morris and Smith were very productive, both having ideas that sounded workable and they supported him when he outlined what he wanted to do, they wished him the "best of British" in dealing with Sword and Andersonn as they left him to it. Precisely on time both the divisional Chief Inspectors were admitted to his office and sat down. Chavender asked them if they wanted a drink, gave them a coffee each as requested, and sat down himself. He then asked about the differences between the two towns and why such territorial claims still existed - surely they should be one big happy family?

Sword, a local Plympton man, explained, "Well, it basically goes back when Bryantsand-on-Sea was first made, oh, how shall we put it best? Border contact just after the war, when two opposing developments joined. Ever since then we have both continued to grow gradually and rapidly at times, becoming more like one big town with many sub-boroughs, swallowing up smaller outlying towns and villages as we marched outwards. Like a devouring horde of hungry army ants, the developers descended on us, with more and more green belt being put to concrete. Plympton losing its identity to its newer neighbour as it became more fashionable and becoming more like what London is, a vast collection of boroughs, and still it grows. The two towns are like an ever hungry devouring dragon and are only ten miles away from Middlechester and fifteen away from the next resort, whilst inland the urban sprawl is fifteen miles deep.

"Plympton is a working port, although, more accurately, half a working port; the ferry side and import area are situated on the far side of the river and bay in a large industrial complex, but due to lack of deep water and ever-increasing bigger container ships, the town side of the river, where the warehouses used to be, and some still are, have been converted into ultra modern and very expensive flats now, and of course there are the marinas along this side now. The RNLI uses the bay behind the ferry side on a site dating back to Roman times. Apparently, they have proven that occupation or settlement has been going on for several thousand years here, whilst Bryantsand is a mid-Victorian or early Edwardian seaside resort.

"I'm sure John agrees with me that both towns bring just as much revenue into the county as each other, but the county town takes a lot of the credit that it doesn't warrant and tries to influence, or have an influence, over matters that don't concern it. Of course you have Middleshire County Council, the Plympton Borough Council, alongside that Bryantsand Borough Council and then all the local parish or town councils that have been swallowed up, yet still retain control over certain small areas of interest. This all leads to a confusion of issues and clashes over who has what authority, over what and whom?

"It will be much better when the two larger Borough Councils merge; they may just have enough muscle to take control of the parish and town councils then, as I say it's a total confusion of interests."

As Sword stopped to take a breath, Andersonn added "Yes that's about the size of it. I myself am not local but, like you, a newcomer or 'wally' as they call us. As you may know, Middleshire is the fourth smallest shire in the UK, it has some seventy odd miles of coastline" - here Chavender nodded - "and three major towns with several smaller, yet quite still large towns/villages, along with plenty of small villages and hamlets. The counties main source of income is from its thriving tourist trade, which means that we have a seasonal peak in crime, when the population of the county virtually doubles in size. The local councils should really cooperate more, and they do to a certain level, especially now that the two biggest local councils are on the verge of merging, trying to save money they said. Both football teams have only recently been in the same league, and the old rivalries have broken out again, it really was a good job that they drew on Saturday!"

Chavender then explained his idea and hoped that they would support it. After mulling it over for a while, they all agreed in principal to give it a trial for six months. Chavender thanked them both and told him that all CID men and a sergeant from each main subdivision would be meeting tomorrow and that he would be speaking about this and some other subjects then. Seeing that the time was late, Chavender walked with them to the carpark to go home. They saluted and went their separate ways.

For Wednesday's meeting, Chavender managed to get the canteen for an hour, so he could fit everyone in and provide enough tea and coffee, and by ten am they had all assembled. Six DIs, six DSs, and eighteen DCs, as well as Inspector Carr and the two uniformed sergeants, he thanked them all for attending and outlined his proposal that for the next eight months they would all rotate round the three main police stations getting to know the various areas covered. He went on to explain that the rural CIDs, having different theft problems to solve than those in the town, citing when was the last case of a stolen tractor in Bryantsand investigated, whilst he had as yet not heard of a pickpocket in the countryside. There was slight amusement and sniggering at this comment, which was hushed by him saying that he would ask for volunteers for the first round of temporary deployment, if not he would just choose them at random.

For the time being, investigative teams would be no fewer than two men, which allowed for continuance in investigation. He thanked them all for turning up and would answer any questions they may have the next time he met with them in the local police stations, he asked for Inspector Carr, DIs Pearce, Small, Harrier, and Molly-Fergus, DSs Wootton and Carruthers to stay behind and meet with him in his office. He spoke to the two uniform sergeants, thanking them for attending and again reiterating that he would speak to them when he visited them at their stations.

This was part of Chavender's plan, it was to get them talking between themselves first and not ask silly questions that he could not expect to give the right answer to. He thought it would keep them on their toes for a while, and off his back whilst the new plan was implemented. Once all were settled in his office, he asked Carruthers if he had the lists yet and if not yet completed could he expand the search to include the county as a whole. He then spoke at length to all, about the scheme to integrate the detective force throughout the county and that they must all be prepared to work in any part of it without petty-minded nitpicking differences as to which town was the older or whatever argument they could think up at the time. That was why he dismissed the others before it got into, "it's not my job," "I'm not paid enough to do that" or "can't someone else do it". He asked Carr to stay and let the others leave; he continued talking for a few minutes and asked if he was busy on Thursday, if not could he take him around the older town and police station again, Carr said he was free and okayed meeting him at 8.30 in the morning. Chavender thanked him and after Carr had left, carried on with the ever-present paperwork.

The stroll round Plympton the next day was rather pleasant with the late February sun bursting through a very pale blue sky which gave the coming spring a boost. They chatted on the way in, and parking the police car at one end of the high street, got out and walked towards the old port. The high street was the usual mix of shops, cafes and street vendors, shoppers stopping them every so often to ask a question. Partway down the high street they came across market stalls.

Chavender stopped and looked at some with interest but what caught his eye was an old, what he called a 'rag and bone' stall. He had not seen one since his childhood, the tabletop was a mix of everything you could possibly think of, kitchenware, books, knick-knacks, tools and some electric goods. Chavender spent a few minutes looking through goods on the table.

"You won't find no 'ooky stuff guv, it's all legit that is, got receipts to prove I 'ave, look as much as you want, go on pick something and I'll prove it with a bill, I can ya'know."

Chavender replied, "I bet you can, but I am not on the lookout for, what was it you said, 'ooky stuff' - just having a look, okay?" and carried on his way.

Carr spoke. "He used to be the local villain as a lad, burglaries, joy riding, and criminal damage, not like his ol' man."

By this time, they were walking beside the old port that had been rejuvenated by the conversion of the old warehouses into modern 'des-res' flats and the docks into marinas.

Here they stopped and Chavender said, "See, Carr, if the CID based in Middlechester don't spend time here, how will they get on when someone nicks from a boat moored here? Bet half of them couldn't tell port from starboard!"

"You're probably right on that score sir, but before you carry on its best to tell you that a tractor was stolen from Bryantsand a few years ago, it was the one used to sweep the beach each morning, so some clever clog might try to catch you out sir."

"Oh," laughed Chavender, "thanks for that, Carr; let's head back."

Slowly they headed back up the high street, both enjoying the sunshine as much as the rest of the general public. Passing the rag and bone stall the lad shouted out, "'ere Plod, I've got bills for all of this stuff, nowt nicked 'ere, ya know, all legit this is, bloody victimisation that is, trying to earn an 'onest living I am, why don't you go and solve some proper crime and leave us alone, ta."

Further on they bumped into Sergeant Jenkins and a constable doing foot patrol, stopping to return salutes and having a word with them. They found that Inspector Pearce had been called to another suspicious death. They thanked Jenkins and asked him to call through to find the address so they could go straight there.

"Oh it's not far sir; I'm sure Inspector Carr will know where it is," and he wrote it down for them.

Chapter 9

Chavender and Carr easily found the address, and saw Pearce, who explained, "No one had seen the deceased for a few days probably no longer than a week, and were concerned, so they called the police. On entering, the sickly sweet aroma of death had greeted the first constable, who then phoned for me and a doctor. The doctor has just left and puts time of death at about three to five days ago, the cold weather of late helped slow down decomposition somewhat. We think the cause of death at the moment is a heroin overdose, but the autopsy will reveal more. Preliminary enquiries have turned up nothing out of the ordinary, but I'm not sure. He was known to take cannabis and other such drugs, but was not known to be a heroin addict, that's why I think it could be suspicious."

"Hmm, yes, thank you, Inspector Pearce. It has been known for drug addicts to 'upgrade' you know! Do we know how long he's been taking, and who his supplier is? Perhaps he could help? Did he have a mobile phone? Get that to the tech boys see what they gleam off it I suppose, anything else that may be a touch odd? No? Then keep me informed would you? Thanks."

With that they both left and headed back to headquarters.

On the way back they talked a little about Chavender's first few weeks and that thunderstorm.

"Good for farmers and gardeners alike, that storm cleared the air," said Carr and carried on, "released a lot of nitrogen that did and topped up the water table, bet the water companies will still try and claim it will be a drought this year."

Chavender let Carr talk on as he tried to learn the route back, only half listening or "copping a deaf 'un" as he was known to do with his wife and girls when it got a bit too much for him to take it all in.

They arrived at headquarters. Chavender thanked Carr for his time and asked if he could he possibly be available to take him to Bryantsand around midday tomorrow and arrange for him to go out with a uniform patrol on Monday, if that was okay. Carr thought it would be, and would let him know in due course.

On his way to his office Chavender bumped into Carruthers.

"Ah, glad you're back Sir, I have that information you require."

"That's good," said Chavender. "Let's go to the canteen and talk it through, I'll get us a coffee."

Chavender often found that a coffee relaxed the younger detectives and they were more willing to express their ideas. He paid for the coffees and sat down with Carruthers. Compiled on several sheets of paper were the lists that interested him. Carruthers then went through the various lists saying, "Deaths above average for time of the year, but if no more deaths occur in say, three weeks, it would be average. Burglaries average, slight rise in drug offences and car crime, darker nights I suppose, and several attempted burglaries, here the intruder was disturbed as they tried to break in or had just broken in, probably trying for car keys! Usual Saturday night drunken brawls and no increase in domestic violence, male or female, one arrest for impersonation, and several cases of theft by distraction, mainly on the old, but not solely, which we think is related to the impersonator in some way, he may have cased the joint and gave or sold the names and address to others in the trade, so to speak. Pick pocketing is down, but that will peak in the summer.

"Traffic report a slight increase in drink driving offences involving accidents and drink driving over all, but that would be normal for the time of year. On average these driving offences are down slightly, along with other misdemeanours such has nuisances caused by teenagers, graffiti artists and petty vandalism. Several illegal immigrants caught at the port and detained and two lorry drivers arrested in conjunction with trying to smuggle illegal goods, ten kilos of mixed drugs and several firearms of various calibres, theft from farms and farmers up a touch but not by much and that's about it sir. In all respects, pretty much the average or run of the mill figures for us."

Chavender thanked him for his hard work and took the report from him. They continued drinking their coffee whilst he looked at the reports.

Ah well, he thought, *it had to come.* Leaving the hustle and bustle of London with its soaring crime figures that would keep Sherlock Holmes busy for a few hundred years with the variety of crimes committed, and coming to the peace and quiet in the countryside, ah, rural life. *I hope Tiff and the girls really do like it here and are not just saying so for my sake*, Josh thought; perhaps he'd better 'grill' them all tonight to see what they thought - after all it was only six weeks since the move.

The next day, Carr took him to Bryantsand Police station and after chatting with Chief Inspector Andersonn and DI's Lister and Small and finding only routine investigations under way, thanked them for their time and left to go back to headquarters. Once again he thanked Carr for his time as they entered the building.

Carruthers came up to Chavender, "Hello sir, message from DI Pearce, he will call you later today sir, and nothing added to those lists yet, so it looks like average. Even the latest drug related death did nothing to spike the figures, we have probably about six a year, most recent one only takes us up to five, sir "

Thanking Carruthers, Chavender got up and went back to his office. He was pleased to see that, finally, they had installed the computer. He had to rearrange all his pictures to fit but he did, making sure that Tiffany was in the prime position. Switching the computer on, he then spent the next two hours setting things up, transferring diary dates, syncing phone data, creating an email account and sending several emails letting his colleagues know that he was online, wishing them all a good weekend and he would see them Monday. Just as he pressed the power save button to shut it down, his phone rang.

"Hello Chavender speaking. Hello DI Pearce, any progress with the latest death?"

"Hello sir, we have just completed preliminary enquiries with the neighbours and nothing is sticking out sir. They think someone called a week ago, but are not sure, they think they saw a strange car but, again, they're not sure. They think he had started to do stronger drugs several months ago, but none of his friends could actually pinpoint to any strange incident, probably too stoned to think straight. Drug paraphernalia was scattered all over the rooms, from basic cannabis to a few used syringes and a couple of wraps. Sir."

"Well," said Chavender, "it looks like a drug overdose doesn't it? Don't spend too long on it - it is the weekend after all. Let's wait for the forensics and autopsy report, we should have them by Monday hopefully. Have a good weekend Pearce, bye."

"Bye, Sir."

Chavender sat for a while, thinking three deaths, two incidents, one an accident, one a possible overdose, still just above average, as Carruthers pointed out, that would level off if no more deaths occurred. Still, he thought, don't let it bother you old son, pack up and go home, enjoy your weekend.

The weekend passed in a blaze of glorious early spring sunshine and Josh, Tiffany and the girls took the opportunity on Sunday to go walking along the coastal path. Chavender explained to his children that the oldest period represented in Middleshire was the Jurassic, and that was behind them, so walking forward they were 'time-travelling' into the Cretaceous period and during this time, which was about 200 to 140 million years ago, the Jurassic seas had inundated the old land masses and marine and swamp conditions were found. Later came the Cretaceous period of 140 to 65 million years ago, a period initially of salt flats, then later of lush swamps and finally of a great sea. Chavender made it sound interesting, just, and he then sent the girls looking for fossils along the beaches.

Once home, the girls washed and sorted, swapped and generally were amused by the fossil finds for at least an hour, announced it was a great place to live, then they reverted to type and watched a Disney DVD for the afternoon. Josh and Tiffany took the time to have a nice long chat over a cup of tea and, finally, Josh's mind was put at ease about the move.

The girls bedtime came around and the normal Sunday night clamorous fight for first bath and last to bed was made easier by the girls being worn out from the long walk. Consequently the usual before sleep chatter was very short, and they soon were sound asleep.

Chapter 10

The Monday after the Chief Constable's weekly update meeting, Chavender called for Inspector Carr and was taken to the Traffic Division's area, where he was introduced to the Inspector on duty. After introductions, Carr left them. Chavender and Donaldson had a coffee and chatted for a while before they set off on patrol. They spent several hours driving round the A and B roads, listening in to the police radio and meeting other patrols at rest stops. During this time they talked about police work and what it had become, driving offences and why they were so unpopular with the public who saw such offences, especially the static speed cameras, as cash cows for the police force and the police safety speed cameras, why? They concluded that it always appeared that the poor old motorist was being caught, but then, they decided, if you speed you are breaking the law, after all, you chose to speed, you chose to drive around without a driving licence or tax, insurance and or MOT, no one forced you to do that. They agreed that, nowadays, with ANPR and all the wonderful gadgetry at our disposal, car driving offences are the ones people are most liable to be caught out on. Burglars are not taxed or MOTed and certainly don't need insurance, and, as of yet, technology has not been invented to track or catch burglars like the Police can with drivers, although CCTV helps, it's not quite Big Brother yet; no, they concluded, it's down to the police to use good old fashioned detective principals and of course modern technology where it exists.

They thought about it for a while before Chavender said, "Perhaps we can bar code the regular suspects or chip them so they can be tracked; I wouldn't be surprised if they claim it's an infringement of their human rights! That argument cuts both ways for me, what about my rights not to be burgled by some thieving little scroat who just fancies my belongings? Detective work is slow sometimes, checking alibis, sorting through reams of statements, looking out for any inconsistencies and nine times out of ten getting nowhere and starting over, uniform and Detective Constables working away but always the same, a gut instinct that something doesn't add up, if only… If only."

Soon they were back at headquarters. Chavender thanked the inspector for his time and the interesting conversation they'd had, and saw DI Pearce.

"Coffee, Pearce? Let's head towards the canteen, that face tells me the reports aren't what you wanted?"

"No, sir, not at all what I thought, but that's the way the cookie crumbles sometimes. Thanks for the coffee."

Sitting down with their coffee Pearce and Chavender read the reports. Again, forensics couldn't help, all they could say was that the needle was used for heroin, fingerprints indistinct, no forced entry. Autopsy said much the same thing. Doctor thought it could have been a heart attack brought on by the overdose putting too much strain on the heart and with no one in a fit state to help him, he died.

"That's it, sir. So, again, if we suspect foul play we can't prove it, it's just you, your - our - suspicion, but pretty remarkable don't you think - three deaths and all by a sort of natural causes killed them?"

"Perhaps we could meet up with the police surgeon," said Chavender, "see if he is free this afternoon and let's go have a chat with him - arrange that for us please, Pearce. I will hold my afternoon open, so any time would be good."

"Okay, sir." Pearce got up to arrange the meeting and Chavender went to his office.

He had to wade through several long emails before he started to sort out the rota for the temporary assigned Detective force transfer. Pearce called him shortly after to say that the police surgeon could see them in half an hour.

"He's at the hospital in town at the moment and we can catch him before he leaves," he added.

"Right," Chavender responded, "I'll meet you down in the car park, we'll take my car, you can show me the way."

Very shortly they were at the hospital and met with the police surgeon in a spare office. Pearce showed him the doctor's report of the suspected heart attack brought on by overdose of heroin' if the overdose did not kill him the heart attack certainly did. The surgeon mulled the report over for some time before speaking.

"Um… yes I can see that it's all very probable, not much wrong in that report, although… It would be hard to say for certain, you would need the needle for testing, You must think it's suspicious, otherwise why would you ask questions? Ah… Yes, I seem to recall a case about some ten odd years ago now where someone committed suicide by injecting potassium chloride. Now an injection of potassium chloride causes a heart attack and is bloody well-nigh on impossible to detect, see, yes difficult for the coroner or doctor to realise it was induced and not a natural heart attack - after all, a heart attack is a heart attack when all is said and done. You see, an excess of potassium chloride in the blood interferes with nerve signals, and stops muscles and nerves from working. So when it reaches your heart, the heart stops and you're dead. As it stands, it is very hard to detect because the potassium chloride, and I would say a strong solution of it, would be fatal."

"Why is it hard to detect?" asked Chavender.

"Oh that's easy," replied the doctor, "because potassium chloride is a naturally occurring substance in the body and thus is assimilated into the body as a natural compound. Yes very hard to detect, need the needle for that to prove it was anything other than natural causes, say murder or suicide. Sorry, but that's it, can't help you any more I'm afraid."

Chavender pondered for a moment before asking, "One more thing, doctor, how easy is it to get?"

"Oh, quite easy," the doctor said confidently. "Off the web or in a weaker concentrate fertilisers, freely available, I think is the term I would use."

"Interesting. Thanks for your time doctor, it's appreciated," said Chavender as he shook the doctor's hand and they said their goodbyes.

Chavender and Pearce drove slowly back to headquarters.

Chavender, thinking out loud, said, "So, hard to prove otherwise unless of course we find the needle, the only needle we found and had tested had traces of heroin, no other chemicals, so another case is closed and another sorry chapter in the life of a drug addict closes with his funeral. Oh, and I suppose no connection with the other couple? No matter how remote… Oh what were their names… Yes, not hard to forget the Joneses."

"No, sir, no connection at all, did not even move in the same circles sir!"

"No, the only thing that might be a connection is the strangely natural way they died, if you know what I mean; we suspect foul play but the facts are against us!"

"Yes, sir if it wasn't for the fact that we couldn't find where the ammonia or potassium came from, we wouldn't be so suspicious now."

"Yes I see, still we tried, but if the evidence is against us the only thing we can do is hope that if it is murder, the murderer will slip up. At the moment the search area is too vast to pinpoint where he would've bought the chemicals from, no pharmacy records to go on, the WWW, well we haven't got the time to search the world, and many thousands of outlets that may sell ammonia or potassium. No, if we do catch the offender it will because he or she slipped up. Patience is now the game. If I were Conan Doyle I would be writing a paragraph about Holmes doing some heroin or disappearing to a drug den for a few days, just to keep the plot on the boil, it's been quite an interesting first few weeks."

Chapter 11

Wendy hesitantly started to explain. It was hard, very hard for her, here she was a very attractive, tall, blonde, early twenty-something slip of a woman, a successful press reporter having the hots for a policeman, admittedly a handsome one, especially in his uniform, but still a policeman at that. It did something for her, she was not sure what, but it did!

She thought she could see what his wife saw in him once you got past that nose of his; probably his dry sense of humour, his manners always correct or was it the ability to make her think she's the only thing that matters to him, the centre of his universe and he would lay down his life for her at the drop of a hat, his medal proved that for her? Wendy sighed, she knew he was a happily married man, with children and very much out of her reach… yet? She dreamed on; she could see the beginning of grey in the hair on his temples and some worry lines around his steely blue eyes but she could not help feeling like a schoolgirl having a crush on the strict history teacher, like she had had, she sipped her coffee quietly for a while. Suddenly Chavender interrupted her musings.

That look had not gone unnoticed by him; after all it was one which his wife used much to her advantage, he knew that with one look and saying his name, Josh, in a certain way he was done for, whatever she wanted… She… he was disarmed, putty in her hands, now it was his turn to blush a little and quite rudely for him ask, "Come, Miss Blaise, spit it out, I do not have all day to stare glassy eyed into my coffee cup; if you have something to say then say it!"

She snapped out of her May to December fantasy about him and begun to talk.

"Well, we've been doing some digging into the merger of the two councils, to be able to give the townsfolk the heads up on it. Well, one of our guys was looking into some past buying applications from some Bryantsand and Plympton councillors, and we think that we've found some irregularities. It concerns the joint planning committees who were responsible for the future parcelling up and selling off of council land, more specific the leaders of these committees and three local developers, it seems that backhanders may have been involved and we think that a front company, called Eco-Developments, has been set up, to buy council owned land at knock down prices. Directors are Grey, Schonebeck and List, but they all own their own development companies here on the mainland, although Schonebeck is in liquidation at the moment. Prices are sometimes as low as peppercorn price.

"It seems they have bought up small sections of land called Ransom Strips, not large tracts, which, when the rest of the land is sold by auction, these little strips could be could be worth millions; this of course did not raise suspicion. So when outside developers try to buy the land behind, they may be put off, or be charged millions, for what amounts to something the size of a small garden. This company is registered offshore and the CEO is Schonebeck, so it will not be linked to the councillors, or the others directly, but bank details are proof that financial dealings happened between these people. Furthermore we have proof, although it was obtained probably illegally by a hacker, the council's web security is hopeless, never choose a password that is so simple to guess! He managed to get into all the council's records, past and present. Something to be said for the paperless office, otherwise we would have had to have done a Watergate.

We are going to run the story this weekend, and are giving you the chance to investigate them."

"May I have a look?" She handed the file over and Chavender started to read. "Um… Yes… Aha… You know we may need to know the hacker's name, but if what you say is correct then I think it's a case of fraud!"

Wendy replied, "You may have to give immunity to the hacker, but if you are going to investigate can you do that without the name for now?"

"Well, I'm not sure, but let's see shall we? Please follow me, we may need to see the Chief Constable on this."

They both got up and went to the Chief Constable's office; after knocking and being asked to "come in," they entered.

"Hello Chavender, hello Miss Blaise, what can I do for you?"

Chavender explained and showed the report and asked for advice; it was agreed that the people mentioned would be invited to help the police with their inquiries, so to speak, and that he should arrange for this to happen the next day, which would give him time to arrange the personnel. He asked Miss Blaise not to print anything that may harm the future investigation into the alleged offences.

"We're not trying to muzzle the press," he said "but help to keep it out of trouble!"

Wendy agreed, and then said she had planned to attend the next joint planning committee meeting for 2pm tomorrow, would that be okay? Featherstonehaugh and Chavender said nothing, but thanked her for the information, and she was shown out of the building.

Chavender informed the other senior police officers of what was going to happen the next day on a conference call from the Chief Constable's office. They all agreed on a rough plan and on Chavender's suggestion that the investigative teams should form their owns plans, and have them approved by him, and about his idea of keeping clear from the initial operation, it was seen by the

Chief Constable as a sound tactic. Chavender called Lister, Smith and Carr, asking them to attend a briefing at 4pm that day without fail, and told them to bring a detective sergeant and two constables along each. He then called Molly-Fergus to arrange for all members of the divisional CID to attend the meeting. He obtained the location of the planning meeting and arranged the briefing room, with the list of names and address were they would be and what time to arrest them.

Divisional CID arrived on time and Chavender got down to the briefing. "Lister and Smith were to invite the two councillors to an interview, whilst the sergeant and constables would provide the necessary muscle, they should do it after the meeting."

He would leave it down to them how to do it; he then turned too Harrier and Molly-Fergus, gave them the names and addresses of the three developers, one was not in the country at present, and told them that any time during the meeting they could collect them and bring them to divisional HQ. He would take no active part in this investigation, but would like all preliminary enquiries over quickly.

"This may wrongfoot them later, but for now they were to keep the interview to about three hours or so or else they may get restless. Remember, it's voluntary, hopefully, the only thing I will say, is take the mobile phones off them. They can make a call to their lawyers from the police station. The lawyers will certainly make sure they do not incriminate themselves, okay, but you must ask for their passports as well, get permission from them too, to confiscate them, in writing, if needs be." Chavender went on. "Then I want your recommendations on how to proceed, if it's a case of fraud or not, but always stress its voluntary, any statements made are voluntary, unless you caution them, but I'm pretty certain that we will get next to nothing from them. I'm sure their lawyers will push for the interview to be over sooner than later, I'm not worried on that score, basically I want to rattle their cages a bit, trip them up into making mistakes; you can caution them that investigations will be on going, they may or may not get in touch with each other, or make contact in some way to concoct stories. I'm not really worried about that, they can do what they like after we release them the more freedom they have, the more likelihood of them digging themselves into a big hole, we will get so much more from the peripheral information we gather now, like from phone records, papers or harddrives."

He told them that the Chief Constable would be seeking a search warrants for all the known addresses that morning and he would rely on the team led by Inspector Carr, with sergeants and Constables to execute that warrant at the same time as the suspects are in custody.

"We are not arresting any one at the moment, you must make that clear at first but if they give any sign of... Oh, how shall I put it? - a reluctance to cooperate on their part, you must caution them and add, under the suspicion of, or conspiracy to commit fraud, then you can drag their sorry asses in. I want no 'get out of jail free' cards to be played by any of them, okay? If it is a case of fraud, naturally fraud charges will follow, and, by the way I do believe the press may be present, which is one of the reasons I do not wish to get involved, the other is that I was informed of the situation and I do not want to be prejudiced against any of them, okay? Now sort out your timetables, who does what and where."

Chavender then turned to Carr. "Could you arrange for some uniform help to be available tomorrow afternoon, just in case we need to seize reams of papers and computers? I make it about nine hard drives need looking into plus any bank statements, letters, mobile phones, and anything that may prove of interest. We may have to contact phone companies; they should have kept records of local and international calls for billing purposes. I think yourself, a sergeant, two detective constables and four uniform constables should be enough. Liaise with Molly–Fergus and Harrier. If needs be split your force up with three vans and a car. You could collect them round-robin style, it's up to you Carr.

It would be hard for them to destroy any evidence on the hard drives, and our tech boys can retrieve most things from the most damaged of drives."

Carr looked at Chavender and asked, "Excuse me, sir, but why isn't DI Pearce being involved in this operation?"

"Oh that's easy Carr, and a good question, I may need someone with no connection to the initial investigation to read the reports along with me, and I don't want to be seen to be biased in any way. It will need someone totally separated from the initial investigation. I don't want the worms to wriggle off the hook for any legal reason. You can bet they all have access to top class lawyers, who could make a hole in any case big enough, in this case, to put a housing estate through."

Carr replied, "Thanks sir, you know the last DCI kept us uniform jobs out of such shouts, and if we were involved we were treated like mushrooms, kept in the dark and fed bullshit, so any screw up could be blamed on us!"

Chavender thanked them all and hoped, he said, that they were not just mushrooms but team players, and the reason for letting you choose and plan your own mission would help him immensely in the future. "Involving uniform in the initial stages will also help; it will help with the mundane work of any big investigation, the reading and collating of statements, the sometimes endless search through masses of files, which at some point will overwhelm the resources available and mistakes could be made, I cite that Lincolnshire case, the final suspect was interviewed several times and went on to commit several more offences before being caught by, as luck would have it, by traffic police on a routine patrol stopping the vehicle for a broken light. Hearing a thumping noise coming from the boot, opened it to find the next victim neatly trussed and gagged laid in the boot of the car. Now that was just a lucky stop, but I don't want to rely on luck or any form of good fortune to get results. I wish to give uniform a better understanding of detective work and it may lead to more uniform trying for the CID department."

He then dismissed them and left to inform the Chief Constable of the plans being made and that another briefing was arranged for 12.30 the next day and could he attend, to which he agreed.

Chapter 12

At 12.30 the following day, they again assembled, plus those other ranks chosen to assist, only this time the briefings were done by the DIs and Inspector Carr, and all plans were finalised. Chavender went through the plans again with everyone; arresting officers for the councillors were Lister for Councillor Walker, Smith for Councillor Melbourne. For the developers, Harrier for Mr Grey and Molly-Fergus for Mr List, Inspector Carr said he would go with DI Molly-Fergus and start collecting information whilst a team led by a sergeant would be with DI Harrier. All plans were given final approval by the Chief Constable, and they were then given the off by Chavender.

Chavender motioned to Wootton, and spoke quietly in his ear and sent him on his way and then phoned his wife saying he would be very, very late probably he would not be home till the next day.

Carr was provided with the search warrants and left with his team. The Committee team left in three unmarked cars, and a marked police car, and as they drove slowly into town the excitement in the cars was intense. To some this would be their first public arrest, and they were understandably nervous. Lister and Small, in separate cars, were reciting the lines they thought they would use. "Excuse me, Sir, would you mind accompanying me to the station to assist with our enquiries" - an old-fashioned line of many jokes, but it seemed to work every time. If that failed the caution would be read with the line 'conspiracy to commit fraud' and they would have no option but to come to the station, but as Chavender made it clear, he wanted cooperation on their part.

Meanwhile, Carr was waiting with Molly-Fergus near one of the developer's houses. They were waiting for the "go" over the radio and listened in as the committee team moved up ready for the off. The signal would be given when the Councillors left the meeting. The meeting drew to an inconclusive close and gradually broke up, Councillors Walker and Melbourne walked out with Councillor Ireland, the Leader of the Committee, but were all stopped in the foyer by DIs Lister and Smith, who approached the respective Councillors and, almost in unison, asked if they would like to accompany them to the police station.

Both Councillors started to protest quite loudly, "What for, why, what have I done? I want to call my lawyer. Why are you arresting me?"

It started to get a bit tempestuous, with people coming and going, or just stopping to stare, and with the milling members of the public, press and council officials, it was beginning to disintegrate in to a farce. It was then that Lister decided to arrest Councillor Walker, and Smith followed suit. They were both cautioned and asked to surrender their mobile phones and informed that they would be allowed to call for their lawyers from the station.

They continued to protest until they were both handcuffed and led away to the waiting police cars. The press, meanwhile, had a field day, they had something to report. Miss Blaise and her photographer, along with curious onlookers, followed the little procession to the cars, whereupon Detective Sergeant Wootton spoke to Miss Blaise saying quietly, "Excuse me, Miss, but I have orders from Ol' Beaky to arrest you, he wants a word with you," Wendy Blaise was wide eyed and gobsmacked. She was being arrested!

"By whom did you say?" knowing full well that that nickname fitted only one person at divisional headquarters.

"Oh, sorry, Miss, but DCI Chavender has asked me to arrest you, so I must caution you. You do not have to say anything, but it may harm your defence if you do not mention when questioned about something which you later rely on in court. Anything you do say may be given in evidence."

Wendy Blaise started to protest her innocence, pouted, and suddenly stuck her hands out, wrists together, "You'd better cuff me then."

She made no fuss when she was handcuffed, but she made sure her press photographer got many, many pictures of her being arrested along with the Councillors. Wootton did not understand the need to arrest Miss Blaise, but, orders is orders he thought. He made sure she travelled with him and a woman detective constable on the drive back to the station, with no one else in the car. Both Councillors were placed in separate cars for the drive back and the convoy, after twenty minutes or so, sped off.

Molly-Fergus, once the 'go' was given, drove up to the developer's house, knocked and waited, when the door was opened she produced her warrant card and, confirming that it was Mr List, cautioned him and arrested him. Inspector Carr, produced the search warrant and informed Mr List that they would be seizing computers and his phone and any records he may have on the premises. They moved with some speed, collecting and bagging evidence and carrying it out to the vans. Once Carr thought he'd got it all they left to go back to headquarters. Harrier and his team did the exact same with Mr Grey and his property. Soon all the vans, bar one, were heading back. Inspector Carr and two uniform officers went to the address of Mr Schonebeck, they knew he was not there, so had brought along the police's "Universal Key". After two resounding thumps the door gave in. They quickly gathered the items required and Carr left a uniformed Constable on site until the company used by the police to make a property safe, came and secured the door. All arrests had gone smoothly, and within three hours were all back at base with a vast amount of papers seized, but it was the computers that Chavender wanted the most. Papers, if they had missed any, they could pick up later.

At the police station more photos were taken of them all being led into the building. Apart from Miss Blaise, the duty sergeant booked them all in, cautioned them again and allowed them to phone for their lawyers. Miss Blaise was put in an interview room and when she requested to phone for her lawyer, she was told that the DCI would see her first, then she could phone for her lawyer if she wanted. She was left in the company of a woman police constable. Some moments later Chavender and Wootton entered the room.

"Right Wootton, de-arrest her please!" said Chavender.

She looked bemused and started to demand an explanation, "Why did you arrest me? Why have I been brought in like and treated like a common criminal? How could you do this to me after that nice article I wrote on you, why?"

Funny, thought Chavender, *I know no common criminals*, and he started to say his bit. "You were brought in under arrest, you have now been de-arrested, so you're free to go, or you can stay voluntarily to make a statement which DS Wootton will take down in the presence of myself and this woman police constable. I stress, once again, you are not under arrest, you are free to go. What is it going to be Miss Blaise?"

She looked at him and Chavender once again saw that look as it drifted across her face. She was startled when he slapped his hand on the table, boy did she have it bad, she thought, glad he can't read my mind or else! Wootton too was startled a little, but did not see anything amiss; he just thought Chavender was trying for effect.

She decided to stay and for the next three hours gave a rather long winded statement. Basically, what she had told him the other day, but this time she was pressed to give the name of the hacker. She was released without being charged, but thanked by

Chavender. He then, due to the lateness of the time, decided to ask Wootton to take her home, which he undertook willingly.

The four men in different rooms all asked to call their lawyers and said nothing until they were present, this Chavender expected. As he stated, if any wrong doing was going to be found, it would be in the computers and papers that they kept, and what he could get from the hacked files they would all strenuously deny any involvement in wrong doing or fraud, no matter what you asked them. He made it clear to the investigating officers to just probe generally, nothing specific, some odd dates, who bought what and when, after several hours the interviews were over, and they were released without charge, but had to agree to surrender their passports. They were informed that an investigation into alleged malpractice, or fraud of the council's planning regulations, would be ongoing, they were all then allowed to go home.

Chavender called the investigating officers in to the canteen for a debriefing, which lasted an hour or so. He then thanked them for their time and said that he hoped wives and girlfriends would be understanding that they had to work till the early hours of the morning, but they could have the next day off. Chavender thought about going home but decided against it, seeing that it was nearly 3am. He went to his office and started to read through all the statements. All pretty general stuff, denials of the allegations, 'don't know what you're going on about', etc., but he knew it would be the information on the computers that would make or break this case, and that meant good old-fashioned detective work of reading reams and reams of figures till your eyes nearly popped out of your head with the strain; looking for that one bit of information that would be the spark to the gunpowder trail that led you to the motherlode. Of course the press had a field day. In the paper the next day Miss Blaise's picture topped those of the other arrestees, she had half the front page. A picture showing her being handcuffed with the other four below, the headlines, screamed out in bold type 'Police Oppression of the Press'; again it was a curious fact that the press can criticise the police at the same time as praising them and the article intimated an ongoing investigation into the four other offences relating to town planning. The next few days went slowly whilst the investigative teams probed into the financial dealings of the respective companies, checked bank statements and phone records and waited for the information to be pulled of the hard drives.

In fact the rest of the week passed slowly routine police work was, and is always a slow and laborious business, and by Thursday the tech guys had copied all the hard drives, which amounted to at least fifty discs for each hard drive, times by nine, made about 450 discs full of information to wade through, each labelled, catalogued, date of extraction and who by, had been delivered to Chavender office in nine boxes clearly marked with the name of the suspects computer on; in fact the tech guys had labelled up and subdivided each section of information by a simple colour code at his request, green for bank statements, red for phone bills, blue for planning, and black for interface or cross matching with the others on the list, these discs he asked them to leave blank, his investigators could copy and paste files on to them. This would help the teams to cross reference any items that they thought might be interesting or germane to the investigation, also clearly printed on the labels of, and on each of the cases, was a set of letters and figures. Chavender thought that if the coded set GB#1MrGreyF#20, represented; G = *BANK*, B = planning = #1 and #2, #3. #4 et, and a F#20 = file number and so on for Mr Grey, so a simple X added to the end of the coded sequence meant a cross reference to another file, the information was subdivided into files. He wanted this colour coding so that if any discs went adrift they could be easily found and put back in the correct order, this same code was used on all the discs of the suspects, Chavender hoped it would make things easier to cross reference once a match was found. By Friday he had worked it all out into as to who would do what, when and where; "where" was easy, that would be here, "who" could be DIs Lister, Small, Harrier, and Molly-Fergus, "when" next week, but he did not want them staring at computer screens all day, so he limited the time to two hour blocks for four hours a day, with an hour joint discussion in his office. It would be slow, very slow, but, as he thought, they were not trying to catch a murderer and no one was going to die from the snail like pace, so he was not worried. It would be a drain on resources if he made the team too large, and something vital might then be missed. At the senior officers meeting on Monday, once again, Chavender found himself hogging the entire time, outlining his plan to all and getting approval in principal, at least. In this way the process would be transparent, well as transparent has he could make it, if the press report was to be believed it could amount to millions obtained fraudulently by five people, although the fifth person had not yet been interviewed. Then there was the problem of the hacker, so far left alone by him. He wondered if he could get Miss Blaise and DS Wootton to bring him in? Now, there was a thought! Perhaps after the weekend, he would arrange it for Monday, he called DS Wootton and asked him to liaise with Miss Blaise to bring her and the hacker in on Monday about 2pm.

Chapter 13

Early that Saturday morning, the girls were playing in the garden, Josh was sitting at the kitchen table talking to Tiff about how things were going and, in general, how well they seemed to have settled in, especially the girls, what with making friends at school, and Tiff and Sue. He wanted to bring up the problem with Miss Blaise, he could think of no easy way to say it, so he just started clumsily.

"Er... Tiff, you remember the reporter who did that article on me, you know um... Miss Wendy Blaise, well I think she fancies me, you know!"

"Oh," said Tiff surprised, "what makes you think that dear?"

"Well you know that look you give me sometimes, when I'm being a bit reluctant to do as you wish, then you say my name a certain way, that sort of sets the hairs on the back of my neck on end and I cave in! Well she tried that the other week and I could see... Well... to put it bluntly, I'm sure she fancies me!"

Tiff did not answer but put the kettle on, sat down and took Josh's hand, looked into his eyes, smiled and said, "Well I can see why she does, you know you press all the right buttons for me, sweetheart, even now, oh yes you certainly do, especially now you have to wear uniform, you make me and the girls feel so secure and that all is right with the world... You sexy hunk of a man," she purred. "*My* man, understand?"

The last bit was said more like a threat and he just nodded his head, "Perhaps," Tiff said, and then stopped and did not finish her thought, by now the kettle was boiling and whistling away screaming for her attention. Josh felt that he had got off lightly without too much of an ear bashing, not something you do every day is to confess to your wife that another woman fancies you! Tiff, after making a cup of tea for Josh just the way he liked it, then "felt Josh's collar" some more, to use an old police term, to corral her man into getting started on some redecorating, and to take his mind of that other subject, she said they would start on the spare bedroom, and work their way down and round the house. She also thought it was about time she started to look for work, not to go back into the police force but something else, after all she took that Open University degree course in Law, perhaps she could teach Law or work in a solicitors office in town?

Josh's sigh of relief was very audible, as his wife changed the subject without blinking. He started to reply, saying that that would be a good idea and ok with him but, she did know that he loved her and only her didn't she, and his girls? Tiff left Josh in suspense for a while and turned her attention to paint colours for the spare room, she thought pale, sky, or baby blue in silk emulsion would be good for the walls and a deep Prussian blue gloss for the woodwork for contrast with white gloss for the window and sill? Josh drinking his tea in silence, waited for an opportunity to continue, when Tiff burst out laughing and sat on his lap and put her arms round his neck, looked into his eyes and said, "Josh" which immediately made the hairs on his neck stand up, she rubbed noses, kissed him lightly, whispered, "yes" and got up. Josh still none the wiser, did not comprehend what had just happened even though he was a relatively good detective, but actually understanding his wife even after all these years of marriage left him way out in the cold; he was still not sure, what, if anything, Tiff meant, apart from the fact that they were going to redecorate and that she still loved him, she had offered no advice on how to deal with Miss Blaise.

Sunday was spent buying paint, rollers, brushes and dust sheets, with the girls taking an absolute delight in choosing colours for their rooms along with murals, lampshades and new matching bedding, Josh started to mutter something about deep pockets and short arms, when Tiff elbowed him sharply in the ribs and pointing said, "Isn't that Miss Blaise? and who's that guy with her?" Josh took his cue from the direction of her finger and spoke. "Yes that's Miss Blaise, and one of my Detective Sergeants with her, c'mon, let's dart down here!" said Josh rather embarrassingly and started for an aisle in the opposite direction but Tiff took him firmly by the hand and practically dragged him towards them.

"Now come on Josh, don't be a wuss."

With the girls in tow they managed to accidentally cross paths. "Hello Wootton, Miss Blaise, this is my wife Tiffany and my daughters - just getting some decorating supplies" he added, but not sure why.

"Hello sir," said Wootton.

"Hello Josh," chimed Miss Blaise, "Nice to see you and your lovely wife, my and your daughters too", adding, "I bet you're glad they took after your wife's side of the family," looking at him and ignoring Tiffany.

Tiffany holding Josh's arm tight almost to reaffirm her claim to him, looked at Miss Blaise, "That was a really nice piece you did on my husband the other week." She stressed the "my husband" part and rounding up her brood said "Come Josh, time we paid for all of this, nice to have met the both of you," then turned and walked away. Wootton, looked somewhat askance at what had just occurred; he knew something was wrong, but could not quite put his finger on it and carried on with their shopping. He would ask Wendy later what it all meant.

Out in the car park loading up her Land Rover, Tiff said to Josh, "I see what you mean dear, she certainly has the hots for you! I guess we will have to do something about that, won't we?"

Josh nodded in agreement, marvelling at how easy it had been to spend £300 in as many hours! And they drove home, the country lanes sported nice yellow drifts, as the daffodils made a valiant display with a backdrop fresh green grass, interspersed with the white of snowdrops, spring was definitely in the air. Passing warning signs for 'Farm Traffic' and a curious home made one of a farmer saying 'SLOW MUD', Tiff asked Josh, "Look I know I now live in the countryside, so I expect farm traffic, just like I expect to drive through horse muck on the road but you don't see any signs in town saying town traffic do you! And what in heaven's name is slow mud? Political correctness gone wrong I suppose."

Josh tried to make sense of her arguments, "They put signs up just in case you forget I suppose, and as for mud in the road, have a look in your highway code sometime, it will tell you its illegal to deposit mud on the road. Well, what did you make of Miss Blaise, Tiff?"

"Oh not a lot, but you're right about her, it definitely looks likes she has a crush or complex on her part, I'm glad you told me, Josh, and from your reaction I know it's not reciprocated on your part love, so that's okay."

Josh heaved a great sigh of relief and said, "Thanks Tiff." As he felt a great weight being taken of his chest. The girls were watching a DVD on the new system hanging off the back of the front seats, and were too engrossed to listen to any of the conversation between their mum and dad.

Once home they all helped to unload the car and put the stuff in the spare room for now. Tiff plated up the pizzas they had bought and they sat down in front of the television and watched yet another cartoon film about a princess. Soon it was bedtime for the girls. After a bubble bath, they went up to their bedrooms and chatted for some time before dropping off to sleep. Josh and Tiff cleared away the empty plates and sat in the kitchen having a cup of tea before Josh said, "Tiff, I think that detective sergeant we met today knows about the nude photos of you!"

Tiff looked a bit thoughtful at the revelation but said, "So what, its nothing to be ashamed of, and I got paid really well for posing for them, but I see what you mean; perhaps it would be best if we invite them both over to have a word. You're already meeting with them in the afternoon in an official capacity, so get them to come in the evening, it will give me time to get the originals out and we can take it from there."

Josh replied, "Is that the best way to deal with it love? I mean I'm not a prude but I'm not sure I want naked pictures of my wife all over the station!"

Tiff reassured him, "That won't happen Josh; we are going to disarm them both, okay?"

The Monday afternoon interview with the hacker was informative to say the least. Wootton showed Miss Blaise and a rather young fellow into the interview room, got them some tea and coffee and waited for Chavender to arrive. He finally arrived some twenty minutes later, and apologised for making them wait. He then had Wootton caution them both and asked if they wanted a lawyer present. He gave then ten minutes private discussion time. Outside the room and much to Wootton's surprise, Chavender asked him to bring Wendy over to meet with them at 6pm tonight.

Back inside Chavender asked if they wanted a lawyer and both said "no", he then asked the young man to outline the process that he used to hack the council's computer.

"Ah well, that's easy, because all computers are connected to the world wide web, you find the computer you want to hack by using special programmes to find the mother ship, so to speak, or by sending out viruses or even better still, something called a Trojan".

He talked rather excitedly about his expertise in hacking computers. He had first thought of sending an email to the Town

Council's office with a Trojan Horse in. He went on to say, "but the really good ones are the ones that build themselves, these are so called Frankenstein viruses and are small bits of information that come in on the tail end of safe downloads, in little bitty bytes. The antivirus software ignores because it doesn't recognise bits of programmes, or this programme, as a threat. Now, these build themselves up in stages in your start up software or programmes on your computer until all of a sudden it's there, no matter how many times you run your protective scans it won't be recognised as a threat, because it's attached itself to the core programming of the computer. Now, sometimes when you start up your computer and go to the programmes start up menu, you may see something, an odd or strange icon possibly, a bunch of grapes or something like it. Once you have it, anything you type, such as passwords or letters, can be remotely accessed by the mother computer, it is virtually untraceable. Once inside the host computer you can then find what you want very easily, passwords are not a problem and are quite easy to guess. I guess, take for instance Miss Blaise's computer, I reckon her password is something like 'Modesty' and some police computers have "nine nine nine" as a password, how silly is that! What you need is a password that is hard to hack, something personal, something I will not get in a million years of trying. Something like your favourite food when you were nine, but again if you have the wrong type of virus on your computer the moment you type in any password it will be sent back to the host computer and from there it's plain sailing. You can remotely access that computer if you want, transfer money, buy stuff, all quite legally because you are using all the right passwords, it doesn't recognise it's a strange computer or strange addresses. Take for instance, if you invent a programme that you attach to a bank's mainframe computer, telling it that at midnight, it has to transfer a single penny from everyone's bank account into a special account, then at midnight it will carry on doing it until someone notices it. In the meantime, you empty that account every day! Simple really. How many times do you query spending a penny? Not many I bet, but by then it's too late."

Wendy Blaise thought for just a second, damn, better think of a new password, he was too close to mine for my liking! Wootton who was taking notes, stopped the young lad every so often to clarify points, which gave Wendy a chance to study both men, she must admit she liked them both, but for different reasons.

Chavender she saw as much as a father figure, strong, kind, loving, in an authoritarian sort of way, someone who would not hesitate to put you over their knee. Woodley was the standard type male of the early twenty-first century, capable and virile, reasonably attractive but a bit dim towards female desires or needs, even though he thought he knew what she wanted, but could be trained very easily, like she had done in the three days since they started going out. He was putty in her hands, whereas Chavender would still resist her trying to change him until she gave up on him and they would live as happily ever after as one could in such a situation. From what she saw of him and his wife on Sunday, Chavender was not exactly under her thumb, he still showed an independent rebellious streak that his wife had yet not cured him of and probably would not want to, part of his authoritarian loving charm, along with his nose. It then dawned on her that she had no real hope of trying to peel him away from his wife; the ties that bind in this case were much too strong, in fact, four ply strong! She had been daydreaming for some time, when Chavender spoke to her.

"Miss Blaise...! Miss Blaise, you with us or with the Woolwich?"

She broke from her reverie, "Oh sorry must have drifted off," she said blushing, "are we done?"

"No, not quite, we just need to read through the statements, get them signed and you can be on your way. Thank you young man for your time. I guess I had better go and change my passwords now!"

When Wootton and Wendy Blaise arrived at Chavender Mansion that evening after work, the four off them sat in the kitchen, where they discussed the centre fold murder case. Chavender again claimed his wife's right to privacy and felt that what was said here was not to be repeated and private information only. Tiffany pulled out the A4 glossy photos of her and explained that afterwards, due to the lack of support from the top brass in the Metropolitan Police Force, she had had a terrible time adjusting back, especially after the metropolitan police tried to discipline her when the photos appeared in a popular men's magazine, after all she had signed a waiver and had been paid very handsomely to appear partly dressed in her uniform and it was mainly down to Josh that she managed to come through relatively okay. He had defended her at the cost of his own career in the tribunal that followed, supported her when she went a bit doolally with depression, and they held up promotion from him for years. It was only the fact that he applied for and got this position that he made DCI.

The phone rang and Chavender got up to answer it, he called for Wootton to come out and listen to the call on speaker phone. The call was about the ongoing investigation in to the Councillor's alleged fraudulent activities, leaving the girls alone in the kitchen. When the call was over, they both returned to the kitchen. After another half hour of chatting, they got up to go, at the front door they both said their goodbyes, Wootton and Wendy left.

At the door waving them goodbye, Tiff grabbed Josh's hand and whispered in his ear, "It'll be fine now, dear," kissing him on the cheek. "I had a private word with Miss Blaise; she now understands that you're off limits."

Chapter 14

At work the next day, after DIs Lister and Small arrived, Chavender explained to them what he wanted them to do, how it was to work and left them to it. He found Wootton and Carruthers in the canteen, got a coffee and sat down with them.

"Hello you two, nothing worse to do then?"

"Hello sir, no not really just going over those reports you asked Bill to compile for you, not much in them that sticks out as they say, but why are you so concerned about three accidental deaths?"

"Ah yes, Detective Sergeant, remember that first meeting we had. Well, something is well out of place about these cases that does not fit with the facts that we have. See the accidental gassing, the overdose all very plausible, in fact, so plausible as to be very, very ordinary, mundane even, that it's not a happenstance event, yes they seem to be such a mundane way to shuffle of this mortal coil, an everyday occurrence so to speak, not so far removed from reality that would make us immediately suspect foul play, see what I mean?"

"Yes I think so," said Wootton.

Chavender went on by saying, "What proof do we have? None! But we have three people dead, so we either accept the findings of the Coroner's Court or we have to find something that will link them to a murderer!"

Wootton butted in, "Which will be that leap of the imagination you spoke of sir."

"Yes it would be, Sergeant, yes, it would be!"

Chavender got up and, collecting two cups of coffee, he went to see how Lister and Small were getting on - *good name for a double act* thought Chavender - opening the door with his elbow he managed not to spill any coffee. Inside the two Detectives were having a breather away from the screens.

"Ah. Bless you sir! You're a lifesaver! Just what the doctor ordered."

"I thought you might need something to drink about now," Chavender said, handing each a cup of coffee. "How's it going?"

Small replied, "Slow sir, very slow, but so far nothing."

Lister said the same, but added, "I'm glad you thought up this method sir, I don't think my eyes could take an all day sitting, looking at the screens certainly gives the eyes a workout, strain wise, sir."

"Yes, I know," agreed Chavender, "I've started to wear reading glasses nowadays, sign of getting old I presume! Anyway give it another hour and come and see me, okay?"

With that, he turned and left them to it.

By the time he got back to his office, Molly-Fergus was waiting for him; he asked her to come in, and as they sat down he said, "Well, Molly-Fergus what can I do for you?"

"Nothing much sir!" she replied, "but when are we going to get our hands on that Schonebeck fellow?"

Chavender was thoughtful, "I was thinking of giving him another week to come back voluntarily; after that, I thought may be one of us will go and either pick him up, or interview him in Germany, we have his home town address. I'm just making contact with the local police chief and awaiting his reply. Don't worry, if any wrongdoing has happened, they won't get away with it. I suppose you're angling for that trip abroad then?"

"Well yes sir, I am, it would be a good chance to practice my German, sir."

Chavender looked at her sharply. "Yes well I would rather you spoke English, remember no mistakes, but I will consider your offer, Molly-Fergus, okay?"

"Thanks sir," she said, and got up and left.

Meeting the other two detectives outside, they exchanged pleasantries and went their separate ways.

Lister and Small stood outside Chavender's office and after knocking on his door, waited to be called in. They entered and he beckoned them to sit down, then de-briefed them for an hour or so, Thanking them he said he would see them in the morning for day two, they got up, saluted, and left just as his phone rang.

"Hello sir, Pearce speaking. Looks we have another unusual death, sir; it's at the library in Plympton sir, do you know it?"

"No I don't" said Chavender, "but I'll get Wootton to take me there. See you shortly, thanks, bye."

Calling in on the CID room, he found Wootton, and asked him to go with him to Plympton Library explaining that they had another suspicious death on their hands. In next to no time they were on their way.

When they arrived at the scene, DI Pearce came out to meet them.

"Hello sir, Wootton, not sure about this one, chap just died here in the library, no violence, nothing suspicious about it; he just pegged out sir, could be another one to add to the list, or not. It's got me thinking every death is suspicious now. The librarian saw and heard nothing, but when she came to close up at 3pm, and doing her walking round check, she came across this fellow sat in the reading room dead."

"What's the doctor's preliminary prognosis?" Chavender asked. "Does he have one yet? Perhaps we'd best have a look inside shall we? Has the body been identified and the next of kin notified yet?"

"According to the name on his driving licence, he was called Mr T. Jonas, and I've sent someone round to the next of kin and asked them to formally identify the deceased sir," Pearce replied.

They all entered the building and Pearce showed them the way to the reading room; on the way Chavender asked Wootton to find out from the doctor a cause of death, he would travel back with Pearce. Having a look posed no problem for them. Apart from the chair that had to be moved to recover the corpse, everything was as it was, the paper opened on the sports pages, and nothing else disturbed, apparently, according to the librarian, he would normally come in three times a week, stay in the reading room till closing time and leave when asked. He was no trouble at all, poor man, she added, he was always interested in the local gossip, telling her such things he had read in the papers, about the merger of the councils, about how long some list may well become, about how he remembered his youth, but forgot such silly things like what he had for breakfast that day, or even if he ate breakfast! He would also speak about the depressing news of election rigging, genocide in Africa, fundamentalist groups springing up at the drop of a hat. She thought he was probably a very, very lonely guy. It was all very mundane interesting stuff and yet it seemed like another mysterious murder! But how?

"Do we have the contents of his pockets, Pearce?"

"Yes sir - one brown leather wallet containing; two credit cards, driving licence, twenty pounds in notes, nine pounds mixed loose change, a newspaper cutting about the last local election, one open packet of twenty cigarettes, three quarters smoked - five and a half left, one unopened packet of twenty, one gold plated lighter, one Fusee pocket watch and Albert with charm, betting slips, pocket handkerchief and a comb sir."

"Heavy smoker then by the look of things, maybe a forty a day man," said Chavender. "Anyway not much more we can do here," and they left the library.

Outside Chavender saw Miss Blaise walking up to them. He turned and asked Pearce if he could deal with her.

"Hello Josh, how are things? I hear there's been a death in the library, perhaps you could fill me in?"

"Hello Miss Blaise, um... Detective Inspector Pearce will give you all the information you need; thanks, Miss Blaise."

She sighed, visibly disappointed, perhaps she was not as over her crush yet as she thought!

"Right Miss Blaise, we were called at 15.05hrs today by the librarian here at the Rosemore Public Library, who reported a dead person on the premises; we arrived and ascertained the details of the deceased, called for his doctor and notified next of kin, in this case his wife. The body has been taken to the hospital were we expect the post mortem to reveal the circumstances of his death, and that, at this present moment in time, is all we have to say on the subject, thank you very much."

Miss Blaise turned to Chavender, "Anything to add Josh?"

He shook his head and turned to Pearce, "Best get us back to HQ Pearce."

He had tried to be as polite as he normally would have been, but she noticed an edge to his voice, and they turned and left her standing there openmouthed.

Chavender could just picture the headline in the morning paper, 'Real Life Murder Mystery, body found in local library, Agatha Christie murder mystery acted out in real life in Plympton'. Except that in murder mysteries the body in the library was murdered, but this one could well be of natural causes!

On the way back, they talked about the fraud case, just to clear their minds, and by the time they got back, Wootton was not far behind. They all went to Chavender's office and Wootton gave the preliminary doctor's report.

"Death was caused by a coronary embolism; this caused a massive heart attack and he died within seconds, leaving no outward visible signs that he had had a heart attack. The doctors is pretty sure of this, so no foul play there then!"

"Well, thanks for your time, and I will see you in the morning; hopefully the autopsy will provide us with more answers, goodbye."

Chavender walked with them to car park and overheard Wootton say to Pearce, "Got a date with that reporter woman Wendy Blaise tonight; why don't you and your wife come along, we could go out for a meal or something?"

"Thanks for the offer but I had best check in with my wife first; perhaps some other time. Thanks all the same, see you in the morning. Bye."

"Bye," said Wootton.

"Yes, see you in the morning,"

Parting, they went their separate ways. Chavender's drive home was becoming routine, and in thirty minutes he was stepping over the threshold of his door and was being greeted by his octopi girls in the hallway.

Chapter 15

That morning, Chavender called on Harrier and Molly-Fergus to review the files that Small and Lister had found to be interesting, most were dismissed, but those that interested them they highlighted again for further review. The phone logs and bank statements he gave to Carruthers and Wootton to look through, and asked them to report if they found anything of significance or highlight something that would require further investigation. He did very little in these early stages of the investigation, preferring to have a blank mind when they presented him with, if any, evidence. He did not want to prejudge or draw conclusions that would affect the outcome of the final report, and found that in past cases it always helped. He and Pearce would review the case with the team on a daily basis; sometimes pointing a way ahead for them to look. It would be a slow investigation, something like watching cars rust or paint dry, but it would not help the case if they rushed and missed the smallest hint of a clue, also not having the vast resources of a large police force at hand meant that they still had the normal everyday crimes to investigate, so splitting the time was the best way forward.

On his way to the canteen, he bumped into Carr. "Hello Inspector Carr."

"Hello sir."

"Going to the canteen?"

"Yes."

"Coffee?"

"Thanks sir."

Chavender purchased two coffees and ordered four more to go when he left, he sat down with Carr. Drinking their coffees, Carr thanked him for letting him and his uniform chaps help on the case and said it was a really big boost to them.

"That's okay, Carr, it helped us out a great deal, but I still may need your help. I could do with a final overview of the files that we suspect, and I may need the phone logs checking again, we are not exactly rushed off our feet here but I can't let this case interfere with our on ongoing investigations. So I may need to call on some of your chaps to help out if I may?"

"That'll be fine sir, but give me a day's notice if you could, being undermanned ourselves really doesn't help us, recruitment is down, people are just not interested in joining nowadays, even in the Specials the numbers have dropped, the only number that has risen is the PCSOs."

"Yes, um, well the less said about that the better; if we can clothe, train, and support them, then why can't we employ full time police officers? I know they do valuable work, but I can't help feeling we are getting some stick from Westminster on this. It's a numbers game, people hanker for the old days, when they thought there was a bobby on every street corner. Well, that never happened, ever! We are less noticeable today because we have to use cars in which to patrol. High streets can have a beat bobby or two, just like we had as nippers, that's where we saw our coppers mostly, high streets and markets. That's not a problem, but you can't expect a bobby to walk around some of these housing estates that they're building today, it would take hours, and what if they are at the wrong end when a crime takes place? Just asking for trouble that is. No, we have to use all the available technology and manpower to our advantage, CCTV, helicopters, squad cars and vans, motor and pedal bikes, computers, PCSOs, electronic tagging, and ASBOs, it all helps to keep crime down and our streets safer, but you can bet your bottom dollar that those human rights activists will cry '1984'. What doesn't help is Westminster saying we're not solving enough crime, after all if we solve all the crimes who will make the most out if it? Not the general public; granted streets will be safer, and certainly not the hard working police forces of this country, but that shower in Westminster will get all the credit, they will laud it over everyone by saying that their crime policies are working - poppycock! Still, enough of my rant, Carr, I best be getting back with the coffee for the other four."

He got up, collected his coffee and left. Carr sat and pondered what Chavender had said; most he thought was true but a lot was letting off steam, he felt. He finished his coffee, and felt he had a necessity to do something and decided to walk the high street; he collected a sergeant along the way.

Back with the others, Chavender gave them the coffee and told them to wrap it up in about an hour's time, he would be in his office. He then looked in on the two Detective sergeants and told them the same thing. Passing them the coffee, he had a quick look see how they had got on; it was always hard in these cases to know exactly how far along you were until the very end, but it looked like progress was being made. In his office he telephoned Pearce.

"Hello, Pearce, any news yet about the body in the library? No? Then best come over if you can for the review of the fraud case so far, I expect it to be in an hour's time, no rush, see you then."

Chavender stood by the windows letting the early spring sun warm his face, it was an habit of his to place his face in line with the sun whenever he could, and as a young constable he always walked the sunny side of the street if possible; he liked the sun but not holidays! He looked but, for once, did not observe what was going on. On the industrial estate the daily grind went on as normal, lorries reversing, being unloaded and loaded up again; people doing whatever they had to do. Slowly his mind drifted back to his childhood, when his father used to take him and his brother to the old Covent Garden Fruit and Veg market every Saturday morning, a round trip of some ten odd miles in all weathers to get the fruit and vegetables for the next week. In those days, with no Sunday trading, if the costermongers didn't sell it all, or something was just on the turn in a bag or tray, it would be thrown away, the best time was around midday, when trading was nearly over, many a time they would walk home with bags of spuds, carrots or greens, the hustle and bustle of the crowds, the noise of steel cartwheels on the cobbled road and the shouts of the barrow boys warning people to get out the way as they pushed the overloaded barrows down the road. The picture was so vivid in his mind's eye that he felt like a little boy, ten years old again. He could almost smell the sweaty earthy smell of that hundredweight bag of spuds they used to take turns in carrying home, when, on the odd occasion, they managed to, as they say, 'bag' one! A knock at the door broke him out of his reverie.

"Come in," called Chavender and all five detectives trooped in.

As they all sat down in a semi-circle, they started discussing the findings so far. Molly-Fergus went first, certainly email contact had been made and maintained for some time going back to the formation of eco developments, but, so far, nothing to indicate any wrong doing. Harrier concurred. It then fell on the two Detective Sergeants; again, plenty of contact via both mobile and landline phones between all of them, but unless they could get hold of the transcripts of the calls, they could have been talking about the weather for all they knew! Chavender thanked them and asked them to come back on Friday after Lister and Small did a stint on Thursday for him. He asked Pearce to stay on and they reviewed the progress of the case so far. Chavender mentioned about Molly-Fergus wanting to go to Germany to interview Schonebeck, which he had no objections to, but he hoped he would return here soon. "How's the Library case coming along Pearce?"

"Another impasse I'm afraid to say, I received the coroner's report just before I left, heart attack caused by coronary embolism, a dead end street on that one sir!"

"So, to sum up, in both cases we suspect, or have suspicions of foul play, but we have no hard evidence of any wrongdoing! So once again it's a waiting game; sooner or later something will jibe, and it will become clear for a brief instance and we must be ready for that."

Chavender called it a day and went home, little knowing that later that night, in a quiet street in Plympton, a man would leave the Hornbeam's house at about 11.30 pm, quietly, by putting the key in the Yale lock and turning so as to pull in the latch, close the door and then lock it, leaving behind two dead people. Keeping to the shadows he walked down the street making no sound, 'til, after a half mile or so, he found his car and, opening a small can of beer, which he drank, throwing the can in the road, drove home. The bodies were discovered the next day by the daughter phoning her mum and getting no reply, so she went round to her parent's house to find out why her mum did not meet her as arranged. Opening the door and calling out, "Mum, where are you?" she entered the front room and saw her father, mouth open, eyes staring blankly, head back on the settee, dead. She turned and agonisingly screamed, big salty tears beginning to well up in her eyes, "Dad... Daddy" and then hurriedly, "MUM... MUMMY... WHERE ARE YOU MUMMY?" and frantically searched the rest of the house, calling all the time, becoming more and more hysterical in her shouts as room after room was empty, till she found her mum face down on the bed, dead. Screaming loudly, she rushed over to her mum, shook her and screamed, "MUM... Mum... MUM! Are you all right? Mummy... Oh my God... MUUUUUM!" Panic-stricken, she turned her mum over, shaking her, trying to rouse her but she could not get any response. She left the room more in a daze, terror setting in, shakily, on jelly like legs, practically falling back down the stairs; she rushed back into the front room, tried to rouse her father, but could not, then screaming frenziedly with tears streaming down her face, arms flailing wildly in the air. She rushed out to find the immediate neighbours of the semi-detached house coming out, wondering what all the screaming was about. Mrs Johnson managed to grab her as she rushed down the path to her car and took her into their house while Mr Johnson, getting no coherent response from her, carefully entered the house and took a quick look in the front room. Seeing his friend and neighbour dead on the settee he left, and from his house, first called the police then an ambulance. Mrs Johnson tried to calm the grief stricken daughter, who by now was racked with sobs and trembling, crying, "Mummy" and then "Daddy" alternately over and over again, rocking backwards and forwards, pulling at her hair in despair.

She asked her husband, "How long before they get here? What has happened dear?"

"About ten minutes; its Fred and Beryl, they're both dead I think," he replied with a slight tremor in his voice.

At Plympton police station the call was passed on to DI Pearce, who, after calling Chavender and scenes of crime people, left for the crime scene with DS Wilson. The ambulance sirens echoing in the distance became clearer as they got closer, until finally they burst on the scene with a rather obtrusive air about them, declaring emphatically, "We're on our way, make way, its urgent!" Blue flashing lights reflecting in the windows as, at first, the neighbours' curtains started to twitch and then open curiosity as they came out and stood in little groups asking each other, "What's going on?" Practically at the same time two police cars arrived, adding to the general confusion of the road and as they stopped, the sirens quietened to a silence, leaving only the blue lights intruding on the scene. The police cars contained Pearce and Wilson in one and two uniform constables in the other; very soon they were joined by the green light of a doctor's car.

Chapter 16

Entering the house with a doctor and paramedic, Pearce's immediate reaction was to quickly scan the scene, noting anything unusual but nothing could be more normal than what he saw, apart, that is, from the dead body. The doctor quickly ascertained that the man was really dead and then moved on through to look at the wife. He saw Pearce whom he knew.

"Well Inspector, two bodies, I will have them taken to the morgue for an autopsy, but the wife died from suffocation; the outward signs are quite clear, impression in the pillow, bloodshot eyes, but an autopsy will make certain, but as to how and why, I'm not sure. Not sure what the husband died of yet, but it looks a peaceful kind of death."

The doctor turned to one of the ambulance men and told them to "liaise with the Inspector," for now he would go next door and see to the living, seeing that he could be of no further help here. Next door the daughter had recovered somewhat, but was still in a terrible state; shock was setting in, so on the doctor's advice she was sent to hospital, the paramedic helped her into the wheeled chair they used for ambulatory cases, and carefully took her through the house to the waiting ambulance. He collected his colleague and they sped off, sirens and lights ablaze, into the traffic, defying anyone to impede their progress. The doctor went back and, saying goodbye to Pearce, he too left. The neighbours began to go back indoors and soon the only telltale sign something was amiss was the two police cars. Pearce waited for Scenes of Crime to appear, as well as Chavender, knowing full well what the DCI's first question would be. Before anyone else from the police could arrive, Miss Blaise and a photographer arrived on the scene. Pearce rolled his eyes and strode over to her, he told her that she had missed the initial event, but he confirmed two bodies.

"At the moment foul play is suspected, the DCI is on his way, and it is not connected to the Library Body Case as far as we can tell at this moment in time; thank you Miss Blaise."

And thinking, *I'd better warn Beaky before he arrives here*!

Chavender arrived on the scene at the same time as the forensics team; he allowed them to get on without silly question or interference from him, and he chatted with DI Pearce for a while till Miss Blaise came over.

"Hello Josh, anything to add?" she asked surprisingly calm, for she still felt a certain something for ol' Beaky as she now called him privately in her head.

He replied, "I'm sure DI Pearce has told you what he can, but at the moment we have to treat these deaths as suspicious until proven otherwise. I can confirm, however, we will be removing two bodies, a husband and wife, a Mr Frederick Hornbeam and his wife a Mrs Beryl Hornbeam, the daughter who found them is presently in hospital being treated for shock. We are not sure about the time of death or what they died of yet; thank you Miss Blaise."

With that he turned and went back to speak to Pearce behind the police tape.

At that moment a private ambulance turned up and removed the two bodies; the forensics team left the scene soon after and then it was the detectives' turn to have a good look round.

The house was a typical fifties built semi-detached, with a long front garden and drive leading to a modern plastic porch covered entrance way, put in the same time as it was double glazed by the look of the style. On entering there was a small square hallway with stairs to the left hand side and two doors at right angles to each other, the one straight ahead led to the front room, and the side one led to the open plan dining room and kitchen; this opened on to the garden. The upstairs from a short oblong landing, were four doors; these let you into three bedrooms and the bathroom, two double bedrooms and a single bedroom, a double and single overlooked the garden whilst the other double shared the frontage with the bathroom. Looking into the front room, they could see nothing out of place, no struggle, nothing knocked over, all neat and tidy as it should be. In the kitchen the washing up from yesterday of plates, cups and saucers had been left to dry on the rack but not put away, upstairs it was the same again all neat and tidy no visible signs of disturbance as one would expect in a burglary. In the main bedroom, on the pillow a faint off-colour depression where the wife's face had lain overnight, but nothing screamed foul play to them. Back downstairs, Chavender looked out into the garden, tried the back door but it was locked, looking through the glass panel he could see a neat garden with a shed, small vegetable plot and glasshouse, all that one would expect to see in such a respectable middle class neighbourhood such as this.

Not learning much from his inspection, he and Pearce went next door to talk to the Johnson's. On his way out, he detailed one of the constables to start house to house enquiries, five houses either side would do for now, if they got no information from the first lot then extend down to eight either side. Johnny Johnson and his wife Edith made the two police officers a cup of tea and sat them down at the kitchen table; it was Pearce who asked the questions whilst Chavender listened on. The Johnsons' statement was precise; they heard screaming at about 11.30am, coming out to see what the commotion was about, they saw Judith, the daughter, come screaming down the path, they managed to catch her and Mrs Johnson took her indoors while Mr Johnson went into the front room and saw Fred dead. He left immediately and called the police and ambulance in that order, they did not hear or see anything unusual prior to this. He had seen Fred and spoken to him over the low fence they shared at about 1pm yesterday; they then went out at 2pm to go and babysit for their daughter, who lived in Southampton, overnight, and came back at 10am. That is all they could tell them. The Hornbeams were normally a very happy couple, always pleasant to talk to, and they had helped each other out when or if needed. Thanking them for the tea and their time, Chavender and Pearce left. Before going back to headquarters, he asked Pearce to keep him informed, but as it would be a couple of days before any reports came back, to keep up with the door to door enquiries and doing background checks.

Outside, Miss Blaise was talking to neighbours, when spotting him she walked over to him just as he was getting in his car, "Anything to add, Josh?" she said, kneeling down at the car's door so her face was level with his.

"No, nothing really Miss Blaise; I do wish you would stop calling me Josh in front of my men, it doesn't help you, you know!" he said politely, but stressing the Miss.

"Oh I know that Josh, but you're such a handsome devil I can't help it," she said smiling at him. "Anyways, I've now got Woodley."

Getting up she lent in and quickly kissed him on the cheek and said "bye." Chavender was dumbstruck by her impudence, blushed a little, and, like a little boy being kissed by his aunt for the very first time, wiped the offending area with his hand several times as if trying to wipe the contamination from his face. Luckily for him, no one saw what had happened. On his drive back to headquarters, he kept looking in the mirror just to check he had removed all traces of lipstick.

Back at headquarters, he first went to the gents to wash his face vigorously, and then he checked in on the fraud teams to see how they were getting on, asking them to be ready for a debriefing with him in the hour. Again then, same as yesterday, some links but at the moment nothing that says or screams fraud at you. Thanking them for their efforts, he then told them about the suspicious deaths that had been reported. As they left, Chavender started to review the files that they highlighted for him. He found it hard to concentrate, the time passed slowly, until finally 6pm came around and he left for the day.

Chapter 17

That day at work, Chavender couldn't get 'with it'; everything seemed to be a chore for him, from setting the Detectives to work on the fraud case to getting in touch with DI Pearce. Something was on his mind, troubling him, something personal, but he couldn't quite put his finger on it, it was nagging him deep down. He sighed. *Ah well, perhaps in time it'll come to me*, he thought. He then phoned Pearce again asking whether the door to door enquiries had produced anything yet, and how the daughter was. Perhaps she was up to being interviewed yet? If so he would like to sit in. He would come across now if Pearce could arrange for her to be picked up and brought to the station in an hour's time, if that was okay? Pearce could see nothing wrong in that, after all Chavender was the boss. He managed to get two constables to go and collect the daughter from her home. The interview with both of them was just a formality really; they had most of the timings from the neighbour, they just wanted to clear a few little details up; like when was the last time she spoke to her parents, was anything amiss when she entered, did she touch or move anything apart from her mother, was the front door locked and did she know the state of her mother's mind? Were they in the habit of taking sleeping pills?

She answered these questions, hesitantly, signs of crying long and hard showed in her eyes and sadness etched in her face as she replied, "I spoke to my mum the morning before to arrange for us to both go into town and get something for Dad's birthday. We agreed to meet in town at 10am. I got a little bit anxious by 10.30

when she didn't show up, for it wasn't like her to be late. I tried ringing several times and got no reply so I decided to go round. I left town at 11, just in case the bus was delayed and got to my mum's at about 11.25. I put my key in the front door lock and opened the door. I went into the sitting room first and that's when I found my dad, there, dead in the front room, on the settee, and I started to look for my mum and I found my mum on the bed, face down in the pillow, arms bent and palms flat either side of the pillow, as if she was going to push her face up at any moment, you know like when soldiers surrender."

She showed them what she meant, arms level with the shoulders, elbows bent, and palms open and face outwards. She went on, starting to cry a little, dabbing her eyes with a handkerchief.

"Oh it was shocking, such a sight; yes it shook me up all right, I guess I panicked, I mean *really* panicked. I've never seen a dead body before, only on TV, not in real life, and the shock that it was my parents, who... who were the dead bodies really threw my mind and I ran out of the house and into next door. The rest you know."

As far as she was aware her mum was sane; they both were. Sleeping pills?

"No," she said, "Not that I'm aware of. I can't really be sure, I've not lived at home for some ten odd years now, and you know how older people are; they don't like to admit they have to take sleeping pills, or any other such pills like painkillers, you know, in case you worry about them, even though that would be the least of your worries. Why?"

Chavender replied, "Well in such cases of unexpected death, we have to ask all sorts of strange questions. We found an empty packet of sleeping pills in the house; the questions may seem strange to you but it gives us a fuller picture into the state of their minds." He quickly added, "You know if they were happy or depressed; it will have a bearing in how we proceed with the investigation!"

"Oh," was her noncommittal reply.

She had made it through the interview barely without crying that much, but the emotional struggle of the last few days was clearly etched on her face.

"Well, thanks for your time, Mrs Julians, and I am sorry for your loss," said Pearce sympathetically, placing an arm on her shoulder. "Please take your time to compose yourself."

He added that when she was ready, he would get the constables to take her back home. He led her to the front waiting room, sitting her down with a cup of tea and getting the lift organised for her back home with the duty sergeant. He went back into the interview room where Chavender was waiting, sitting down he looked at his boss.

"Well," said Chavender, "that didn't help at all; nothing from the door to door enquiries, nothing suspicious at all, or nothing seen by the neighbours, nothing about the sleeping pills, all we know extra now is that the front door was locked. Insane people do not plant their faces in a pillow and suffocate themselves, the fight for life takes over and that both were alive the previous day in the morning. Until we get some reports or indications, we can not make any decisions on this case."

"No Sir, we can't, but my gut instinct is that it is connected to the other deaths we've had - but what or how eludes me at the moment."

"I'm inclined to agree Pearce, but what we need is something, a little tiny clue to help us, a creative spark to help leap that chasm of improbability to the probable, and at this moment those previous deaths are accidental, not connected at all, but this case smells like murder to me, but we can't prove it yet!"

With that, he bid Pearce goodbye and headed back to headquarters.

Returning to headquarters slowly by driving along country lanes and bypasses gave Chavender time to think, but nothing immediately sprang to mind; still he had the fraud debrief yet to come, so perhaps something would come to light; after all he had put all four of them on it today, so maybe progress would be made! He called them all in at 2.30pm and asked them what they had so far.

Molly-Fergus spoke for them all, saying, "Still not a lot really, some obvious tie-ins with the emails, but no real proof again. Looks like they were loath to put any of it in writing. All we can prove at the moment is that they all appear to have a part share in Eco-Developments Ltd.; this the parent company was formed when the other companies closed down. All of them have exactly a one-fifth ownership, each having put in, or promised, half a million pounds in stake money. It looks like they were about to buy something, but what is not specified! We have only done about a quarter of all the files so far and have yet to get a look at the planning files from the council - that may tell us more?"

Chavender look puzzled. "A half million pounds each? How did the councillors get or have that sort of money? Perhaps a backhander?"

Molly-Fergus replied, "No sir, the two councillors are part of the deal, but it's more like on a promissory note with them, they have, has far as we can tell, have both together only put in about £400,000, so they are well short of the half million pounds that the others have stumped up."

"Um, well that's a start," said Chavender. "Perhaps they've made the rest up by giving tip offs to the developers, that's what we need to find, lady and gentlemen; that will be the key to the case, I feel; but it will be hard linking them to any wrongdoing if all we can prove is email contact, or the occasional meet for a meal. What we really need is for one of them to have made a slip, a miscalculation, an opening of some sort and then we may have a chance! One last thing - Mr Schonebeck, he has not bothered to return as of yet, so, if he is not back by Wednesday next, I will arrange with the German Police to have Molly-Fergus go and speak with him in Germany. I have passed on a request to present himself here, purely voluntary, to assist with our enquiries by 10am Thursday. If he doesn't, then you're to go over on Friday next, so long as your back to work Monday morning, any time after the interview is yours."

Molly-Fergus nodded in agreement. *Great,* she thought, *a weekend away with my boyfriend, get back for Sunday night and back on Monday morning.*

"Anything else? If not, have a good weekend and I'll see you all Monday morning bright eyed and bushy tailed, fit for another week." Thanking them, Chavender then dismissed them all for the weekend and went wearily home himself.

That Saturday morning, after a good cooked breakfast, Josh was in the spare bedroom ready to start the redecorating. He had a CD player and some of his favourite music; he was ready to go on the offensive, ready to remove the layers of old paint and wallpaper. It always fascinated him that, after the seventies and eighties' paint and woodchip boom, patterned wallpaper was making a comeback, along with the dado border, styles go and come and come around again. Now here he was removing the old woodchip and paint, so he could paint and paper, but it was just what he needed. An NTR job, removing the layers of wallpaper, the steaming and stripping of the wallpaper, could only be carried out with any of the heavy classics. Best of all was Wagner's 'The Ride of The Valkyries' followed by Offenbach's 'Orpheus in the Underworld Overture' and many such others, they all had the same theme, a good rhythm, some fast and furious sections and even better slower sections to have a rest in, in-fact as he was want to put it, "music to strip by". He could switch his brain off and work as an automaton, so long as he didn't put too many dents in the plaster that needed to be filled later it would be okay. Tiff every so often would send one of the girls in with a pint cup of tea, hot and strong, sometimes with biscuits, and to get a progress report. The girls would come out soon afterwards screaming with bits of damp wallpaper stuck to their heads and clothes, as Josh made like some mythical steam breathing monster. By early evening, all the wallpaper was off the walls and in black sacks, ready for a tip run. The old faded carpet was cut up, rolled and tied up. Josh cleaned the last remnants of stubborn wallpaper and decided to call it a day, even though it had been a long day, it was worth it, for Josh had managed to start to clear his mind of clutter. Another day of NTR and his brain would be freely thinking again! After cleaning himself and changing, he went and sat in the armchair; a fatal mistake for within minutes he had dropped off, being woken by Tiff an hour or so later to say tea was ready. Sunday, apart from the tip run, found Josh sanding all the wood work and using sugar soap to clean the last bits of grime and dust off, and he was finished. Stage one complete, he reported, when he sat down for a cup of tea. He had managed to clear his mind, put cases in to some sort of perspective and logical order for ongoing investigating, and decided that after the Chief Constable's senior officers' meeting in the morning, he would go and see Pearce.

Chapter 18

After Chavender appraised the senior officers of the County
Constabulary on how progress was going, and looking in on the
fraud teams, he called Pearce and informed him he would be with
him within the hour, and asked if there any news or reports yet.
Receiving a negative answer, he set off for Plympton. At
Plympton Police station he bumped into Sergeant Jenkins.

"Hello sergeant, how's your wife and daughters?"

"Fine sir," he replied.

"That's good, mine are well also, but the wife has me
decorating the spare room, spent all weekend on it, good job
really as it helped clear my mind! Still I'm here to see DI Pearce.
Let him know I'm on my way up, will you sergeant? - thanks."

Chavender found Pearce looking at the photographs taken at
the scene of the double - what? murder? - placing them in some
sort of order that made sense. Chavender joined him and took a
turn at looking at each photograph as Pearce finished with it.

"Nothing leaps out does it, sir? All looks pretty normal as any
day would look. Place tidy, washing up done, cups, saucers and
plates, it probably would have been put away if they had not died
so suddenly, really nothing out of place; well, nothing that sticks
out."

They looked for about half an hour when Chavender asked if
they could go and see the Scene of Crimes Officer, see what he
could add. They walked the short distance of the corridor to his
office, knocking, they entered.

"Hello Arthur," said Pearce, "this is DCI Chavender, our boss; got anything for us yet?"

Arthur replied, "Not really Pearce, old chap! Sir, just nothing of a muchness you know, we've not found any strange finger prints anywhere or fibres that don't tie in with what's already in the house. No strange objects and no forced entry on any door or window, in fact as a crime scene it's barren in its ordinariness, but then by its very barren nature it could prove it has been tampered with!"

"Oh," said Chavender, "the lack of evidence is evidence in itself of wrongdoing - is that it?"

"Smart chappie, you have for a boss there Pearce, not many would have picked that up so quick; last bloke you had was as dim as a torch with a flat battery. But yes that's the point of it, the perpetrator had time to clear up, if indeed it was foul play and indeed if there was a perpetrator. Still don't know cause of death yet?"

Pearce answered, "No we are still waiting for the autopsy report to come in."

"Well as I say, depending on the findings, the facts I have at the moment can be made to fit either scenario! Its not that clear cut at all, either the chappie who did it is very clever, or there was no chappie!"

"Damn it!" blasted Pearce, "another unsolved case, I can do without that, there must be something so trivial, overlooked by either us or the perpetrator that it is staring us in the face?"

"Well, whatever it is," said Chavender, "will have to wait, perhaps if we went to the coroners in the morning, he may help us? Arthur, thanks for your time, and you will let us know when your findings are complete? Bye for now."

"Goodbye you two."

With that, they left. Chavender said to Pearce, "I'll come back in the morning, hopefully by then we'll have something from the coroner to work on. I'll see you about 10ish. Okay, Pearce!"

"That'll be fine sir, I'm going to go round once more to 140 Mulberry Road, just for a final look over, then off home. I'm heading out with Wootton and his girlfriend Wendy Blaise for a meal; she knows my wife from her university days!"

Chavender looking quizzical, remarked for him to be on his guard in case she tried to wheedle something out of him.

"No, don't worry sir, I won't let anything slip. When I asked my wife the other day about going out with Miss Blaise and DS Wootton, she remarked about it then." Chavender popped in to see Chief Inspector Sword to say goodbye and left for headquarters.

When he arrived back at headquarters he went straight to his office; from here he called the fraud investigative team in for a debrief. Small and Lister entered, but the look on their faces said it all, another session drawn a blank. Chavender thanked them and asked if they could return on Wednesday; they nodded approval and, leaving the cross-referenced list on his desk, got up and left. He collected the lists and read through them, noting that Councillor Melbourne's name was the dominant one, it came up twice as many as did Councillor Walker's name, perhaps he thought if he concentrated on him, he would prove to be the opening that they required, but they still needed to check the rest of the discs first, perhaps by the end of the week - yes that would be best. Now, where was Carruther's report into the recent crime figures? Finding them he looked over them again; pulling one page out from the rest, he got up and went to see if Carruthers was in. Entering the CD room, he could only see a detective constable; he quickly scribbled a note and left it with the file in the intray. Saying "goodnight" to the young officer, he left and went home.

The next morning Chavender was all action. He met with Carruthers and saw that he got the list and instructions, requesting it to be completed at the earliest possible moment. He wanted a full list so suggested he drive to both police sub divisions to get the details.

"I want times as near as possible and dates okay? Thanks." Leaving him, he went to see Harrier and Molly-Fergus and indicated that Melbourne was a name that may crop up more often than not, but don't overlook Walker, or the developers, to Molly-Fergus he told her that the German police had replied "that they had passed his message on". Having set the troops in action he drove over to Plympton, collected Pearce and headed for the coroner's office.

By 11a.m., they were sat in the Coroner's office waiting to see Dr Thomasson, the coroner. His secretarial assistant provided them with coffee and told them that he would be in shortly. Chavender had never quite forgotten his first experience of seeing a body dissected, as part of his training as a police cadet, the entire class had to go and see one being performed. It fair turned his stomach, especially that first long cut from the groin area to the throat, opening up the entire chest cavity, then the removal of various bits and bobs for analysis as he remembered. A shiver ran down his spine and his hand jerking in spasm nearly spilt his coffee.

"You all right sir?" Pearce said. He replied, "Yes, Pearce, someone just walked over my grave, that's all!"

At that moment the coroner walked in and they started to get up; the coroner said, "No... No please don't get up, finish your coffee first." He walked round his desk and sat down. "Now what can I do for you fellows?"

"It's the Hornbeam case sir, have you any news for us?" asked Chavender.

"Yes I suppose I have; let's start with the easy one first. Mrs Beryl Hornbeam died of suffocation and it's entirely possible that she did it deliberately - suicide in other words. There was no sign of a struggle, no bruising of the throat or any signs of trauma - ie a blow to the head; it seems she may have taken the same sleeping pills as her husband then placed her face into the pillow; she did this when she was sufficiently drowsy enough not to have attempted to save herself and slowly she suffocated. The husband, Mr Frederick Hornbeam, I suspect was given enough sleeping pills to have killed him; it looks like his heart stopped, just stopped working; they both died peacefully, not knowing, painless and peaceful. We are examining the stomach contents to find the drug in question that the sleeping pill contained, and I would put time of death at about 4.30 for him and a hour or so later for her. The packet that the sleeping pills came in were not prescribed by their doctor, I checked on that for you, so I can only assume they were bought over the internet. Damn dangerous way to buy sleeping pills if you ask me, no telling what you're buying, the pharmacy abroad probably don't care about exact quantities of, or how well mixed, all depending on how cheap you can get them for, pay for what you get I suppose! Anyways, back to the Hornbeams; I'm fairly certain he died of an overdose, not sure how many were administered, probably with a cup of coffee or tea. I'm checking in the digestive tract and stomach so an exact dose I can't quantify yet, but enough to kill, that is certain; maybe as little as two but could be up to five or six. She on the other hand took three, which would have made her extremely dopey, enough to paralyse the body's muscles but not the action of breathing, enough, probably, to slow the breathing rate down somewhat, hence face down in to a pillow; she simply suffocated, all the signs and symptoms are correct - no foul play with her or him; a probable scenario is, she could have killed him and then herself in some form of fit or rage, it would be hard to administer the drugs in sufficient quantity to kill by a person unknown to them! My educated guess for the drug in the pills would be Amitriptyline, which is a powerful sedative type drug found sometimes in sleeping pills. The test should be back in a day or so, and when it does it will probably confirm what I've said to you. Can I ask a you question now please?"

"By all means," Chavender replied.

"Were there any signs of a disturbance in the house; you know a break in or broken crockery as if there had been a fight?"

"No, Nothing like that, it would appear that the crime scene may have been cleaned up afterwards or not as the case may be; on your current verdict, and our physical evidence, it would give the appearance that she murdered him, she then committed suicide!" replied Pearce.

"You know," continued Pearce, "we either have a very clever murderer on our patch, or a series of very remarkable coincidences, that have now left five, possibly six people dead in a few short weeks! I don't buy into that theory at all - no my gut feeling is murder - but as of yet I can't prove that anyone has actually died of anything but, or by, natural or suicidal causes!"

"Um, I see your predicament young fellow, but I can't help you, you know, if the evidence points me towards, and I say strongly to these conclusions, I have to go with that, unless you can prove to me otherwise that is; I will be releasing the bodies in the morning. I have kept certain samples back just in case you may find your mythical murderer for further analysis, but at the moment my findings are as I indicated to you; she murdered him, she then committed suicide, whilst the state of her mind was unbalanced; those are the conclusions as presented to me by the facts. Thank you"

On their way back, Pearce exclaimed, "That's a crock of crap! Sir, I don't buy into his cause of death theory, no, not by a long chalk; something is not sitting right. Five maybe six people dead, since you've been our boss."

Chavender looked indirectly at Pearce. "You're not suggesting that I'm the murderer, are you Pearce?", rather tongue in cheek.

"No sir, nothing like that; after all your alibi is as watertight as the Titanic or what one could hope for." Pearce carried on his theme of baiting his boss. "You have several high ranking police officers who can vouch for your presence at any given time, and a very beautiful wife and four lovely girls for when you're not at work, sir."

Chavender half rose to the bait, but stopped in his tracks, and said instead, "Remember the Titanic sunk on its maiden voyage. Oh by the way, how was it when you went out with Miss Blaise?"

"Oh absolutely fine sir, my wife and Wendy almost hogged the whole night reminiscing about their Uni days. Wootton and I felt left out, sort of neglected, but it gave us time to talk; he certainly is smitten by her, but I'm not sure of her yet, nor is my wife. I hope she's not using Wootton sir, you know in a journalistic sense to get at someone, you know what I mean, sir."

"Yes I do," came back the short reply.

Back at headquarters, they both made for the fraud room. Pearce went and told them to shut it down for the day whilst he went and got some coffees; they all assembled in his room sitting down in a now familiar semicircle. They each in turn reported on what they found.

"So far not that much, but one of the developing companies did make a killing when it bought some six acres of council land to build a new estate on. It seems at auction they were the highest bidder, but it sold for well under the market value, this was about three years ago; that may well be worth looking into. We are about three quarters of the way through and so far, this is the only evidence of possible wrongdoing we have found - not much to go on is it?" said Harrier.

"Okay thanks for that, best if you get back to your other investigations."

With that, Chavender dismissed them all. He sat for a while looking through the reports again, for the last few hours of his day before heading for home himself.

Chapter 19

The next day, Chavender asked if they could set two pinboards and a whiteboard up in his office. On one he set out the dates and times of the six deaths they were investigating and on the other the fraud case. The fraud board was practically empty apart from the reference to the land deal. The other one, however, had plenty of information on, whilst the whiteboard had connections written on it or should have had. The six dead people were not known to each other, they were total strangers, not related or connected in friendship in any way, shape or form; it was so unrelated as to be remarkable he thought, six unrelated deaths. He added another column under the heading causes of death; again nothing, two suicides, two heart attacks and two accidental gassings. All pretty natural ways to die, nothing quite like having a murder weapon to go on, a knife or guns, something tangible that can be felt, examined, tested for clues, here nothing, Nada, zilch, apart from one empty bleach bottle, one syringe, on empty packet of sleeping pills, all common everyday objects. Okay, if it was murder?

"What can we say against that list?" he spoke out loud, taking a sip of cold coffee, and continued with his musings. Chewing over the known missing facts, no ammonia bottle, for the first couple who died, significant or not? - probably most likely, find the bottle we may find the culprit, the drug overdose or heart attack, find the needle with a mix of Potassium Chloride and heroin in, again we have the culprit, the heart attack in the library, I don't think its connected but at the moment we can't rule it out, would be very hard to find the culprit - we have a very good witness by the way of the librarian; the last couple, she murdered him then killed herself with sleeping pills, no suicide note, empty packet of pills bought from a web source, find the source may find the culprit. Web source - best check with Pearce to see if the couple had a computer at home, but could have used a public one in a library, also not every suicidal person leaves a note!" With that he sat down in his chair and looked at the whiteboard for some time, before being abruptly awakened from his meditations by his phone ringing.

"Hello, Chavender speaking."

"Hello, Josh," answered Tiff, "Mum's had a nasty fall at home and broken her wrist and bruised her face, the silly, silly old sod she is, and do you know what? She has only just rung me from the hospital, three hours later, but they won't let her home without someone to look after her, so I'm going up to London to collect her, she can stay with us, right dear? I've asked Sue Jenkins if she could pick our girls up and you can pick them up from theirs when you leave work, okay? You'll find their house quite easy, okay, it's on the old estate next to the new one just outside of Plympton, on the main road in, got a pen dear? I'll give you the address."

Writing down the address, Josh asked if she could arrange for her mum not to have so many sausage-based meals whilst she stayed with them, adding, "Please Tiff!", almost pleading with her before adding, "Okay love, I'll see you when you get back, I don't suppose it'll be till later on will it? I'll have everything ready, the girls will have to bunk in together for the meantime seeing as the spare room is out of action."

"Thanks Josh you're a real sweetheart love, bye, see you later, love you and the girl's bye."

"Bye," and he put the phone down. Pondering on his fate, and dreading the sausage diet he would have to endure for the next few weeks, which sent a shiver up his spine, perhaps they could wean her onto something less sausagey for the interim? They could only try, thought Josh, he got up and left for the canteen to see Sue and get a cup of coffee. In the canteen, he managed to speak to Sue. She had just got in touch with Bert who was on night shifts this week and told him he was to collect the Chavender children also, he was supposed to pick her up after, but perhaps Josh would give her a lift home, at least that way he wouldn't get lost. He agreed and arranged to pick her up at 4pm, and he then went and spoke to the Chief Constable about leaving a bit early.

Collecting Sue on the way out from the canteen they made it to her house inside the hour. On the way, Sue talked about lots of things, girls growing up things, school uniform things and finally pointing out the new estate that had just been finished within the year. Originally it was earmarked by the council as recreational land and she could not understand it, first how they managed to sell it and then how they managed to cram so many houses in to such a small area, also why they had to pull down two houses to get onto the land to be able to build. Chavender listened half-heartedly, but vaguely remembered that this was on the way to where the first couple died. Stopping outside the Jenkins' house, Sue ushered him in, only to be greeted with a hue and cry that the Jenkins had not seen before, his girls all rushed him at once, chattering away, only quietening down once a hug and a kiss was both received and given.

"Cor blimey," said Bert, "that happens all the time does it, Sir?"

"Yes, Sergeant, I'm afraid it does; it's like being engulfed by a very noisy octopus sometimes, but I've got used to it."

The girls had chatted wildly until Sue shushed them in to the front room to continue watching a DVD.

"Thanks for doing this, both of you, really, it is kind of you both, I know what my girls are like, but to the uninitiated it could be overwhelming."

"That's okay, Josh, it just goes to show you how much they love you that's all. Bert gets the same reaction but nowadays only when he brings in the pizza." Looking at her husband and smiling, he just nodded his head as if to say, that's it, pizza delivery boy, that's me! "Now sit down won't you, Joshua; Bert will want a cup of tea before he goes and I'm sure you could do with one. Go on, take the weight of your feet, grab a chair, I wont take no for an answer; and anyway the film has at least a half hour to go, and the girls are quiet for now, shame to disturb them."

Josh, sitting down at the table, waited for his cup of tea. Bert asked him about the latest suspicious deaths and then spoke about how the place had changed since they moved in some fifteen odd years ago. He was a young constable then, Sue, a bank girl; he went in one day to cash a cheque and he fell in love with her, courted and married her, then nine years ago the twins came along and he could not be happier. Josh nodded in agreement; he could almost say the same thing except he had two sets of twins so perhaps he was doubly happier.

By this time the DVD had finished and all six girls came at once into the kitchen. Taking his cue, before the clamour could start, Josh thanked Bert for picking his girls up. He prompted his girls by saying "manners" to thank Bert and Sue also. They said their goodbyes and left. Getting them settled in the car, he suggested fish and chips for tea, to which they all readily chorused "YES" in agreement; the background chatter of the girls in the car was like one of those black and white jungle films at night, when the crickets chirruped incessantly, so stopping at a chippy was a relief for him. He bought them all fish and chips, which they ate, sat in the seafront chippy.

Once home, they made short work of moving bedrooms around and getting gran's bed all set up. Happily tired and full, the girls went to bed without complaining. Josh sat up to wait for Ma and Tiff. He had called her earlier to see what time she was likely to get home so that he could have the kettle on, ready to make a cup of tea. By 10.30pm, both women arrived; he helped carry the cases in and made them all some tea.

"Now Ma, what have you been doing? Fell over chasing that young window cleaner of yours again? I told you before, just say the word, I still have some friends in London, they will help you catch him." He looked at Ma and smiled as he said it.

"No, you cheeky devil, it wasn't that Josh; I slipped on some mud whilst talking to Henry, you know my neighbour, the old ex-head gardener; you know he still grows vegetables, he lets me have some sometimes, fair takes me back, vegetables straight out of the ground onto the plate, very tasty too. I took him out a cup of tea and slipped on my path going to him." Josh agreed with her; nothing nicer than fresh veg, he said.

Tiff couldn't help a yawn and said she was tired after the drive to Ma's and back, so with Josh's help they cleared up. Josh washed up the three cups and left them to dry on the drainer, and they settled Ma in the spare room and went to bed.

Chapter 20

The next morning saw a general hullabaloo from the girls when they saw Gran with her arm in a sling and cast, awkwardly trying to do things left handed and generally being fussed over, she eventually submitted to the indignity of having her cast signed by the girls with magic marker. Josh, making sure that Tiff could cope with Ma, left for work.

Something was wrong, something was troubling him, he had had a very disturbed night's sleep, something was praying on his mind but he could not place it, or think what it might be; he tried to think about it, but it only submerged the thought deeper in to the recesses of his brain. He sighed in semi despair; he knew from past experience it could take days or weeks to explode in to his consciousness. He remembered once trying to think of the male lead in 'Dr Doolittle'; now you would have thought that that would be easy enough to recall, but oh no, not for him, three days it dwelt on his mind, three days of trying to remember Rex Harrison, oh how it bugged him, just like something was bugging him now! Consequently his drive in to work was over before it had begun.

Parking his car, he saw Sue heading in; he caught up with her and thanked her and her husband again for getting the girl's, Ma was safely ensconced in one of the girls' rooms and then added, "Tiff has asked me if you and your family would like to come over Sunday for tea, nothing fancy, maybe my turn to be the pizza boy this time, she was thinking about three would be nice?"

"Well thanks Josh, that would be lovely. Bert gets off nights Friday, so he should be back to sleeping at night okay by then. Bye, Josh."

"Bye, Sue," he said as they parted inside the building.

Absentmindedly, Chavender walked to his office. When he got there and had just opened the door, he realised he had passed the CID room, turning round he headed back. Carruthers sat at his desk beavering away at those reports he wanted so badly, Wootton, crosschecking files on the fraud case, two detective constables, suddenly finding work as he entered and walked over to the two detective sergeants.

He casually sat down and looked at Wootton, and asked, "How's it going Sergeant?"

"Not so bad Sir, slow if you know what I mean, but I think progress is being made; I can definitely tie the two councillors to one of the developers, but it don't make it fraud, Sir!"

"No it doesn't Sergeant, no it certainly doesn't."

With that, he sighed, got up and left. The two constables relaxed a bit too soon and stopped what they were doing and began to lark about a bit; Wootton told them to "pack it in", and they were just about to give it some lip, when suddenly the door flew open. Chavender's head popped round the door jamb, looking at the two of them and said, "You two. My office, twenty minutes. Sergeant can you make sure they attend please?"

"Yes Sir," said Sergeant Wootton. When he got back to his office he called Inspector Carr, arranging for him to sit in. They all duly arrived, the two young constables, Wootton and Carr. Chavender did not quite tear strips off them but asked Carr if he could do with some extra help for the rest of the week. "Split them up and put them with a sergeant will you Inspector. Now clear off the two of you before I change my mind and make it permanent! Go on! Get! Skedaddle now!" The two young constables left with Inspector Carr to serve out the rest of the week in uniform.

Their leaving left Wootton alone in the room with Chavender. He thought it would be his turn for the next roasting for the lack of discipline in the CID room. Chavender then spoke to him.

"That might hopefully teach them. I can't stand lollygaggers, especially when others have got to work; looks like I may have to look into the staffing levels of the CID branch here if two men can stand around idle for most of the day! Now Sergeant Wootton!" Chavender said it with a touch of menace and he could see Wootton turn a bit paler, thinking he was for the chop now. "Well, what does my modern day Casanova, my Lothario, have to say?" He paused for effect, and before Wootton could blurt out an excuse carried on. "What's this link you may have found? Will it lead us to the mother of all fraud cases or be a damp squib?"

Wootton looked quizzically at his boss, and with a smile said, "Excuse me Sir, but, Casanova, Lothario, lollygagging? Swallow a dictionary this morning, Sir? Anyway thanks for dealing with those two; they were warned both by myself and Molly-Fergus, to get on with some work; the shock you just gave them might just put them back on the rails Sir, they are both decent detective constables when they put their minds to it.

"The link involves a bit of insider knowledge; List Developments built the new estate on the edge of town on previously owned council land which was sold at auction. It went for well under the market value for such land due to poor access to the site. The older estate was built on half of the finger of land that this farmer owned, he continued to access it by the old farm trackway shared by the neighbouring farms. These two farms and the estate effectively cut his field off from the farm that owned it. It could only be entered by foot from the older estate through a narrow strip of land about three metres wide owned by a pair of houses. This was entirely due to the lie of the land, behind the houses was a strip of land some 30m deep, running the length of this boundary, at one time behind these houses was the entry way in to the field so here it was at least twenty metres wide and no trees because of the hard standing underneath. The wooded area was designated a SSSI by the County wildlife trust, as the woods, farm land and track way on the other three sides effectively cut the field off, thus six acres of allegedly very poor farmland was cut off when the older estate in the eighties was built. The then farmer held out against the developers and basically kept his land intact. He died sometime in the nineties and the council purchased the land from the deceased estate due to lack of probate. The two sons could not agree with what to do with the land, so sold it to the council, to pay for the death duties. They still made a tidy sum out of it though! Well, five years ago a private landlord paid well over the odds for the two houses with the right of way. He immediately sought a court order banning people from using his land to gain access to the land beyond, put a fence up and that was that, he then put some undesirable tenants in the houses, drug addicts and the like. They basically trashed the places inside of two years, they fell into disrepair and then they were left derelict for a year until the land behind was sold. He then sold the houses and the right of way to List Developments, Sir."

"Right Wootton, well, so far, not much wrong in that, possibly insider trading but it will be hard to prove. What you need to do now will be to see if the landlord had any connection to any of the people or companies under investigation. And get me a map of the area please. Thanks Sergeant."

As Wootton was leaving, the phone rang, it was the desk sergeant informing him that a Mr Schonebeck and his solicitor had arrived to have a word with him. "Thanks Sergeant; put them in an interview room and tell them someone will be with them shortly." With that, he went and found Molly-Fergus.

The interview did not last long; Mr Schonebeck had nothing to add and would say nothing, so after a frustrating hour or so, he and his solicitor were allowed to leave. Chavender asked for Mr Schonebeck's passport, he refused on the grounds that he needed it to travel abroad, and they had to let him go with it. Molly-Fergus was very disappointed, no trip abroad this weekend; Chavender saw it on her face and was about to say "hard cheese" when he stopped and looked thoughtful for a moment; he nearly remembered what was bugging him so, but it went again in a flash.

"Nevermind, Molly-Fergus," he said, "We'll get them eventually. Best wrap it up for today, get your results. You and Harrier, better come to see me okay." Collecting Harrier and the reports they entered his office, sitting down they talked it over for an hour or so, but again nothing was coming to light.

Wootton called by, he had managed to get hold of an old map of the area in question. Chavender pinning it to a pinboard saw that it was roughly square in shape, but had one corner cut across, it was here that the two houses abutted the field, then the woods filling out the two large triangles and the farm track, it showed the older estate trapping the land behind, to the far north and north west of the map he saw why it could only be accessed from the old estate side; there was a tidal estuary and mud flats to contend with, to the north and northeast good arable farm land, with only the farm track leading to three farm houses, and quite a few miles from the nearest road, he saw immediately that anyone buying those two houses, had the field at the back, in his back pocket so to speak.

He thanked them for their efforts, dismissed them and decided to call Pearce. "Hello Pearce, any updates from the coroner yet?" he asked.

"Yes Sir," Pearce replied. "We now have the report but it basically states what he told us; without visible evidence of foul play, his verdict stands at she killed him, she killed herself! He won't budge on that Sir, no matter what our objections might be, unless we can prove or have proved the existence of a third person in the house at the time of death, who administered the sleeping pills and how, he cannot go against the evidence of his own eyes."

"Look Pearce, best if you come to headquarters in the morning; bring Smith with you okay?"

"Yes Sir, see you in the morning, bye."

Chavender then put a call into Bryantsand-on-Sea police station and left a message for Lister and Small to join him in the morning; after a final call to Harrier and Molly-Fergus, asking them to attend, he had decided to have a review of the cases so far, just to see if they had not missed the blooming obvious!

Chapter 21

That morning at the revue meeting, they all painstakingly went through all the evidence so far, which amounted to "diddly squat" as far as he could surmise, looking through the files so far had revealed a tenuous link, in that the fraud, and the deaths were "all over the shop". No pattern unless you call the randomness of the deaths a pattern, the way they died, the lack of evidence of foul play. That thing from the other day was still bothering him, as he passed the pictures of the Hornbeams house round for a final look; what he hoped to gain from this exercise he did not know, but when all else fails "spit in to the wind" his gran used to say, and filling your mind with trivia helped. The DIs passed the pictures round, looking, chatting but not really knowing what they were looking for. When the one of the kitchen drainer was passed along, Harrier said, "Three cups, two plates and some knives and forks, all pretty normal stuff to find on a drainer!"

It was then that that bugging feeling that Chavender had had exploded; he asked for that photograph, looking at it and said, "Well I think I can say, quite confidently, and contrary to the coroner's statement, that the Hornbeams were murdered!"

Pearce and the rest looked at him puzzled. "Please explain Sir? You're only seeing what we are seeing and we cannot make such a confident statement as that!"

"It's easy, I was at home the other day, my wife had gone to collect my mother in law because she fell and broke her wrist, before we all went to bed we had a cup of tea, I washed up three cups, three people, three cups! See? What's in that picture but three cups! So it's got to mean three people had a cup of tea doesn't it?"

Looking at Molly-Fergus, "Can you pick any holes in my conclusion, please?"

Thinking silently for a while she replied "No Sir, but it is a very long stretch of the imagination isn't it? I mean one person could have had a cup of tea by themselves and then later two people together, thus three cups."

"Um yes I see that, but that doesn't wash with me; how many of you use a fresh cup for every cup of tea, you may rinse out the used cup, but generally you use the same cups all the time! I certainly don't use a fresh cup; I mean if we have a cup of tea at home my wife normally sends for my cup, she doesn't get a fresh cup each time or else I would need ten clean cups per day! I bet most households have spare cups, yes, but not twenty spare cups I'm sure?"

Pearce interjected, "Well if it is murder, then how can we prove it? No evidence was found at the scene that was not deemed abnormal by the scenes of crimes and forensics! All our enquiries so far have found nothing out of the ordinary - true, our best witnesses were away that afternoon and night, the neighbours, but it would be even more of a strange coincidence for our murderer to be so lucky as that!"

"Well Pearce, let's think of what we know so far, five possibly six people murdered, we have absolutely no concrete proof of murder, how much more luck do you need? No I tell you they were murdered, but now how to prove it? That is going to be the next problem!"

Thanking them for their efforts, he dismissed them; going over to his whiteboard he wrote three words and put a question mark after it in big bold black letters: "WHO ARE YOU?"

Having done that, he sat down and smiled to himself, it was not the biggest revelation, but it may just prove to be the start that they needed; he then got up and went to the CID room, to see how the other parts of the investigation were coming along. He saw Wootton and Carruthers pouring over the reports that the two subdivisions had sent in to them, nodded and asked them to wrap it up so he could update them on the Hornbeam case. They all went into his office and sat down; it was Wootton who noticed the whiteboard and what had been written on it.

"So you think its murder then Sir?"

"Yes I do," he replied and told them about the cups!

Carruthers then spoke. "I think I see what you mean Sir, two people equals two cups, yes, yes!" He then repeated almost verbatim what Molly-Fergus had said.

Then Wootton spoke. "Yes, I think I know what you're getting at; this is one of those leaps of faith isn't it Sir?"

"Yes sergeant, it is, but I'm absolutely positive that I'm right in this instance; I can think of no other reason for three cups than for three persons!"

He then went on to ask if the reports would be ready by Monday to which they both said "yes". Thanking them he dismissed them and departed for home himself, he was relatively happy that evening, that at last, they may have a way in to one of the cases.

Saturday at "Chavender Mansions" saw Josh masking up the walls and windows. He applied some deep base coat paint to the skirting and doors and some light base coat paint to the windows. Pleased with himself for still having the better part of the afternoon free, he left the paint to dry. He sat in the kitchen with Tiff and Ma having a cup of tea and discussing what was going to happen Sunday afternoon, and how Ma had agreed to a less sausage based diet, but she would not eat that pasta stuff that they liked so much!

Sunday saw Josh put the Prussian Blue gloss paint on the undercoated woodwork and the white gloss paint on the windows, before cleaning himself up and going out and to get several large mixed pizzas, garlic bread and lots of fizz. The Jenkins arrived just after three and after introductions; the girls went into the front room to watch a new DVD, whilst Ma, Sue and Tiff sat in the kitchen. Bert and Josh went into the conservatory.

Bert said, "I don't know how you cope Sir, being surrounded by that many females, I don't mean it in a sexist way, but boy, it must be difficult on you. I love my wife and kids you know and I can just about handle the three I've got - but six, you must be overwhelmed sometimes. I mean at home I'm allowed to use both toilets, but in one of them I can leave the seat up, but if I use the other I have to remember to lower the seat afterwards, if you know what I mean Sir!"

"Ah, yes I do, we have not reached that stage yet here, thankfully, but sometimes Sergeant I cop a deaf un; I listen but not really listen, if you know what I mean, but I'm afraid I do it more and more of the time now, must be getting old, so consequently I miss things, annoying little things, like the other day, when I drove your wife home to pick my flock up, your wife chatted on about this, that and the other but you know what, I can't remember a thing she said, even though later that week, some of what she said had a direct bearing on one of the cases we are investigating!" he replied.

They went on to talk about the garden and how Bert thought that he could get a sizeable vegetable plot in one corner, and how he was on the council waiting list for an allotment; in the meantime he would make do with the little bit he could do in his own garden and then went on a bit about decorating and other such mundane stuff, before Tiff called them in for the pizza tea.

Tiff and Sue plated up some pizza, cheesy garlic bread, glasses of fizz and took it through to the front room for the girls to eat; they had started on another film; putting the pizza and fizz on the coffee table they left them to it, saying, "There's more, once you demolish that lot if you want it, girls." A chorus of

"Thanks Mummy," came from the girls, as they barely diverted there attention from the large TV screen; the two mothers smiled as they left, at least they would be quite for a while. In the kitchen Bert and Josh sat down, having more tea poured for them, both had a smile on their faces as they tucked into the pizza.

Sue said, "And what have you two Cheshire cats got to smile about?" whilst Tiff finished the sentence, "Come on, spit it out you two!"

Ma added, "They look just like the cat that's got the cream!"

Josh answered, "We pair, this most noble and noblest band of police brothers, this great put upon manhood, these servants to your magnificence, grace and beauty, have just marvelled at our great... I must say our most excellent good fortune to have landed a pair of lookers like you two!"

Bert added, "Who can cook as well," as Josh ducked the tea towel that was flung at him. Bert collected a thick ear from his wife and they all laughed, Ma looked on a bit puzzled, and said, "Can't understand you young people these days! Bah, call this cooking, buy ready-made food in, put it on a plate and you say it's cooking; generation lazy I'd call that." Josh was about to reply but Tiff caught his eye, a slight shake of her head and he let it drop. Soon it was time for the Jenkins to leave, and saying their goodbyes, they left for home.

Tiff whispered in Josh's ear, "That went well, thanks for that love."

Getting the girls ready for bed that Sunday night was a chore. They were overfed on pizza and fizz and were not in the mood to sleep, let alone stay in bed; they all started to play up in turn, first one wanted to go to the toilet, then another one, round and round it went until Tiff put her foot down. "Enough girls, that's four times you've all been to the toilet, now bed, or I'll get your dad in!" But when they were all in bed they still chatted and chatted and chatted some more. First Josh and then Tiff looked in on them and told them to "Be quiet, you need to go to sleep!"

Finally Josh at 11pm looked in and they were still wide awake and chatty, not tired at all. "Right you lot, if you don't pack it in and get to sleep now, there will be no more takeout food for quite some considerable time! It will be sausages all the way until Gran goes home, okay?"

Scowling at them, Josh thought that was fair, he was not like his father; he had made that point to Tiff when the first set of twins was born, he would not be the strict disciplinarian that his father had been, he would be firm but fair minded, not like some of his and her generation! Finally around midnight the only sound coming from the girls room was silence. Josh lay awake most of the night thinking how could he take that next leap of faith that the Hornbeam's case seem to demand of him, and where would it lead him to.

Chapter 22

The Senior officers' meeting on Monday was mostly led by Chavender explaining how he thought a murderer was on the loose, but he also stated that the link was very tenuous indeed and that it, and he, could be proved wrong by the evidence as it stands. In fact, none of the other DIs were totally convinced that he was right, apart from DI Pearce that was, who suspected, but like Chavender could prove no wrongdoing. Featherstonehaugh looked quite puzzled by what Chavender had said.

"So your supposition is that persons or persons unknown murdered two people, in their own home, and no one saw or witnessed any wrong or wrongdoings being carried out, or in fact the perpetrator then leaving the house - is that correct Chavender?"

"Yes; I'm afraid to say, it is on the flimsiest of circumstantial evidence that I have based my case on Sir. Three cups on a draining board and that is it; nothing else from any of the experts backs my theory up, in fact, they contradict it so much that sometimes even I doubt it, Sir!"

Sword then spoke, "Well that's a pretty kettle of fish you have there Chavender, no evidence, hard evidence of anything illegal going on in my patch, but you say I may have to be aware that a murderer is on the loose?"

"That's right Chief Inspector, but as I say no proof."

Andersonn then interjected, "What about my area then? Anything I should know about."

"Not for now, so far you have escaped, but why I don't know, unless the murderer is one of those fanatics from Bryantsand, killing the good people of Plympton, which I don't buy into for one second."

"I should hope not," Featherstonehaugh replied, "it looks like you've got us all jumping through hoops, but I agree the evidence is too flimsy, so for now we bide our time; nothing to the press, we have to wait and see what happens next; if there is a murderer on the loose we just have to hope he or she makes a mistake. Now what about the fraud case?"

"Nothing much Sir, a small lead which may improve the more we dig, but again not hopeful on that score Sir. We still have a vast amount of information to sift through yet, probably another two weeks worth at our current rate, but I feel slowly, slowly, catches the monkey Sir."

"Yes I agree with you on that premise Chavender; well thanks to all of you, for your time this morning, it has been most productive and certainly informative. I will see you all next week if not beforehand at your divisional headquarters, I shall be doing a tour of inspection. Thanks and goodbye." He then dismissed them and they left. Sword and Andersonn walked with Chavender to his office.

Once seated Andersonn asked, "Right, Josh, what can we do to help out? There must be something you need help with, I'm sure Robin will agree with me, we can't have someone loose on our streets killing people at will. I mean I know manpower is tight, we can barely cover what we have at the moment, let alone all the extras we seem to be getting, like when they build those two new massive housing estates. For a while I will have to deal with the problems of drunken labourers doing their best to smash up the towns nightclubs on a Friday and Saturday night. You know we are going to be one of the fastest growing towns along the south coast for a while; it may well upset our neighbours."

Looking at Sword as he said this, "Yes it may well, John, but you're right we will be stretched once they start the building works, just trying to keep the peace will be hard enough, let alone look for a murderer!"

Chavender asked, "What developments are those, do you happen to know the names of the companies John?"

"Not really Josh, they are only proposals at the moment, it will be ratified when the two councils unite; they are allowing or having to expand into otherwise green belt land, this is so they can meet central government's targets for affordable housing. New housing that is anything but affordable to many a young person. I know my eldest and his girlfriend just tried to get a mortgage, for one of the shoeboxes they are building at the moment, even with my help lending him half the money, he just made it and he still struggles to find the repayments, and he is reasonably well paid, not like one of our young constables!"

Chavender thanked him for the offer of help and reciprocated the offer; he had some young detective constables who needed a little discipline, a night or two back on the beat would benefit all concerned.

"Yes I heard what you did the other day, Inspector Carr and I were having a chat when he popped in the other day," said Sword.

"Still," said Chavender, "we will have to keep an eye on those developers, just in case it's linked to my investigations. It's a wonder the council have not looked into it; perhaps I should have a word with the leader of the council?"

"Yes, that might be wise Josh" said Sword, adding, "I'd best be off, better make sure my station is up to the mark, if the old man inspects he really inspects, lockers, toilets, canteen, duty rooms, waiting rooms, cells and point of contact for the public, you can bet it will be a white glove inspection. Yes, shiny boots and two pairs of laces that sums him up, but I do agree with him, it gives the youngster a sense of pride. Well thanks Josh, it was very informative. Anything to add?"

"Yes Robin, and you too John. I think you will both need to detail a sergeant to tidy up the posters in the point of contact rooms, little bit higgledy-piggledy if you know what I mean; he made the duty sergeant here do the same last week, fair tore a strip off of him about the state of the posters he did, gave him twenty minutes to sort it he did, stood there whilst the sergeant did it just in case he tried to delegate it, poor sergeant, went beetroot red."

"Thanks for the tip off" said the pair, leaving Josh to his musings over "how, what and why" in the Hornbeam case.

Chavender then made an appointment to see the leader of the council for Tuesday afternoon and then went to see Carruthers, to see if he had anything for him yet. On entering the CID room Chavender was pleased to note that the previous lassitude was gone and he was met by a hive of industry. Speaking to Carruthers, he asked how far he was from completing the task.

"Oh not far sir, another day and I should be finished."

"Good, good when you're done come right in with it please."

"Okay, will do Sir."

Just then, Wootton came in and Chavender asked him to come along to the meeting he had arranged with the leader of the council, at 2pm the next day. He then left and went back to his office, where by now Lister and Small were waiting with today's conclusions.

"Right you two, astound me with your wit and wisdom!" They both looked at odds with him until he said, "the reports please!"

"Well Sir," said Small, "it's like this; we think we may have a connection between the landlord and one of the developers. It's a man called Fitzgerald, Peter, a right nasty piece of work Sir, a regular on/off guest at Her Majesty's Pleasure, several counts Actual Bodily Harm, Grievous Bodily Harm and theft Sir. Well apparently he was, a long time ago, one of Mr List's site agents when he owned List Developments, who upped and left to go back to the Republic of Ireland about five years ago, where he set up the parent company, since gone bust, called Fitzgerald Lettings. They owned the two properties, and only those two properties, that were eventually sold to List developments later at a knock down price, literally! The whereabouts of Peter Fitzgerald are not known at this moment in time, but we can contact the Garda to see if they have heard of him lately and we can check on those "In-Custody" lists if you would like us to? It all seems a bit fishy, but again what do we prove? A developer would appear to have had a lucky break. Now of course if we can prove that Mr List was the money behind Fitzgerald Lettings and that somehow the two councillors were involved; it would be a pretty good start, but I'm sure Mr List's accountants will be able to account for all his money and or expenditure over the past decade, Sir."

"Yes I see, thanks for that; perhaps when we get into the bank statements we will unearth the link, but for now we continue with the current files. Only when these are done will we move on; it's painstaking I know and slow, but better slow than miss something very important that may help us."

With that he dismissed them, asking them to come back Wednesday morning. They got up and left the pile of reports for Chavender to look through; he briefly skimmed the summary pages, drawing the same conclusions of Lister and Small.

Looking up at his three boards, he turned his attention to them; he stared intently at them for several minutes, but nothing sprang to mind, except the three cups, of that one fact he was very sure. The next morning he sent messages round that six detective constable from Monday next week were to report to different police stations, he would listen to any objections on Wednesday, but he warned them, that he would only postpone the temporary assigned duties once and once only, after that you went no matter what. The same would be applied to the Inspectors. He also warned everyone that if uniform needed extra hands he would only be too willing to supply them; if he caught any member of his department slacking, it would be up to the senior Inspector in charge to make sure that everyone was working to their best ability. From now on, he would spend at least one day every two weeks at divisional police stations, or as much as his workload would permit him; he said he did not see himself as exempt from such deployments. He then called for Detective Sergeant Wootton and left for the meeting with the leader of the council.

Chapter 23

The meeting with the leader of Plympton Council was informative for Chavender. He asked how the merger of the two councils would be set up and the leader, Councillor Langton Boyshill, explained, "Some three years ago we set up a joint committee to look into and study the feasibility of the two towns merging, we finally reached an agreement one year ago that the merger would happen before the next round of local elections this year. At these elections a reduced number of councillors would be elected, including some newly created extended wards, some of which will cross over existing boundaries between the two towns. This would reduce the number of councillors by a quarter, from two hundred between the two towns down to one hundred and fifty, they then would elect one mayor, one deputy mayor, one leader of the council, one deputy leader and then the councillors. On the workforce side they would employ: One head of services, one deputy head of services and departmental heads for the various departments and one other department Without Portfolio, a catch-all for the interim period of two years, when it would then either close down or continue until the teething problems are sorted. By doing this we will be employing nine possibly ten heads of services rather than the twenty-odd heads of service that both councils are currently employing. We anticipate that this will save both councils about three million per year, allied with the drop in pensions and allowance payouts. The front line work force will remain roughly the same, while it must be said redundancies will happen, most redundancies will occur in the upper and middle management rolls and through natural wastage including those attaining retirement age. Are you with me so far?" The two police officers nodded in unison that they had followed him so far.

He then continued, "We will leave the two town halls as they are, they will become two satellite town halls, with reduced staffing and within the year we will relocate some of the service heads to a new building and a new town hall, yet to be built. Again, although not a direct saving, we will be able to rent out the empty floors and offices, thus increasing our revenue from such a venture, all told this will reduce both councils budgets by some three to six million pounds without affecting our services or commitments for at least the foreseeable future. Some council owned land will have to be sold to allow for the increase in numbers of affordable housing limits as those that have been set by Whitehall, this will include some green belt, some recreational and some other demarcated or set aside land. Also it will go some way to make up the pension shortfall, when we, like some other councils, invested wisely or so it was thought so at the time in foreign banks, we of course lost a lot of money when they folded without warning. We have since then been trying to recover some of it but all to no avail! On the down side as far as I can tell, initially some waiting list will increase, we are not sure which ones yet but certainly some will lengthen, the only one we know for sure is housing. The housing list will immediately double when the waiting lists join but once the housing stock, in council, housing association or private, has increased, these will come down quite significantly to below normal levels, other lists will take a few years to settle down but we expect them to do so.

"Whilst this was going on, we looked into land that could be sold without affecting the look, feel or nature of the two towns, areas that were under used or derelict, the relocation of council offices and depots, this would free up some forty to fifty acres of land; we had to have included some green belt land, but we looked at it in such a way, so as not to destroy natural or specific wildlife habitats and heathlands. This green belt land, really amounts to so little. It's either in small blocks, thin strips or small parcels up to four acres in size of land that its use as green belt is seriously compromised, because it is situated between us, Bryantsand and the neighbouring villages and towns, which, due to the pressure of the expansions over the past two decades from all of us, are beginning to join or touch at various points, so much so, that one can now drive in a urban situation from the Port out to the nearest independent town some fifteen odd miles in one direction and ten in the other. We are fast becoming too big and ungainly for our own good! At the current rate of expansion, we will join ourselves to the county town in twenty years' time. That, gentlemen is a fact, and we cannot avoid it! Pressure from immigration, population growth and the job market will determine the eventual size of the conglomeration or metropolis that will over come us all. Any questions so far? Gentlemen."

Chavender asked, "Who was on the original review committee please?"

Boyshill replied "Myself, Councillors Walker, Ireland and Longbottom, plus two outside independent advisors; it then went to both full sessions of both councils for ratification, were it passed the majority mark by thirty votes for Bryantsand and twenty-five for Plympton. We then sent the report to a constitutional expert for checking and then announced a timeframe for the merger. Once that was done we sent letters to every household in both towns outlining our proposals, requesting feedback and several public meetings later we were able to agree the merger as it stands."

"Who decided on what land to sell please?" asked Chavender.

"That was initially done by independent sources but went through to be ratified by both planning committees three years ago; the breakdown of land is roughly forty percent Bryantsand and sixty percent Plympton's; this equates in total to an area some seventy acres of mixed use land." The leader went on to say, "You see, in the eighties the watch word for local government was de-centralisation, the spreading of services across the boroughs especially in London; this was in a way to make them seem unattractive to private companies; we were just seeing the start of privatisation. The councils wanted to retain control of as much as they could and saw de-centralisation as way of doing just that. All it did was make it easier for private contractors to pick off the council services in small itsy bitsy parcels. Nowadays the watchword looks to be amalgamated centralisation of services, this primarily is to help keep costs down, but only time will tell if it works or not!"

Chavender then asked if he could get the breakdown of names for both committees for him, and any other relevant information on the merger and to send it over to police headquarters.

"Yes, I'm sure we can do that. I will ask the Town Clerks to provide you with the names, you should have them by the weekend. Anything else I can help you gentlemen with? I do have another meeting to attend, with the press."

"No thank you Sir, you have been most helpful; thanks and goodbye Councillor Boyshill," said Chavender and with that he and Wootton got up and left.

On the way out they were met by Wendy Blaise, who asked Chavender, "Well Josh, nice to bump into you! What are you and Woodley doing at the town hall; did it have any bearing on the investigation in to the fraud case?"

"No Miss Blaise it did not," he said, trying to put her off the scent. "We are here to ascertain some facts about the merger, that may bear or have some correlation to the fraud case but not directly, thanks."

"Well! You just said yes and no in that answer to my question Josh."

"Did I?" he replied nonchalantly and carried on walking. "Goodbye Miss Blaise."

"Bye Josh, Woodley... Oh Woodley will I see you later still?"

"Yes Wendy" Woodley replied quietly, being embarrassed by her personal question, "about 6pm when I get off work."

Chavender was a bit upset by the allegedly accidental meeting and he was not so sure that Miss Blaise did not have prior knowledge of the meeting from Sergeant Wootton! Still, it did not bother him that much as he thought that Wootton could be sent to Bryantsand police station next week; back at headquarters Carruthers was waiting to see him.

Chapter 24

"Well Carruthers, what have you got for me? Anything interesting?" he asked.

Carruthers replied, "Well Sir not much; none of the places our friendly impersonator visited are connected to any of the deaths, robberies or even related to any other type of doorstep cold calling! Sir, in fact, so far as I can ascertain, none of the dead people even remotely crossed each others' paths. In fact, the nearest we have to a meeting is possibly to the body in the library, Mr Jonas, the Hornbeams may or may not have known him sir, they were both members of the County Library and, or at least, used that library that he was found dead in sir."

"What was our impersonator nicked for Carruthers?" asked Chavender.

"He was nicked for impersonating a clergyman Sir! With probably every intent of passing on details to the distraction burglars, that's how they normally operate. The gang pick a likely area, one with more than its fair share of elderly people, someone calls beforehand, they leave it a week or two and then the other two chancers come along and try their luck, maybe one in ten times they get lucky and walk away with a tidy haul Sir."

"Um yes, I see... The worst type of criminals we have to deal with, hard to catch them at it but it normally goes quiet once the word gets out; perhaps that is what has happened here and, of course, you managed to catch the fake clergyman."

Just then Chavender's phone rang; he answered with his usual, "Hello, Chavender speaking."

"Hello Sir, it's DI Pearce; looks like we have another suspicious death, it's at Flat 9, 141 London Road Sir."

Thanking him for the call Chavender grabbed his hat and coat and turned to Carruthers saying, "Right Carruthers, come with me please, we are going to Flat 9, 141 London Road."

Arriving at the scene, Chavender was met by DI Pearce.

"Well" said Chavender, "What is it then Pearce?", to which Pearce replied, "His meal delivery people came as usual this lunchtime and as he didn't answer the door as usual, they assumed he was out. See that box Sir, they would put his meal in there if he was out, it's insulated and lockable. They came again at 5pm to deliver his evening meal and found the midday meal still in the box. After knocking repeatedly, and fearing the worst sir, especially since those meals delivery people up in Lanchestershire let one slip by for a week before calling the police and getting that flack in the press over it, they called us in. We forced an entry and found the poor bloke was dead in his bed Sir; it's got to be definitely murder this time or I'm a monkey's uncle!"

"Well let's not jump the gun, Pearce, but I do agree with you, we are getting jumpy; every time someone dies now, we think its murder. Let's think otherwise until proven otherwise, if that makes sense? Or we could read into the evidence what the hell we liked, especially if we go in with preconceived ideas!"

"Yes Sir, sorry Sir, but its getting a bit much, if you know what I mean Sir!"

"Um yes I do, Pearce, but let's wait to see what forensics and the coroner have to say, first! Do we have a preliminary cause of death yet?"

"Yes Sir, another heart attack the doctor thinks, no sign of forced entry, no sign of a struggle, no sign of anyone other than the deceased in the house, Oh and before you ask only one cup on the drainer sir!"

Chavender looked at the young DI and rather jokingly said, "Am I getting that transparent now young fellow me lad?"

"No Sir, but seeing as how your leap of faith in the Hornbeam case led you to think of three people, I have looked on the drainer here, just in case."

"Well, you do know it might be something else now don't you? Something that doesn't tally with the surroundings, something different... yes very, very different. Have door to door enquiries begun? Better do them just in case, but being flats I doubt that any one would have seen or heard anyone coming or going, the stairwell didn't echo too badly as I came up, so anyone with soft shoes on would have, or could have, left virtually silently, and once on the street would have become invisible to the houses on the other side. Until he or she turned that last corner, he or she could have come from anywhere!"

Once the forensics and doctor had finished, and the body removed to the mortuary for a post mortem, the three detectives went in. The heavy aroma of stale pipe tobacco smoke hung in the air, which, strangely enough, the three detectives could feel as well as smell. The walls of the sitting room were stained a mottled sepia brown from the nicotine, but the flat was neatly furnished in what one could only say was "Bohemian" in style. What furniture there was, was practical and plain, reminding Chavender of his childhood when utility furniture was still around from just after the war. *Why?* he thought. The living room, kitchen, bathroom and bedroom all still very neat and tidy and all smelling of tobacco smoke, some rooms fainter than the others of the occupant's desire for pipe tobacco. Only the kitchen and bedroom retained some colour other than the sepia yellow nicotine stained walls and ceilings. His keen eyes saw no hint or sign of a struggle that one would expect if the murderer had had to use force. Chavender checked the kitchen cupboards, but only found two extra cups and enough crockery for one person, food was on the sparse side, not surprising seeing that he had his midday and evening meals delivered. The bedroom was furnished with a single bed, bedside cabinet and angle poise lamp with a chest of drawers along one wall and an old-fashioned antique bureau desk, stuffed full of letters, some books on gardening and some more letters in a box on the floor. Beside the bureau sat an easy chair, behind which a wall light hung. On the flap of the desk was a book on *How to Prune and Train Fruit Trees*, along with another book *Gardening in Small Spaces*. They all took this in, but they all ignored the significance of the books, thinking that it was a reading interest of his. In the front room was a pipe rack with four pipes in, tobacco and several full ashtrays, in one, a partly smoked large bowled pipe, similar to the one that Holmes smoked, was left, several burn marks on the small coffee table could be found were he had tapped out his pipe and some of the hot ash had fallen on the surface. Several tins of empty pipe tobacco and two full ones were found in the sideboard and all in all, pretty normal items one would expect to find in a pipe smoker's house. A set of home made shelves, made from scaffold planks and breeze blocks along one wall showed a varied interest in reading matter. Chavender asked Carruthers to go to the nearest paper shop and see if they sold that particular brand of pipe tobacco. On his way down he bumped into Miss Blaise and her photographer.

On the landing a young constable prevented Miss Blaise from going any further, as her protest increased in volume, Chavender put his head out the front door and was about to ask what all the commotion was about when he saw Miss Blaise. His face fell, but manning up he beckoned her to come forward, the constable duly obliged.

"Twice in one day; we have to stop meeting like this, Josh, people might begin to talk!" she said loud enough for Pearce and the Constable to hear. "What have we got here then, Josh? The paper grapevine says it's another mysterious death, is that the case?"

"Not at the moment, no, we don't know for sure; a Mr Graves, Robert, was found dead this afternoon shortly after 5pm, the police were called in by the meals delivery company when Mr Graves did not answer the door after repeated knocking; we gained entry and he was found on his bed, dead, at the moment of a suspected heart attack. His next of kin have been notified and we are awaiting the coroner's report. That is it I'm afraid, Miss Blaise, nothing spectacular or sensational for your paper to print."

She then asked whether it was connected to the other deaths. "That makes a total of seven people now in a few short weeks, do we have a murderer on the loose?" to which he replied, "As far as we can tell the deaths are unrelated, although it must be said that three have now died from heart attacks. I understand from medical sources that these have been, so far, naturally caused and do not raise suspicion of the medical examiners, otherwise..." He let go of that train of thought and said "Thank you Miss Blaise." He turned and went back inside. "Right, Pearce, we will wait for Carruthers to come back and then we will clear off, okay?"

"Yes Sir," Pearce replied.

They continued looking through the flat, but nothing stood out. Carruthers came back shortly and said, "The local paper shop did not sell pipe tobacco, he said that that particular brand of pipe tobacco could be bought from the tobacconist in town, our man could have bought it from there Sir."

"Okay, we'll check that out in the morning now, it's getting on a bit, it's been an intense day and I'm ready for going home. We'll pick this up in the morning. Could you give Carruthers a lift home, Pearce, if that's not too much of a bother?"

"Yes Sir, can do, goodnight Sir." with that he left for home.

Chapter 25

The next day the local paper carried two headlines: 'Police baffled in mysterious deaths of several local people' and 'Police continue investigating Plympton Council', both from 'our star reporter Wendy Blaise'. In both cases the articles were by any one's stretch of the imagination far fetched in their conclusions, as they invariably are. Chavender was unable to speak to Pearce during that day, due to his ever growing pile of paperwork. It was surprising how fast it grew, even if left for one day. With Small and Lister on file duty again, Chavender wrote out the transfer list and emailed them to the stations requesting as of Monday the following personnel will be temporarily assigned to these stations, he would allow reasonable travel expenses or travel time but not both."

That done he then went in search of Molly-Fergus, he needed to check something with her. Finding her in the canteen he bought a coffee and sat beside her.

"Nice bit in the paper Sir, looks like we don't know our arse from our elbows Sir! Running round like blue arsed flies, chasing shadows or whatever you would like to call it, it makes my blood boil, they don't know half the story, yet they make out they know all of it, and who the perpetrators are."

"Don't let it get to you Molly-Fergus," said Chavender, "if I were to believe half the tripe they wrote about me, I would not be able to get in my car, cause my head would get in the way! So, what's bugging you? Incidentally, if you don't mind me asking, how come you ended up with a name like Molly Molly-Fergus?

Which of your parents lost the bet?" he said, trying to take her mind off whatever was bothering her. "I thought my name was bad enough, you know its other meaning is "Chub" don't you. So I could have had either one of two nicknames, "Chubby" or "Beaky." But come on, come now... Molly... Molly Molly-Fergus." Stopping and without thinking he carried on by saying, "That's almost as bad as "Major Major" in *Catch 22*!"

"Yes Sir," she said, "I know, it could have been worse, far worse. You know, it could of been "Milo Minderbender"! Well, the answer is you see, my father was a Scottish Fergus, my mother was an Irish Molly; they could not agree on the best married name to use, so in the end they decided to keep both and it became double barrelled - my brother, and I, bet you can't guess what they called him Sir?" Looking at him and smiling.

"Um... Well... Let me see... Is it... No... Could it be... Fergus Molly-Fergus?" Chavender replied tongue in cheek.

"Yes sir, my brother's first name is Fergus."

"Well now, Molly your turn to guess my brother first name."

"Is it something that sounds like a fish sir?" He nodded, "Well let me see, it's not something like Kevin Chavender?"

"What a good guess Molly, but that hardly sounds like a fish now, does it? But no, he was called Grayling Chavender, another fishy name admittedly; the only reason I got stuck with Joshua, was because I looked like a great Uncle or someone, it was his name, who along with me, had this fine beak of a nose." As he said this, he tapped his nose with one finger, "My brother missed out on that and thankfully so did my four girls. So I got the nose and a fairly decent first name, my brother got no fine nose and was stuck with the name of another fish as a Christian name; my old man was potty on fishing, or more likely just plain potty! In the end we called him GeeCee."

They both laughed. He finished his coffee and got up and left, completely forgetting he was going to ask her about something.

At the canteen door he remembered what it was he wanted to ask her, so he turned round and went back. "Hello again Molly-Fergus, I forgot to ask you," tapping the temple of his head and shaking it, "did you check the information that Lister and Small found out about the landlord who sold up and went back to the Republic of Ireland?"

"Yes Sir, a small time crooked person, one time supporter of the IRA. The Irish police and our Immigration records indicate he is still in the Republic of Ireland, Sir. Why?"

"Oh just wondering that's all, it's so I can cross him of my list of suspects for murder - just a passing fancy it might have been him! Anyways, you might as well come back with me, we can collect Lister and Small on the way. I'm sure they're going to be happy that I've cut their session short!"

Picking up the two DIs on the way to his office, they entered only to be confronted with another two whiteboards. Lister sarcastically stated "saving on curtains and pictures Sir!" Sitting down he avoided the look that Chavender gave him. "Right you two, what have you got for me?" he asked, and Small replied, "Well sir, we continued following that lead about the landlord and it looks like he owns another agency, an employment agency called Navvies for you. From what we can gather, he uses it to supply the labour to the developers from Southern Ireland. The developers buy houses on the cheap, and let them to the labourers at a very reasonable rent, they then turn a blind eye to some of the shadier practices going on, on the construction site, you know bending health and safety rules, burying left over or waste materials under the gardens."

Chavender looked at him and was just about to interrupt him, when Small carried on, "Oh nothing dangerous, brick rubble, wood, cement and plaster board off cuts, generally they would dig a hole three to four foot deep, a foot of rubble and two to three foot of soil on top, just in case someone was to dig that deep sir! This would have saved them on average probably three to five thousand pounds per site by not using skips or muck away, this then went into the navvies fund as a bonus on completion of the works. At the end of the construction they would all go back to Ireland sir, the houses that they rented could either be renovated and sold, if modern enough or demolished and the land sold for building on, just for your information sir, this happened to about twenty bungalows in the Rosemore area of Plympton some ten years ago and the land is still derelict and still owned by Grey Developments. This money would disappear, ready to be used again, probably written off as a tax loss. It seems ok apart from the burying of rubbish!"

"These houses that they bought for rent, can we look into that please?" asked Chavender. "Well, what's next?"

Lister replied, "Well Sir, that's the councillors and developers files done we now move on to bank statements for all of them."

"Good, good, perhaps we are getting to the light at the end of the tunnel! Now about our suspicious deaths, any thoughts? Anyone?"

"Well Sir, the only thought I had and you may not like it Sir, is that all the deaths have, as they have been found out, to be natural or accidental; it is only the police or more specifically you, that seem to think anything is wrong or suspicious with these deaths so far. We have no hard evidence at all, no witnesses, in fact zilch! It's only the fact that they have all occurred in our county, which is a small area and not nationwide, that has raised the death tally here; taken as a whole I would have thought that the cause of death is not out of proportion to national figures, Sir," said Lister.

"That may be so, and I do take your point Lister about local and national figures. Insofar as it goes, we don't have two brass beans of evidence to rub together, in fact even this latest death I would not be surprised if it came back as natural causes that he died of!" Chavender remarked, "Still not a lot we can do until someone makes a mistake and lets us in, and if my hunch is correct, that could well be not be for a long time; if we do have a murderer on the patch he has been very clever so far. No or very little usable forensic evidence, so what is he doing to make it appear that it's the invisible man doing the killings. Well for a start, no direct evidence of any wrong doing by choosing a type of death that appears to be hard to trace, looks like natural causes and he times it, or is lucky enough and chooses people, so as to have no witnesses to his grim deed. I don't for one thing, think we have the invisible man killing people, or even aliens, it must be someone and that someone *WILL* make a mistake eventually. You may ask why I think so?" Answering his own question he carried on. "It's that little thing called 'lack of evidence" that's been bugging me for a long time now. This lack of evidence in my eyes is evidence enough that something just doesn't smell right, six possibly seven people just don't die and leave nothing behind. Let's look at what we have so far." saying this he went over to a white board and started to write. "One, two people die from gas poisoning, evidence pretty slim only one bottle, yet two liquids mixed, Two, drug addict, heart attack could have been chemically created by Potassium Chloride injection, evidence, very hard to detect in the body because it is naturally occurring and no trace of the needle used to inject chemical only the one showing signs of heroin use. Three, now this could possibly be natural causes, but with no evidence what so ever yet, it will remain on the list until proven otherwise! Four, two people die, one from sleeping tablets bought over the web possibly and possibly administered by the wife in a fit of rage, or whilst the balance of her mind was disturbed, who then commits suicide by suffocation and sleeping tablets, evidence, no previous sleeping pill use, no quarrels, no computer at the address, no witnesses but three cups on drainer! Five, one man dies in his sleep, no evidence whatsoever yet, could be heart attack again! Now! Can you see that evidence is beginning to emerge isn't it, all pretty slim and circumstantial, but evidence enough for me, that is three possibly four heart attacks, two gassings and one suicide in the space of, oh... I would guess around... Say starting about five maybe six weeks ago weeks so far as we can ascertain."

Soon all of the new whiteboards were nearly full; the DIs looked on as Chavender put the final column in relation to or known to each other; against each set of deaths he wrote 'none' and said, "not even as far as we can tell at the moment even remotely connected, but connected they must be, and that is the burning question at the moment." He then went on to say, "I know it is pretty feeble so far ladies and gentlemen, but what else can explain all these unrelated deaths, not much except, and I say this with absolute conviction, that they must all be related in some way, find that and we will be halfway to proving the cause of death either way. Don't you agree?"

The Detective Inspectors all nodded in agreement, although they really did not quite see what he was driving at with the lack of evidence is evidence in itself bit. Until he went on to say, "Look I know it is hard to grasp, but what if I said the same for extraterrestrial beings or 'aliens', no evidence yet of their existence but people believe in them, so therefore they must exist! As of Monday next, the following inspectors will swap stations, Molly-Fergus, will be at Plympton and Pearce will come to HQ; after that, Harrier will swap with Smith, then you will swap with Lister and Small, so in eight weeks we should be back to the start." Thanking them he then dismissed them.

Later that day, Pearce called, "We have the preliminary results sir, it's another heart attack I'm afraid, no... No other cause of death according to the coroner, a heart attack, possibly brought on by the smoking habit of his. The coroner did say that, and to use his term loosely Sir, there was enough tar in his lungs to tarmac the M3 from Southampton to London Sir. He could see no obvious methods or signs of a struggle or bruising from rope marks, no broken skin; only the cut made by the tin of tuna or skin under the nails, I made sure that he knew we thought the death was suspicious but he could not confirm it in any way, shape or form! Same with forensics, they could find nothing out of the ordinary at the flat, although - and they are not sure about this Sir - the heavy tobacco staining and ash could help to mask any foreign matter but again a virtually sterile scene by way of other clues, Sir."

"Right-o Pearce, I think it would be best if we set up a meeting with that doctor again at the hospital; can you arrange that again for us both please?"

"Yes Sir I will make it for Thursday morning, if that's okay."

"That'll be fine, I'll meet you at 9am at Plympton okay, bye."

"Bye Sir," replied Pearce.

Chapter 26

The next day by 10am saw Chavender and Pearce sat in Dr J.M. Mallingson's office, drinking a cup of coffee and discussing the latest death. Chavender asked him to go though death by Potassium Chloride.

Dr Mallingsons replied, "Well, as little as a 20cc injection of a strong solution of Potassium Chloride would be enough to kill someone in a time span of... Oh let's say a few seconds to several minutes; given the correct dosage it will certainly cause an heart attack. This heart attack, which is very painful, may be difficult for the coroner to realise that it was not a natural heart attack or even possibly suicide by self injection. I feel our murderer may have slipped up here, you know; if he had left the needle behind we would have thought suicide, not natural causes, and that would be that, based on that evidence, even less evidence for us to say so otherwise or contradict ourselves, see! Now an excess of Potassium Chloride in the blood interferes with all nerve signals, it is the nerve signals which control breathing and heartbeat as well as many other functions to keep the body alive; a strong enough dose will, and does, stop all muscles and nerves from working, so when it reaches your heart, the heart stops. The coroner will look for clues as to cause of death, facial features, contortion of muscles, as we would in all cases, certain telltale signs give the game away. Take beheading as an extreme example, death is by severing the head from the body, quite easily recognisable I would say, don't you think? So by reading the signs on and in the body we can arrive at a pretty certain cause of death. Of course this would be harder if the body was dismembered, but again I'm fairly certain that given enough body parts a cause of death could be ascertained, if not body parts by themselves could mean death by dismembering. So even that's a traceable death, now back to Potassium Chloride; it will need to be administered as an injection to be certain of working, certain deadly poisons that can kill someone dead in seconds can be ingested into the stomach and have no ill or very little side effects whatsoever!"

Chavender said, "So what you're saying is, it will be hard to identify, unless we can come up with the needle used to inject it with, I don't know about you doctor but I would not let someone inject me with out putting up a fight! But let's say you manage to do so, how do you do that and how could you hide the needle mark?"

The doctor replied, "Well I agree, injecting someone if they are conscious is not easy without their consent; they will invariably struggle and this will leave traces, skin under the deceased's fingernails for one thing, possible defensive injuries, for example, many small puncture wounds or if the person was tied the spasm of the muscles might cause rope marks; no the best bet would be to try knocking them out, possible by a crushed sleeping pill, but again a slight trace, or by Chloroform, possibly no trace, come up behind someone, rag soaked in chloroform only takes a few seconds before you're drowsy enough not to care, then shortly after that fast asleep, once asleep it would be easy to inject someone. The mark left by the needle could be in any one of the soft facial openings not directly on the skin, possibly up the nose, in the ear, in the mouth between the teeth, or even on the scalp - or better still in a wound."

As he said this Pearce flinched at the thought of a needle up the nose, "That must hurt" not realising he said it out loud.

The doctor continued, "Yes it would if you were awake, but remember the person is asleep, actually more than asleep, possibly comatose, so you can do what you like to the body with out the body waking up; it acts more like a Loopy Lou doll - once injected as I said death is certain. I see from the report, a cut on the hand, not a bad cut but never the less a cut, that could explain why he was on the bed."

"Oh - why's that?" Chavender asked.

"Well he could have gone for a lie down to get over shock, you know it affects people in many different ways and it's a killer in the right circumstances!" Dr Mallingson then asked, "Did the medical examiner find any needle marks or any other such possible marks?"

The answer Pearce gave was non committal, "We didn't think to ask the coroner to look for that, apart from, that is, what we already mentioned, the deceased did have a one inch long fairly deep jagged cut to the ball of his thumb, near to the wrist. We're not sure how that came about, evidence suggests by possibly opening a tin of tuna fish, the blade or most likely the tin lid slipped and cut him, as I say it is consistent with evidence found at the scene, a small tin of tuna fish, that we found in the bin, blood stains on the tin lid and on the paper tissue matched the blood of the deceased; the plaster came from the First aid box, which only had his smudged prints on. Blood splatter, which we used the blood detector on, showed us where on the kitchen drainer he cut himself." Pearce stopped and looked at Chavender, "Sir, I've just thought; he has his meals delivered, so why would he want to open a tin of tuna? Unless of course the murderer wanted to inject a lethal dose of Potassium Chloride and leave no trace!"

Chavender nodded in agreement. "Well doctor, could it be as easy as that?"

"Um... Yes I think so, no way of telling how much blood was lost by the cut and it would only take a few ccs worth collected in a syringe to create the splatter pattern, so I would say most likely; but again hard to detect a small pinprick in the wound, but not impossible if you knew what to look for from the off, now might be too late. I think it all depends on what way he did it though; if he injected first, then cut, he could have masked the point of entry with the wound, which is probably why it wasn't found, then collecting a few ccs of blood, easy enough, by using a syringe and plaster on afterwards, any tuna fish found in the stomach, no? What about the bin?" he asked no one in particular. "Yes doctor along with the empty tin we found the contents, he must have dropped them on the sink drainer and threw them away! But it still doesn't add up, why he would want to open a tin of tuna?" This left the two Detectives puzzled.

Chavender then asked how easy was it to get hold of Potassium Chloride and hypodermic needles, feeling that he needed his memory refreshed. "Oh very very easy, from the web, chemists and any number of other places, I'm afraid, probably all untraceable though. Unless of course you had the receipt or prescription at hand, then easy."

"If only," muttered Chavender.

Thanking the doctor for his time they got up and left and on returning to the Plympton Police station, Chavender thanked Pearce and went to find Chief Inspector Sword, to inform him of progress so far. Finding Pearce again, he informed him that from Monday next he would be working at headquarters, so he would leave him to his thoughts till Monday, unless of course we have another death, which he thought may well be a possibility, but he did not expect the series of events that actually happened over the weekend!

Chapter 27

That Thursday afternoon saw him wade through the mountains of reports that the teams had so far thought were at least worth a second look! Bank statements and phone logs were poured over in minute detail but revealed next to nothing, apart from the fact that they knew each other as evidenced by the phone contact log, but without the actual transcripts of the conversation, it needed something to back it up with! Later that day the information he requested came from the Council; the five large boxes came by a Council courier, who requested a receipt for each box and Chavender had to sign for them, plus the contents of the delivery. The boxes contained the minutes of the last five years planning meetings that had involved Councillors Walker and Melbourne and the minutes of the merger committees, along with a request to return or destroy them once done, if they were not to be used as evidence, because they may contain confidential information. The five boxes once safely deposited in his office, added to the general clutter of the now not so barren in nature as it once was when he first occupied it.

Friday morning saw him at headquarters by seven; he wanted the early start so he could catch up with Inspector Carr, who was on nights for the next week or so. He looked in on Carr on his way to his office and asked if he would like a coffee. Carr nodded in agreement and they both went to the canteen. Carr, yawning loudly, sat down whilst Chavender went for the coffee. Returning he sat down, sipped his coffee and thanked Carr for sorting out his wayward constables; the temporary return to the uniform branch helped shake them up a little. Carr assured him the extra help was gladly received, saying he had put them both to beat walking round town with two of the older sergeants, who took no quarter; they kept them walking for five hours each, it served to teach them a lesson.

Chavender agreed and added, "Still I bet you want to get off now so you can get home to bed?" With that he got up and left to look in on the CID room, and see who would be first in. Molly-Fergus and Harrier arrived first a little before their time, both carrying cups of coffee, on time also were the sergeants and constables, all were surprised to see him sat there.

"Good to see that you're all on time. Apart from what we have already under investigation, is there anything new to add?"

Molly-Fergus replied, "No Sir, only the ongoing investigations at this moment in time" using the old police practice of using five words where one would do!

"Good, glad to hear it; are you transferees looking forward to Monday?" he said looking round the room and only seeing semi glum faces, to which he added a halfhearted threat of, "Cheer up its nearly the weekend! You know, you could come round to my house tomorrow and help me redecorate?" Thanking him for the kind offer of extra unpaid work, they each declined, so with a wry smile he got up and left them to it.

On the way to his office he bumped into Featherstonehaugh, "Ah Chavender, just the chap, I'm heading towards Bryantsand police station on Monday at 2pm, for my inspection; please make yourself available. I would like you to come with me, and please don't forewarn them, I will tell Chief Inspector Andersonn Monday morning myself, after our Monday meeting, okay?"

Chavender replied, "Yes Sir" and saluted, as the Chief Constable walked away.

Chavender sat in his office, and he set to and determinedly worked his way through the mound of paperwork he had to do that day, most of which he thought was a vast waste of time, but someone had to do it and, if it came with the promotion, then that someone was him. Every so often he would get up and look over the five boards, but the same conclusions answered him back, facts against him, ninety nine percent, evidence for him one percent, but of that one percent he was dead sure, three cups equals three people to him, even if no one else believed it! By midday the paperwork was done for now at least, he was sure that by Monday another mountain would surely be in his intray. Looking up at the time, he decided to get a coffee. In the canteen he saw Sue Jenkins, who told him to sit down she would bring it over, coming across with two cups and beaming a bright wide smile, she sat down opposite him. She started to speak.

"It was really good of you and Tiffany to invite us over last Sunday, it was nice to meet your mother-in-law and the girls really appreciated it. We've some more good news, Bert got himself an allotment, at last, just in time we think, you know just before the merger. Did you know he had been waiting for three years or more, and rumour has it that the wait will be more than doubled when the merger happens?"

"That'll please him then," Josh said.

Sue went on, "Yes he likes to grow his own vegetables and stuff, and more to the point, it will help him relax a little bit, you know, to unwind, he always potters about at home after a day shift for half an hour, well this should keep him busy at weekends for a while now."

After some fifteen minutes of general chat, he said, "Well thanks for the company and coffee Sue, I'd best be getting back or they might think I don't do anything but chat to pretty sergeants' wives all day!" He got up and left, stopping by the CID room again to check on progress before getting much the same report from the others as they had said all week. With that he said goodbye and see you all on Monday and he left for home.

Saturday morning was warm and fine without a cloud in the sky and Josh really did not want to spend it stuck indoors painting, but Tiff put up a very persuasive one word argument for him to get it done - sausages! So that Saturday, instead of doing something he would liked to have done, like go for a walk, he knuckled down and got on with painting the walls Baby Blue and the ceiling white, by 3pm he had it done, but he knew Tiff would want at least two coats on the walls so the prospect of painting all day Sunday loomed ahead. In the meantime, Tiff took Gran and the two youngest girls out to look for a carpet and do the weekly shop, leaving the two oldest with the instructions "to keep dad supplied with tea on the hour every hour." This at least pleased him, he did not have to go carpet hunting but he knew it would still put an hole in his wallet pocket. They came back just as he was finishing cleaning up and he had just sat down to a cup of tea.

Tiff sent the girls in first to get Josh, so he could help unload the landy, stepping out into the bright warm sunny afternoon. Josh blinked and almost did a double take, the back of the landy was virtually packed full with shopping, bedroom furnishings and yet more paint. Corralling the girls it still took almost a full half an hour to unload; decorating supplies lined the hall, bedroom furnishings stacked on a cane chair in the conservatory, shopping on the kitchen table and work tops. Josh just looked bewildered, could they, did they, really need all this? he asked himself. He looked into the hall and saw himself on decorating duties for the foreseeable future, his faced must have shown some shock as Tiff said, "Don't worry dear, its not as bad as all that, you only have two more rooms to do, after that, we will move mum into the newly decorated room, you can then start on the empty girls' room and once that's done we can move the girls back again, leaving that last room free; by then Mum will be well enough to look after herself and she will return home, so another six weeks and you'll be done!"

Josh jokingly said, "Done in more like, sure you're not trying to kill me for the insurance money, Tiff?"

"No dear," said Tiff, "I think I would make it look more like one of those mysterious deaths you are investigating at the moment, you know, the heart attack ones. I might be kind and do it to you whilst were making love, just so you die a happy man with a smile on your face!"

Laughing, she sidestepped his playful slap to her behind and blew him a kiss as she stepped into the conservatory to sort through the bedroom furnishings.

Sunday saw Josh put the second coat of Baby Blue emulsion on the walls. He was pleased with the results and so was Tiff, so much so, that for a treat, she insisted Josh came with her to select and pay for the new carpet. That afternoon, whilst gran looked after the girls, they went to a carpet shop called Pull the Rug and selected a carpet that Tiff liked, and a date for Tuesday next week was booked for the carpet company to come and lay the carpet, so they would be able to swap rooms later that week. Unbeknown to Josh, that Sunday several people were rushed to hospital with acute abdominal pains; at first it would be mis-diagnosed as simple food poisoning but by Tuesday morning, it would be forming the focus of the police investigations for the next week or so, for five would die by that Monday evening, some later and the others would just make it, but remain critical for some weeks afterwards; it would take a toxicologist some time to work it out.

Chapter 28

On Monday, at the Chief Constable's meeting, Chavender appraised them of the situation thus far and of the unaccountable food poisoning epidemic that had left ten people in hospital.

"The hospital has called in a toxicologist to assist with diagnosis, but until they know what caused it they are having to treat the symptoms as they manifest themselves, the victims are stable at the moment but a few are critical and could die. We have no known lunatic on the loose and all our probationers are accounted for, but until we know for sure what the cause is, we can do nothing, I have constables standing by in case one of them recovers enough to make a statement."

Sword asked, "Are they all on my manor?"

"No, two people are from Bryantsand," he replied. Featherstonehaugh went on to say, "Don't like it one bit, gentlemen, not one bit, we are becoming the focus of the media, look at this diatribe, this dribble that Miss Blaise wrote for this morning's paper." In bold headlines the front page read 'Mysterious Poison Epidemic Baffles Hospitals, Police Investigate!' It then went on to say how the police seem to be doing nothing about protecting the towns' citizens and how it tried to link the previous seven deaths into this epidemic, as revealed by a source close to the top.

"Not you is it Chavender?" the Chief Constable said, "You have been seen quite a lot recently with this reporter woman."

"No Sir, definitely not! But I think I know who it might be, and she might not be too far from the mark about those other deaths; it could possibly be..." Stopping dead in his train of thoughts and continuing with, "Perhaps Sir it might pay us to interview her again; she may have left something out last time or she has some new information Sir. Perhaps Sword and myself or Pearce could speak to her at Plympton? Perhaps Tuesday would be good? "He made a mental note to find out if Wootton had been pillow talking. That morning's meeting seemed to drag on more than usual for Chavender, but at last at 11.30am it seemed to be winding up.

Featherstonehaugh then looked at Andersonn and spoke, "Right Sword lets go, your station will be the first to be inspected." Anderson visibly heaved a sigh of relief, Sword's face dropped, Andersonn knew he would only have a few days respite, best get those last little bits done before the boss comes to inspect, he thought.

"You will drive me Chief Inspector, Chavender can drive me back, okay?"

"Yes Sir." Sword looking at Chavender with despair, and nodded at him, his eyes pleading, thankfully Featherstonehaugh did not catch it, and they were dismissed. On the way to the car, Sword was unable to talk to Chavender, who was hoping that Chavender could guess what it was he wanted him to do!

Chavender thought something might be wrong at Plympton, and that Sword had tried to give him the heads up. *Got it! It's the noticeboard, bet it has not been sorted yet!* he thought and waited till he was in his car before phoning the station on the internal number.

"Duty Sergeant Jenkins speaking Sir, what is it please?"

"Look Sergeant Jenkins, no time to speak, Chief Constable's inspection, we are on our way; make sure that the posters in the front lobby are sorted right away if they have not already been done, get in touch with DI Molly-Fergus or the Duty Inspector and walk round the station quickly, anything wrong put it right, if you can, or make a note in the defects book for rectification ASAP! Okay? We'll be twenty to thirty minutes. Bye."

With that Jenkins detailed a constable to remove the older poster and re-pin the newer posters level, the Duty Inspector was busy in the custody suite, so he got hold of DI Molly-Fergus and informed her of the coming inspection and Chavender's instructions, and they both did a quick walk around. Anything that could be done was, anything that could not be done was duly noted.

"The Chief Constable will probably come in the front door, I suggest you take over the poster sorting detail Sergeant, and if he says anything to you, oh heck you know what to say Sergeant, we best be getting back to our stations." With that they parted just in time, for five minutes later the Chief Inspector's tour of inspection was underway.

Entering the building, the Chief Constable saw Sergeant Jenkins and a Constable tackling the noticeboard. "Good man Sergeant, it seems the Sergeant's grapevine must be working well, yes very well indeed, no bollocking for you then, hey, what, Sergeant!"

"No Sir," Jenkins replied, heaving a sigh of relief; they might just get away with it yet, he was working on that old principle that his father taught him, that got him out of trouble at home many a time - "if it hasn't been done yet, but you're working on it, it will convince most people that you've been working hard, and this was the first opportunity to do it!" "Finish sorting this will you please Constable; can I get you anything Sir? Tea or coffee perhaps?"

"No, no we're fine, later perhaps, you have the defects book here, up to date is it Sergeant?"

"Yes Sir, completed just this morning, as always Sir, Duty Sergeant's rounds when the Chief Inspector or the Duty Inspector is busy, just like this morning Sir!"

Sword looked at Chavender and just nodded his head, breathed a sigh of relief and mouthed "thanks".

Featherstonehaugh looked at Sergeant Jenkins. "That's good, very good, just as it should be right Sergeant? Perhaps you would like to come with us." He then said. "Yes Sir, complete this Constable and then file them away in a cupboard." The young constable nodded and saluted the senior officers and carried on with his assigned task.

Featherstonehaugh then spoke, "Right let's have the defects book, we'll note defects down as we go round the station; you know when I commanded a Regiment of Riflemen, we had an old Regimental Sergeant-Major, who could and often would put the fear of God into the entire regiment from senior officers, all the way down through to the subalterns, the NCOs, and the riflemen on his inspection tours, he hated indiscipline in the regiment, very proud to be a rifleman, as the old saying goes "once a rifleman, always a rifleman", he was and probably still is a rifleman at heart, knowing him, and legend had it that he could spot a speck of dust at twenty paces, a right terror he was, firm but fair, but by golly get on the wrong side of him and you knew it! Yes sir, you knew it. I was not in command at the time but the RSM once had the entire Regiment march round the parade ground all night, because one of the company commanders let his company rule him instead of him commanding them, he took the lead, hardly flagged, even after six hours of parade marching, fit as a fiddle he was; of course I was younger then, he was on the verge of retiring when I took command of the regiment. You see discipline like that would do the youngster of today the power of good, not like it is these days, we must have discipline, must have tidiness and must have respect for yourself and others."

As he repeated his pet mantra, they started to walk round the building for a full three hours, the chief constable poked his nose in everywhere he could, finding fault and giving praise, the faults went into the defect book to be rectified by the next inspection, on the whole Sword was pleased with the way the inspection had gone only a few minor defects and that was it.

"Very good Chief Inspector Sword, yes very good indeed, nice clean and tidy, keep up the good work Sergeant! Trust your sergeants, gentlemen; there the real discipline enforcers, they are the backbone of the force, they should be able to sort out your minor problems for you and leave you free to deal with the major ones, is that not the case Sergeant?"

"Yes sir," Jenkins answered.

"Well thanks Chief Inspector Sword, your station has set a high standard, next inspection in about four months or so, okay? Get those defects sorted Sergeant, I will leave it in your capable hands! Right Chavender, let's get back to headquarters shall we?"

With that, they both left for the return to headquarters. That Monday evening would see five people die and the remaining five become critical cases in hospital parlance and be placed in the intensive care ward.

Chapter 29

Tuesday morning saw Chavender divide his men up into teams to await the reports, so he at least could get them off and running quickly. Of course the press had a field day, headlines such as 'Star reporter to be interviewed again by police in connection with food poison deaths', 'Mysterious Deaths strike in Plympton' as the national papers got in on the act; it even made the local television news that day. Chavender spoke with Wootton about his possible "Pillow talking" but was soundly reassured by him that that was not the case. Chavender thought perhaps she did know something, so got in touch with Pearce and asked him to ascertain exactly what she knew at the interview later that day. He would remain at headquarters waiting to set the ball rolling for the time being, but he would come across later. It was not long before the Toxicologist report from the hospital was brought to him, it made grim reading: Mr B Smith died of acute Taxine poisoning, his wife is in a critical condition, Mr and Mrs English are both dead also of Taxine poisoning, Mr and Mrs Jones both dead from Oleander poisoning. Whilst Mr and Mrs King and Mr and Mrs Waterloo are all in a critical condition with a less than fifty/fifty chance of surviving, it all depends on the constitution of the individuals, but now the poison is known they can treat the symptoms correctly and the greater chance of recovery.

Chavender made an appointment to see the Toxicologist for Wednesday, he would come and see him at the hospital; until then he hoped no more would die. The Toxicologist could not guarantee that, and it now all depended on the care received.

Before leaving for the interview with Miss Blaise, he made sure that the houses of the poisoned people were sealed, so if any evidence was inside it would be left in situ. Driving to Plympton police station, not to sit in on the interview, but to be on hand so to speak, the one burning question he had on his mind was "how?" Sword and Pearce interviewed Miss Blaise but all she said was that it was a guess, they had no evidence of any kind, they were trying to sensationalise the story a bit more for the increase in circulation that such gory deaths and stories bring to the paper by way of revenue. Look at the Dr Crippen case or the John Christie murders, and many others too numerous to mention, and all sensational stories of their time, they all brought in much needed revenue for the papers. "I think it satisfies man's ghoulish curiosity for the macabre!" After an hour or so she convinced Sword and Pearce that she knew nothing more and so was free to go.

Bumping into Chavender on the way out she said, "Hi Josh, any news for the newshound? You are treating the deaths as suspicious, right? Have you any clues yet?" and not waiting for an answer but seeing Sword and Pearce in the corridor, she hugged and kissed him full on the lips and said, "See you later Josh" hugging him again, kissing him on the cheek she whispered in his ear, "That will get them talking, but you're safe now!" and as she was departing she was already formulating Wednesday's headlines in her mind. He turned what only could be called a beetroot red at what appeared to be her offensive activity, and started to splutter and bluster; his hand sought a handkerchief to wipe away the bright red lipstick on his lips and cheek, his colleagues looked on shocked at the little tableau that had just unfolded before their very eyes before Sword spoke, "Bloody hell Josh, your wife will kill you if she finds out, but what have you got that I haven't that catches the eye of such beauties like her and your wife?"

Chavender's facial colour slowly resumed its normal non-flushed hue, as did his power to speak coherently as he started to explain to them both about how she had a crush on him, and yes, his wife does know. Before sitting with Sword and Pearce to discuss the turn of events and what she had said, but nothing directly sprang to the minds of the three police officers, that would or could help them in the case so far.

Tuesday passed slowly into Wednesday for Chavender, expecting the death toll to rise, but those that remained alive had stabilised and although still critical, it was not considered life threatening at the moment.

At Chavender Mansions, the carpet company arrived and fitted the carpet. Tiff and her mum were standing in the freshly painted and carpeted room, Tiff breathing in deep, smelt the freshness of and the newness of the carpet, the faint odour of the baby blue emulsion paint and said, "Nice isn't it Mum?"

"Yes, yes just right!" her mum replied, "So, Tiffany, when are you going to tell him?"

"Tell him what Mum?"

"That you're pregnant silly girl, you can't fool me; I'm your mother remember!"

Looking somewhat shocked that her mum knew, she replied "When this murder case is over, Mum, I don't want him to worry about me as well, especially those weird cravings I had and he had to put up with, and you know how he fussed and went on before the girls were born, so please don't tell him. I will in a few weeks, that's if he doesn't get it from this big clue that I have given him!"

Looking at her mum, she spread her arms wide and did a quick twirl round.

"Okay love but are you sure it's a boy?"

Tiff just nodded her head once and said, "Definitely Mum."

Once again the press did its best to blow things up and out of proportion with yet more outlandish headlines appeared, amongst others such as 'Inspector Clueless bungles investigation into recent deaths and poisonings', showing a stock image of a policeman scratching his head looking at a the white outline of a question mark lying flat on the ground, as one would find at murder scenes to mark out where the body had lain. For the meeting with Dr Solomon, the toxicologist, Chavender took Carruthers. Arriving at the hospital they were shown into a small office and awaited the arrival of Dr Solomon, who, coming from a laboratory, still had a white lab coat on and test tubes sticking out of the top pocket. Introductions and hand shakes over, Chavender asked the burning question on how they could have been poisoned the way they were. Dr Solomon answered "that's easy", and went on to explain.

"Well what you have got to remember is that the poison used is a naturally occurring one; in the ten people poisoned I have identified three poisons; each was self-administered and probably masked in some way. For example, the stomach contents of the those that died of Taxine show traces of a strong Orange and Lime Marmalade."

"Marmalade?" said Chavender in surprise. "Well that does't poison you, let alone kill you does it doctor?"

"No not by itself, but I reckon the marmalade was spiked with an extract of Yew or Taxus Baccata, the common English Yew, in fact, found in practically every churchyard in England. The poisoner must have extracted the oil in some way so as to concentrate it, and to hide its bitter taste, mixed it with the marmalade. All parts of the plant, except for the fleshy red bit of the fruit, contain poisons some good, some bad, for the past ten years or so clinical trials have been underway to see if they can cure some cancers with a medicine or serum extracted from the Yew Tree. Now the symptoms are classic as is for most poisonings, first nausea, followed by abdominal pain, then a lapse into a coma, then death, such as what we saw in the deaths of Mr Smith and Mr and Mrs English. The mode of death is a heart attack which occurs soon after eating sufficient or enough of the poison, the more you eat the quicker you die, but I would say, if you don't die straight away, it could take up to, or between, two to three days after the first ingestion of the poison. Eating enough would lead to a sudden collapse of all your bodily functions, causing death by an heart attack almost instantly, but if it's not enough to kill you outright the symptoms are severe lethargy, trembling or convulsions of the entire body, staggering drunkenly with no awareness of your surroundings, a feeling of muscular or entire body coldness, a dilation of the pupils, along with a rapid pulse that gradually becomes weak, and yet more convulsions. If no heart attack occurs, you'll probably survive as has Mrs Smith. It is hard to estimate the exact dosage required but I would say in concentrated form two maybe three teaspoons full will have the desired effect.

"In Mr and Mrs Jones' case, this took me a while to search for the answer but on first finding that Mr Smith and the Englishes were poisoned by Taxine distilled from a common garden tree, I reckoned and the test later proved, that they both died from another form of shrub poisoning, this time it was an Oleander shrub that the poison was extracted from, most common form of ingestion is probably as a infusion, we found no spiked marmalade in the stomach contents, only toast, so I reckon it was probably administered as a drink, most probably as a tea or something similar; the Oleander contains a poison similar to digitalis. Every part of this shrub is most probably deadly in its own way and highly lethal as well, we know deaths have been recorded by using wood from this plant in fires, and making tea from the leaves as in this case. In a few hours there is abdominal pain, nausea, vomiting, bloody diarrhoea, rapid pulse, and visual effects or impairments. Later, a slow, weak, irregular pulse and fall in blood pressure, followed by failure of the heart. As you can see much the same as Taxine and just as deadly, dosage again varies but a good couple of tea bags might do the trick,"

Chavender winced a little at this, so far his favourite drink and Sunday morning breakfast have been used as cover for a lethal dose of poison.

"Now in the case of Mr and Mrs Waterloo and Mr and Mrs Kingsley, as in the two other cases, I took my cue from the fact that it might be poison from a shrub and found that they had been poisoned by the berries of Daphne Mezereum, again most probably in the form of marmalade. This is because like the Yew poison, it and the berries taste most horrid, but you only need to eat a few to cause death; as with the others, the immediate symptoms are a burning sensation in mouth, followed by nausea, severe vomiting and stomach pains, later on chronic diarrhoea, allied with a general lethargic disposition, a general disorientation or lack of awareness of your surroundings, then convulsions that affect the whole body, and finally followed by death in the worst cases scenario. Again the dosage is hard to estimate but several berries would do the trick I think. Now, that is three natural poisons all readily available from any good garden centre, I would hazard a guess, and all three are extremely deadly, as it has been proven. Now, anything else you would like to know gentlemen? If not I need to carry on with some testing. Well, thank you. Goodbye."

With that he got up and left. Leaving the two detectives certainly a little bit worried as they made their way back to headquarters. Poisons that are easily obtainable and to administer, how many more spiked items are out there waiting to kill?

Once back Chavender gave instructions to search the homes of those that had been poisoned and to look closely at and for any empty jars of marmalade, and open boxes of teabags. If any were found they were to be bagged up and taken to the Hospital for Dr Solomon to test. Chavender decided to scale down the efforts on the alleged fraud case and let it lie for awhile, after all no one had died in the investigation in the fraud case yet! So, all CID's efforts for the time being would focus on the poisoning cases. He called for Wootton and gave him the task of getting statements from the patients in hospital when they came around, he also told him about Wendy's indiscretion at Plympton the other day, Wootton just said, "She had told him about it and it was her way to get back at him for giving me a hard time over the alleged "pillow talking" so no harm done then?"

Chavender was still not certain about that, but he seemed to have bought it, so he let it rest. Back in his office he sat in front of the white boards, looking, staring when suddenly he thought he saw a connection, could it be that the very first couple to die was not accidental but deliberate, by poison gas? If so it would tie in with recent events, but why the long gap! However, not so well with the heart attack victims, but if he could tie it in, it would be a good start he thought, but that gap worried him.

Chapter 30

The council merger was still going full steam ahead, but at a full council meeting it was agreed to suspend Councillors Walker and Melbourne from the Planning Committee, and all future planning applications would have to pass a special planning committee for ratification. This would include any sale of council land in the pipeline now or later. The council was making up for lost time when it should have suspended those implicated in the alleged fraudulent affair. This was in direct response from pressure from the press and members of the public, who bombarded the town halls with letters of protest, especially when it emerged that a previous sale of council land did not realise its full potential due to the possibility of underhand dealings. The date was set for the 4th of March to dissolve both councils and elections to the new unified council would take place on the 5th of March, with the first council session sitting on 6th of March to elect the various Mayoral positions; until then the Councillors would strive to make the transition easier for all concerned. Chavender only half paid attention to what was going on in the civic world, for at that moment he was far more interested in the poison cases he was investigating. The burning question that needed answering was "How? How could five couples have something to eat or drink without knowing it, and that it was poisonous in their possession!"

Standing in his office, looking at the boards and as he was reading through the names and address list, Chavender made his next connection - Mr and Mrs English, of 15 Carew Road. He suddenly remembered that road name, for as a young bobby in North West London, in a certain Carew Road, Northwood, he and a sergeant used to drive down it on patrol, just in case they caught a glimpse of Felicity Kendal who starred in a sitcom, that sometimes was filmed in this road, and that road was on the addresses of the phantom burglaries and rereading the list immediately, served to confirm his suspicions, for it matched the address of one of the poisoned couples. He went to find and speak to Carruthers and Wootton about it.

"Hello you two, I think I may have something for you both to investigate for me. It's about Mr and Mrs English; about six weeks ago they reported an attempted break in one evening, nothing was taken because Mr English disturbed the person whilst he was in the kitchen. Now what if that break in, was not a break in and try to steal something, but a break in and to place or leave something behind? The break in was used, maybe as a cover for placing, oh, say something like a poisoned jar of marmalade or some poisoned teabags. Now if we can assume from this, that it is the same for the other four couples, but they did not disturb or report a break in, that would explain how they managed to poison themselves. It is of course not much of a link or idea, but it's the best one to explain how it might have been done!

"Now it is entirely possible that some people may not have known they had been burgled, because nothing was taken to arouse their suspicions, so no report of an attempted break in, only items or stuff were left! Innocent looking bits and pieces like non-store bought marmalade and teabags, something that would not look out of place to either one of them, you know something along the lines of 'my wife or husband has bought something to try?' and not wishing to appear stupid, did not question it not knowing that either had not!"

"Yes, yes Sir, I think I see your point," Carruthers replied.

Chavender went on to say, "Perhaps you and Wootton had better take a constable with you and check out all fifteen addresses on that list; see if you can come up with something, make sure you do it properly, wear gloves, even take a picture if you must; we want to see if we can get any clear fingerprints from the things you find, okay? Oh, and by the way don't only assume that it was marmalade or teabags; check for anything, and I mean anything no matter how trivial, that the home owners can swear not to have bought in the past six weeks okay, Carruthers, Wootton?"

"Yes Sir" they both replied and he left them to it; Chavender was thinking perhaps this is the breakthrough that we need in this case!

Carruthers and Wootton collected a young detective constable each, divided the list into two and started the searches. Chavender's next decision was to speak to the Chief Constable about considering and in particular, him, speaking to the press. He wanted to get a wide enough area covered with the warning and felt if it came from the Chief Constable's office it would carry the required weight behind it. It was also felt that he should speak to the TV people to issue the warning. Chavender was well aware that they might just be inundated with calls, some phoney, some not, but many would be real and all would need looking into. He would probably need uniform's help to deal with the initial influx of calls, or maybe not; he had a little idea that might just work, and keep uniform on the investigative side rather than answering calls all day long, but he felt that the circumstances warranted it! The Chief Constable agreed, and called for the Deputy Chief Constable so they could discuss it. In the end it was felt that all three senior officers should do the press conference; Chavender could answer any questions whilst he and the Deputy Chief Constable would add weight to the seriousness of the situation. It was also felt that Dr Solomon should be on hand to answer the inevitable medical questions. The press conference was set for midday on Friday and the press were informed to be on hand.

The Chief Constable insisted that full uniform should be worn, making sure that Dr Solomon had a white lab coat on as well, and of course it caught the attention of the national press and news, and although the Chief Constable's bit to camera was central to the agenda, appealing for, as he put it, "people who think they have been burgled in the past six weeks only, from around the first of January say, to call the police, and the police are going to try a novel approach to try and speed things up. In the first instance and to save on manpower, we are going to use recorded message machines - each machine can take sixty messages, timed for maximum of one minute each, each station will have a dedicated number, as can be seen on the wall behind me. Now I urge you to use it please, just leave your basic contact details, like name address and phone number; on the hour every hour, we will exchange the tape or when its full, and we will call you back with in the next hour, and we hope to have someone with you fairly quickly. This way you will only have to wait in queues for a short time, and can expect a call back sooner than later. We expect the volume of calls to be high at first and this will help limit the length of calls to the information the police require at the moment, or you can also call into your local police station. We want to eliminate as many people as soon as possible from our ongoing enquiries; this is so people can get on with their daily lives with the minimum amount of disruption."

It was Chavender who unwittingly stole the show, although it was not his intention to do so. It was Miss Blaise, she put him in the forefront of the news conference by directing all her questions to him; he answered her as best as he could and for a full twenty minutes he was in the spotlight on national news, answering such questions as, "Have the police enquired into the likelihood of more deaths by this poisoner?"

"We're not sure of that, but we can not rule out that more deaths may occur."

"How could and did such a thing happen?"

"We think he broke into the houses to plant either jars of marmalade or boxes of teabags with the poison in."

"Do they know or have any clue as to the identity of the poisoner?"

"No, his identity is still a mystery."

"Can the police be sure they have got all the spiked marmalade and teabags?"

"We are double checking that right now as we speak, two teams are looking into that possibility and that more may still be out there."

"Are these poisoned deaths related to the other deaths that have occurred in Middleshire these past few weeks?"

Chavender's final reply to Miss Blaise was, "At the moment they appear to be unrelated to the ongoing poisoning investigation, but it is to early to tell if some correlation between the deaths might show itself!"

Here the Deputy Chief Constable interjected and pointing to the two large posters behind him of a jar of marmalade and box of teabags. "Obviously depending on the response we get from this appeal, we will employ more manpower on this initial stage, to try and eliminate the possibility of any such poisoned items left, yet to be found or do their nasty deed, okay?"

On question about the type and toxicity of the poisons, he stated that Dr Solomon would answer those at the end; he referred to the Chief Constable's appeal, but at the end he made sure he got some of the other reporters to ask some questions. He then asked for medical and specifically questions about poisons to be directed to, and answered by, Dr Solomon. The police, not wishing for a spate of copycat poisonings to deal with, had agreed with him to give vaguely inaccurate answers but stated they were all plant related poisons; he gave a brief outline of the symptoms and some other gory details, that the press lapped up with great relish.

Then the Chief Constable and his Deputy, answered general questions, and at the end of the press conference the Chief Constable repeated the call for information. Thanking them all for coming, the officers got up and left. The press conference certainly made the national news that night and Saturday morning's local and national papers all led with the poisoning case. On the various news programmes that night, they led with many assorted headlines, and went on to explain, with the help of several respected TV gardeners, the dangers of some plants that are probably lurking in everyone's garden. Miss Blaise's headline for Saturday morning was 'Triffid Killer loose in Middleshire', and the national press had a field day, leading with headlines such as, 'With shrubs like these, who needs Anemones!, 'A Pot of Toxic Tea for two', and 'The Killer in Yew'.

On their way back to headquarters, the Chief Constable said to Chavender, "That went well. I am pleased with that, yes really pleased, novel idea of yours Chavender, yes, very novel indeed, just hope it works! What do you say Jacobs? Any thoughts?"

"None at all sir, I'm sure it will work Sir. I'm sure Chavender thought it through very thoroughly, and would not have suggested it if it did not work! I think you managed to get the message across as did Chavender and Dr Solomon, Sir; it might stir things up for a while but I'm sure they will settle down presently."

"Um... Yes... I think you're correct on that score Jacobs, but if it helps to catch that maniac who is doing the killing, then it will be well worth the adverse publicity we may get in the short term. For the long term good it will do for all of us when we catch the blighter - hey what, what do you say Chavender?"

"Yes Sir, I think you're right there Sir; you and the Deputy Chief Constable certainly made a heartfelt appeal for people to come forward Sir! It might just do the trick!"

Chapter 31

The killer serenely carried on with his preparations to kill again that day, and whilst watching the press conference, he pulled on his homemade skin-coloured elbow length fingerprint less latex gloves, put a fake bandage for his left hand and a comb over wig in the left pocket of a briefcase. He then collected some small homemade phials from his box of ready-made ones, and placed it in the special pouch, which he would set into the palm of his bandaged hand when the time was ready. He added a small bottle of Chloroform and a ready filled syringe with the deadly cocktail of Potassium Chloride. Placing it carefully in a small silver box, he put this in the right hand pocket of a brown leather brief case, along with an official looking clipboard, and he was set to kill. Checking that he had his fake Council ID card, he looked at one of the six lists he had; he was now back to the first list, for he thought he had already killed two people from each list so far; each list contained at least two hundred persons all waiting for an offer of an allotment, they all looked so tantalisingly, so close to an offer, but in reality it was an offer made only when someone gave up his plot, died or took their name off the list, the latter did not happen that often, for the plots of land were highly sort after commodities, and it took many years to get to the top of the list of your choice; now with the merger close at hand, it may take twice as long from now on!

So at random, he selected a preselected name lower down the list. For he had already checked out many addresses for the suitability of him getting away practically unseen, by spying on these houses in broad daylight and by carefully noting the surroundings, and curtain twitching. He left his house, he was going out once more; he was to kill again. He had chosen this method because the other method of poisoning was far too slow and was impeding his efforts. It was, in fact, fast becoming a real liability to him now, that just when he had selected another quicker way to kill, they had all suddenly started to work, but he carried on with his plan, thinking that at least the police would be otherwise engaged, leaving him free to kill. He drove to within a quarter of a mile from the selected house and carefully pulled on the comb over wig and fake bandage. He slowly walked to the house and at around three thirty he was knocking on the door at the selected address; after showing his ID badge he was allowed in; after all he was expected and shown into the front room. He spoke for about an hour or so getting the attention of his victim, then all of a sudden he let out a small yell, and passed it off as sciatica; if only he could walk about a bit, if that was okay, it might ease. "It may get irritating for you if you try to follow me round the room so just keep looking forward, I can write whilst standing still for a bit so it should take no longer than I have already stated. Okay? Thanks." On his walk round the settee or armchair, when he was at the back he would load the pouch in the fake bandage, then on the next trip round he would get closer and closer still until he felt he could make his move. Then he would break the capsule of Chloroform and quickly smother the victim's mouth and nose with it. Naturally, of course, it took the victim by complete surprise and the struggle, if any, was short. It lasted for about ninety seconds or less, but usually they were non-resistant in a minute as was the case now, and fully unconscious in about five minutes.

Once resistance stopped he took out his bottle of chloroform and applied it to the bandage until the victim was comatose, at this stage he opened the box with the syringe in and, carefully choosing his spot, injected the deadly drug in. Once he confirmed that the victim was dead, he would set about removing all traces of his ever being inside the house. He had already called once previously, but only as far as the doorstep, this was to check for the type of clothes the victim wore, number of residents and to make an indoor appointment. This time allowed him to go and buy clothes that matched and would hopefully leave no trace, his latex gloves always worked like a charm, as did the method chosen for the initial delivery of Chloroform. Where possible he would leave late at night, but only at those places where he could do so safely, as it was so in this case. Collecting the front door key he would wait till very late, turn all lights off, slip the latch and put the key in, closing the door silently, placing the key under the front doormat and on his soft soled shoes he could walk away unnoticed. He would always park his car some distance away, carefully hiding the accoutrements of his criminal activities; he would open one can of beer, drink some and throw the rest away, just in case he was stopped - he had to have his excuse ready.

As was to be expected the initial influx of calls came almost at once and by Friday tea time the calls had peaked; it looked like Chavender's idea had worked. The messages were short and to the point, giving only the details required by the police. Of course, sorting through the taped messages and writing the details down took some time, but it also cut out the wasted visits to the crank or hoax called in addresses, for with the modern technology of Satellite Mapping Systems and Post Code Finders, they could eliminate those addresses that proved to be dead ends, literally! Although the one coming from the Cotswolds was taken seriously, because they lived in Plympton at the time, so a call was passed through to the local police, who went and had a look for their colleagues, but found nothing untoward was found at the address. That still left over five hundred calls to sift through but soon it was whittled down to only a hundred, those that fell outside the parameters set by Chavender were asked to bring the offending items in so they could be checked, which cut down the amount of wasted police time, and appointments were made with those callers who more or less closely fitted the parameters and teams were dispatched to check through the contents of their cupboards. Of these only a handful produced any results of noteworthiness.

Naturally the decorating at Chavender Mansions was relegated to the bottom of his list of his things to do; he spent virtually the entire weekend at police headquarters, only going home after spending several hours sorting through and making appointments for his detective force and, with the help of uniform, had managed to arrange everything until Monday evening, although it still left a lot of leg work to do, but he was happy with the way things were going.

By late Friday evening the investigation into the phantom burglaries that were reported was complete, and it produced minimal results; only four homes out of the fifteen on the list provided any concrete evidence of food being left behind instead of goods being taken, so three jars of marmalade and one box of teabags were taken into custody, and immediately taken to Dr Solomon to test, and no homes as of yet had produced any mixed bottles of bleach and ammonia! Dr Solomon took the allegedly poisoned marmalade and teabags away from the constables, and began testing. The test on the teabags was long and tedious; after checking each bag for signs of regluing, then by examining the contents, he confirmed that twelve teabags were made from dried oleander leaves. They were chopped finer and the teabag was reglued well enough to pass casual inspection as they were put either into the cup or teapot. This being said one tea bag in a cup would be enough to give you a very close call with death, but would more than likely give you the symptoms of a really bad case of "Delhi belly". The marmalade on the other hand, whilst looking to be all pure and the same colour, was in fact, clearly and distinctly set as two types. The bottom third or so was the poisoned part and the top two thirds was normal marmalade; it appeared the poisoner made and set the bottom poisoned parts first, and then topped them up with a very good helping of tasty Seville Orange Marmalade; this meant that until the very last bits were used, no suspicion would be aroused as to their true deadly nature. It was this that masked the bitter flavour of the Yew and Daphne Mezereum extracts, and of course, any residual bitterness could be explained away by the sharp tasting nature of marmalade. He most probably used only the extract of Yew Oil and extract Daphne Mezereum, not any of the actual plants which might have given the game away, the poisonous extracts he would have added and mixed in during the cooking process only at the very end, so as not to weaken it by over cooking the poisonous infusion of the oils. These reports hit Chavender's desk Saturday morning and did not make for easy reading. He helped out where he could, but found he spent most of his time organising the routes for the police to follow along with Inspector Carr who then, along with Pearce, selected constables to call on the addresses that most likely fitted the bill, this went on all over the weekend and into the middle of the next week.

Sunday afternoon finally saw Josh sat at home, tired, very tired, but sure now of which direction to push the investigation forwards. He sat in the kitchen whilst Tiff made him a cup of tea.

Ma came in and sat down, putting her broken wrist on the table carefully, and looking at Josh said, "That was a nice bit you did on TV the other day; it looked like that young reporter really put you on the spot, she hardly let you go!"

"Yes Ma, I know; she has a crush on me, don't know why but she does! I'm old enough to be her father for heaven's sake!"

Ma was just about to launch into one, when Tiff diffused the situation, "Why, Josh? What has she done now? I mean, I know she asked you an awful lot of questions, but that hardly equates or warrants that outburst of pique from you?"

She knew that Josh had been brought up in a very strict family and from a very early age where swearing or blasphemy of any kind was not only frowned upon but punishable with a firm spanking; this meant he did not use the more colourful metaphors inherent in the English spoken word nowadays. It was one of his eccentric charms that Tiff loved about him; he would use putdowns of several words that left the other person baffled and scrabbling for the Oxford English Dictionary.

"Oh, she only went and kissed me on the lips in front of Sword and Pearce the other day! Boy did I catch some flak for that from the both of them, you know the stuff I mean, then the Chief Constable said something and no sooner said than it was common knowledge at headquarters - and that's on top of trying to catch this maniac who is intent on poisoning half the population of the county. No, no respite for me and she then does that to me - why I could put her across my knees and smack some sense into her! No I really could." Saying that, he banged the flat of his hand down hard on the tabletop. "Eeeow, that hurt" he said, as the sound of the slap reverberated through the tabletop, making the teacups tremble on the saucers. Shaking his quickly reddening hand to try and cool it, Tiff came over and pulled his head into her midriff and gently patted his head, using that old stock phrase beloved of mothers all over the world, "There, there," parting and kissing the top of his head said, "Is that better?"

Josh just looked bewildered; he was not sure, because the hug did not last long, but he thought he had heard a heartbeat in the wrong place on Tiff's body. He just sat there drinking his tea mulling over things, when Ma spoke.

"So Josh, the reporter has got the hots for you; I know some guys in London who can sort her out for you if you want," throwing back at him what he had said to her.

Josh laughed and the years and cares seemed to fall away from his shoulders, the tiredness now seemed of little consequence.

"That's better love, that's the man I married, not some greying old fogey, worried about his advancing years," Tiff said and finished with, "Now when are you going to start on the next room?"

The rest of that Sunday afternoon, Josh enjoyed beyond measure not thinking about work - only his family mattered.

Chapter 32

The Monday morning routine of the Senior Officers' meeting was becoming tedious for Chavender. For the past few weeks, it seemed that it was he who had the most to say. After briefing everyone on the outcome of the appeal, and how long the search was likely to take, he felt he had said enough.

Featherstonehaugh then stated, "Well Chavender, that idea of yours about the message system certainly worked, yes worked very well indeed! Yes, it seems that asking for the public's co-operation in this matter worked, really well... Yes, very good, good indeed; just wish they could be as obliging in other matters, what!"

It was Jacobs who asked, "How many have you got to go and interview so far?"

"Only about two hundred, but going on the evidence of the investigation into the phantom burglaries, it should come down to under twenty confirmed attempts at breaking and leaving poisoned items behind, Sir."

Sword then asked, "Are they still exclusively in Plympton's Manor?"

"I'm afraid they are, Robin, but we are not discounting any calls from Bryantsand-on-Sea; they are being investigated also, but they only make up a very small percentage of the total number of calls received so far."

Andersonn then cut in, "Strange how it seems to be one-sided, and not out in the sticks either, I mean, local to Plympton, I'm glad that we are not the focus of this maniac, beggars the question 'why?' doesn't it? But it makes you curious as to what his motive is?"

"Yes John," replied Chavender, "if we can find that out, and the other ninety nine things we don't know yet, we should be able to catch the perpetrator. That is all still a mystery, at the present moment, Sir!"

"Well, if that is all gentlemen, thank you, I'm sure you have pressing engagements to attend to. Jacobs, can you stay awhile please?"

The three Chief Inspectors got up, saluted and left the others. They went to Chavender's office to discuss the next phase of the investigation.

The body of the latest victim was found late Monday morning, bringing with it the usual clamour of noisy sirens and blue lights to the quite residential street. The three Chief Inspectors had just sat down in Chavender's office when the call was put through to him; he put it immediately on speaker phone, so they all could hear.

"Hello Sir, Detective Inspector Smith speaking Sir. We have another probable murder; it's at 34 Aldenhants Street, Plympton Sir. Yes, the police doctor and forensics are on scene Sir, anything you would like to add or ask Sir?"

"Yes" said Chavender, "could you make sure that he checks all soft openings on the head of the body, before he moves it and get him to swab around the nose and mouth, okay Smith?"

"Yes Sir, will do, thanks; are you coming over Sir?"

"Yes, myself and Chief Inspectors Sword and Andersonn as well, we'll be with you shortly. Bye Smith."

"Bye Sir."

The three Chief Inspectors arrived on scene fairly quickly, having agreed to let Sword drive them in his car. Seeing the media circus outside the house, they waited for a while to discuss strategy. Chavender called Small and asked him if the specialists and media had finished, and advised that they were just round the corner, waiting for things to calm down press wise.

Small replied, "They all should be done in about an hour or so Sir! I can call you once they have finished if you like?"

Chavender acknowledged that that was agreeable. "Small reckons in about an hour, so I think unless we actually want to bump this into the national spotlight, more than it is at the moment, by three senior police officers turning up, I think we should skedaddle back to Plympton police station - that is if you both agree?"

They both nodded their assent and Sword drove them to his police station.

For that hour they discussed what Featherstonehaugh had looked for in way of defects during his inspection, whilst Andersonn took notes. Small's call came two hours later saying that it was now press free, and once again the three Chief Inspectors arrived on the scene.

Surveying the scene inside, with Small pointing out where the victim had been sitting, Chavender's sixth sense kicked in, for once again, the place looked sterile, too clean, as if the murderer took his time to erase all traces of contamination. He looked for the vacuum cleaner and saw that it still had some dust in it; carefully he opened the cleaner to remove the dustbag, he found a carrier bag in the kitchen, placing the dustbag inside it, he then asked if Small could drop it off at forensics for him. He next turned his attention to the kitchen drainer and cupboards; this time he drew a blank - although he could see several mugs and cups, he could not tell if any had been used this time. Lastly, he looked in all the kitchen cupboards but once again, he found no poisoned marmalade or dodgy teabags.

He looked into the garden, and nothing seemed out of the ordinary, a neat compact smallish garden, shed, vegetable plot and a small shrubbery. Looking at the shrubs, he started to wonder, but he could not tell the difference between a weed and a flower; he would have to send someone round who knew about shrubs and could identify them. All this time Sword and Andersonn followed him round, not speaking, but watching, until finally Andersonn spoke.

"Well Josh, it seems you are certainly thorough, why the cleaner bag, and that search through the cupboards?"

"The place is all too clean, in fact all the murder scenes were too clean, as if they had been sterilised by the murderer; he knew he would not be interrupted, so he had time to clean away any evidence he might have left behind. We did not check the vacuum cleaner bags at the other suspected murder scenes, simply because we could not say for sure it was murder. When the reports came back significantly backing the case for a natural cause of death, we simply failed to check any means of cleaning the house! Which is my fault. Now, in the cupboards I'm looking for the number of cups and the same on the drainer, and finally, I want to make sure that I've covered all the bases. I've had a final walk around. Robin, do you have anyone at your station who knows his gardening, especially shrubs?"

"Yes I do; Sergeant Jenkins is a very keen gardener."

"Great, could you send him round here and get him to name all the shrubs in the garden for me please? Thanks. That's all we can do here for now, best get back to headquarters."

With that, they left and returned to headquarters, where they went their separate ways.

True to his word, Sword sent Sergeant Jenkins round to name the shrubs and inform Chavender, but none were of the type used in the poison cases so far. The only thing Jenkins remarked on was that the small vegetable plot was placed in the prime position in the garden where it could get the most sunlight, just like the one he had. The results from the investigation of the call list was also disappointing, netting only six more jars of marmalade, three boxes of suspect teabags ,and two bottles of dodgy bleach, which on examination all turned out to be suspect and were destroyed.

Chavender's only hope now was this current investigation; he still lacked the vital key to unlocking the truth behind it, but he felt he was part of the way there. It was into this area he next turned his attention, whilst waiting for the coroner's and forensic's reports to come back. To take his mind off the current investigation, he started to look at the council files.

The five boxes of council files sat on the floor in the corner behind the white boards. Fortunately for him, the boxes had a contents label and a list of contents on the inside of the lid. Looking at the largest box concerning the merger, Chavender bit the bullet and pulled it clear and opened the lid. In individual draw file dividers clearly labelled, were all the files concerning the merger, he flicked through the files name tags, there were Housing committee minutes, Planning committee minutes, Council wards (new) and Council wards (Old), number of new councillors, various joint land use and housing stock consultancy minutes and the long list went on and on - and this was just box one.

Looking at it, he decided he needed some extra help to wade through it all, so he stopped and went and looked for Pearce. Finding him in the canteen, he got a coffee and sat down beside him.

"Well Pearce, it looks as though your gut feelings about the heart attacks may be correct after all; we have had way too many, in far to short a time!"

"Yes Sir," Pearce replied, but he was unhappy to be proved correct in such a demonstrable way.

"Finish your coffee, son and come with me; you need a NTR job," Chavender replied after seeing that look of anguish sweep across Pearce's face. He knew that look oh so well! It had upset him many a time. A 'beat yourself over the head', with it look! Feeling miserable, feeling like you've failed! Feeling like you could have done more type look - it would send you potty, if left to gather speed in your brain.

"A what job? What's that then sir! What do you mean by NTR?"

"No Thought Required, Pearce; it's a job where you stick your thumbs up your backside and switch that brain off - it stops you from going mad!"

They got up and went to Chavender's office, pointing to the open box on his desk he said, "There you go, pick a file, any file from that open box on the desk, and read it will you please. It's not exactly a NTR job this Pearce, I do need you to concentrate, but it is the closest I can come up with in such a short space of time. That is unless you fancy a stint as a... Oh, I don't know, an atom counter!"

"No, Sir, this will do fine thanks," Pearce answered with a laugh, and selecting a file at random he began to read.

Chapter 33

The sound of pages being turned was broken only by the deep rhythmic breathing of the two detectives as a heavy silence stalked the room, lingering in the corners, daring someone or something to break its power, the power it had, the power to overwhelm everything in its path. During this silence, the slightest of noise was amplified a thousand fold, such as the footsteps in the corridor and muffled voices outside. The phone rang, startling them and making them both jump; the shrill ringing filled the entire room with noise, chasing the tranquility away until, Chavender picked up the phone and listened. Silence made another attempt to reassert itself but all to no avail, as Chavender and the man on the other end talked, and asked if they could pop down to forensics for a moment.

Leaving open the files, they walked the short distance to the forensics room.

"Ah, glad you both could come, I've arranged a little demonstration for you. Please take a seat Sir, in front of the screen. Can you tell me what you see?"

"I see a smudge, over a partial fingerprint?"

"Yes Sir, you're right, but wrong also; here, let me show you what I mean."

He then went on to take one of Pearce's fingerprints and pressed it on to a glass slide; he put this under the microscope and took a picture of it. He then took a different fingerprint from him and placed it over the first fingerprint, doing the same to it as before. He then took that same fingerprinted slide and asked

Chavender to put on a thickish latex glove and took his gloved finger and pressed it over Pearce's fingerprint on the slide.

"Now let me show you the results Sir; the first slide clearly shows two sets of fingerprints, muddled yes, but definably two sets none the less. The second slide, the one that I over smeared with your gloved fingerprint Sir, is totally different; you get a smudge but its almost obliterated the print below, it's sort of wiped it clean sir. Now I know that it's a bit strange for proof Sir, but it is the only way I can say for sure that two people, different people were in the same room."

Chavender replied, "Perhaps you could get the same result from smearing one print over the other?"

"No Sir, it will still look like a smear and not a smudge; you can see on the first slide where lines cross over and at the edges where you see only one set of lines. With the smudge, Sir, the fingerprint below is wiped out so to speak, and you are left with the edge bits of the fingerprint!"

"Okay," said Chavender, "You got me on that one; so it's two people then!"

"Yes Sir, I think so, from this evidence which could be backed up with the next item. Now with fibres, it was a bit harder, on close inspection they both look the same, both blue denim, but examine them not as fibres but as density of colour Sir. I'm sure you agree they don't match."

He had replaced the slide with one showing several strands of denim; you could clearly distinguish deeper blues against the more faded blues.

"This can only come from two pairs of trousers, one newer than the other, fade and wear - patterns don't lie Sir; for example, the pair on the victim, being older and more worn than the other one's fibres."

"That's good," said Chavender, "Very good, but why only now, why not for the others that you looked at?"

"That's easy, we followed the direction that the coroner's report led us in sir, I know it's a poor excuse, but when the coroner said heart attack, we stopped, due to the lack of evidence that did not fit in with the report from the Coroner's office! Not an excuse, I know, but we still have some of the evidence from those early deaths, but unfortunately not evidence that matches this, such as clothes fibres and smudge prints."

"Anything else you have got to show me?"

"Yes, the dust from the cleaner bag, mostly what you think dust is made up of, but we did find a few strands of white fibre; we think it may have come from a bandage, maybe the bandage he used to smother them with!"

Chavender sat and pondered what this new evidence meant to him. It certainly tied a few things together. Perhaps the Coroner's report would help to clarify things further still.

"Well, thanks for that demonstration. Could you go back over some of the older evidence, just to see if anything else shows up please?"

"Yes Sir, that I can do for you, but I'm not sure what we will get, if anything, but I will try Sir."

Saying their goodbyes they got up and returned to Chavender's office. Returning to the council files, neither could concentrate properly, until Chavender let out a "Damn and blast it! Does that mean every time we saw no fingerprints, we should have been looking for no fingerprints?" He got up and went to the whiteboards and wrote against the names, "No fingerprints!"

"Look how easy it is now, apart from this last case, when we can actually prove no fingerprints; I wonder how many other clues we have missed? Probably all of them! It's that lack of evidence, is evidence in itself? Ummm, now I wonder if it is the same person doing the killing; perhaps he got a little bit, oh how can I put it, annoyed with the lack of success with the poisonings, so he found another quicker, but more direct way of killing, up close and personal. So if it is the same man, these deaths all must have something in common, But what, and WHY!"

Standing for a moment in front of the boards, looking intently before returning to his desk, where he carried on reading the council reports. Close to home time, the coroner called asking if could meet him in the morning at nine am, to discuss the latest death, Chavender agreed.

Chapter 34

The next morning, at nine am precisely, Chavender and Pearce arrived at the Coroner's office and were invited to take a seat; they both sat down. The Coroner started to speak.

"Now, it is exactly the same as in past cases, death was caused by a heart attack, but because we now suspect foul play and also have an idea of how the Potassium Chloride injection is administered, we can now look for possible evidence. In the case of the latest victim, the Potassium Chloride was injected into the deceased's mouth; it clearly left three needle prick marks, which, at first glance, could be mistaken as the marks left from a visit to the dentist. On checking with the deceased's dentist, this was not the case, so we can safely say with utmost confidence that the deadly injection was administered into the mouth. This is not an area that a sane person who was awake would let anyone inject into, just the pain and fear factor from an actual dental visit would be enough for someone to struggle or at least put up a fight."

As the coroner finished speaking and started to drink his coffee, after taking a sip he was just about to continue when Chavender put his cup down and said, "Well, that ties in somewhat with the forensics report, but that has set the old grey matter working. Since yesterday I've been thinking of how - not the why but how. Now then, I'm going to give you both a likely scenario based on my experience and the evidence we have so far of how it was, or possibly it could have be done. You may correct me if I'm wrong at any point, but I must stress this theory fits the facts we have at the moment, and may get blown out of the water by subsequent events or of more evidence coming from our investigations. Do I make myself clear on this point?" The Coroner and Pearce nodded in agreement, as Chavender began to talk to them both.

"First is the reason most often thought of by the public, to be the most common way to administer Chloroform to someone." The two other men began to listen as Chavender went on to say, "In the past Chloroform has been reputed to be used by criminals to knock out, daze or even murder their victims. This plainly is not the case!" Continuing by answering his own question he said, "The use of Chloroform as a quick and simple knock out drug has become widely recognised by the book-reading public, especially those of the murder mystery book readers genre, so much so that it is now bordering on the ridiculous and as such it as been clichéd unto death and beyond; this is primarily from its overuse in many, many, crime fiction novels. Now, it is these authors who would have us think that the murderers make use of a Chloroform-soaked rag to render victims unconscious or even comatose, in a mere matter of seconds. However, it is totally erroneous because this is nearly impossible to do so in practice, am I not correct doctor?" "Yes," the Doctor replied, "this is because you cannot incapacitate someone using chloroform in this way without that person's consent, for they would start to struggle, or at least put up a fight. In the real world it takes a minimum of five minutes of inhaling an item soaked in Chloroform to render that person unconscious, but at around thirty to sixty seconds, I suppose it could make a person reasonably relaxed, enough, at least, so as not to care!"

"Thank you doctor", Chavender replied, and he returned to his theory. "Most criminal cases nowadays involving Chloroform also involve another drug being co-administered at the same time, such as alcohol or a crushed sleeping tablet of some kind, as is possible in one of our cases - for instance, the Hornbeams. This of course takes time, but it has been found in the past to be one of the most effective ways to make someone complicit in its administration. After a person has lost consciousness due to the Chloroform inhalation, a continuous steady volume, must be maintained?"

"Yes" confirmed the Coroner, "That is so; to keep someone 'knocked-out' it would need fresh Chloroform every time the Chloroform had evaporated away, or else the patient wakes up, sooner or later," he continued, "but with an adjuvant or a subsidiary secondary means of making someone pass out, this will keep the person in a state of unconsciousness until the person is totally unconscious, it is at this stage that in the olden days operations would be performed."

"That's correct for an operation," said Chavender, "but what if the murderer only needs him to be compliant enough to administer the Potassium Chloride injection, so in reality only a smallish continuous dose is required, of say, and here I would hazard a guess, of probably a further two minutes or so? That brings the total number of minutes up to about four or five, so we are getting close to that magic figure of six minutes!"

"Yes you are," said the Coroner and added, "About or around five minutes should do the trick nicely, to render someone to a near comatose state. The use of a carrier drug is well known to most murderers, simply put, in my expert opinion, unless you incapacitate someone first, Chloroform don't work as the majority of members of the public thinks of the way it should work!"

Chavender went on to say, "Secondly, and this is, in my considered opinion, possibly the way or how he, or she, could possibly commit the crime. If you can I want you to try and imagine the following scenario. His sole aim or purpose is to gain the victim's trust, the aim of which is, in the first place, to get the victim to self administer the drug, so he gets drowsy enough not to care. It is with this in mind, and to this end, that I'm going to take you back to the good old days of Quack Medicine in the Old

Wild West, or anywhere in fact, but I like the Wild West best! Oh, let's say to around 1870, that should do, yes, when quacks were rife and patent medical remedies were all the rage. A foul smelling, brown sweet liquid in a medicine type bottle would be proclaimed to be a cure all for everything from cancer to baldness, it usually went along the lines like this. The quack would turn up at a town with his sidekick in tow, set up and proclaim the new wonder medicine of the age; he would offer to let someone try it, his sidekick almost bent double and obviously in pain would come forward, beg to try some and be miraculously cured. Thus setting the stage to sell what only could best be described as a brown foul smelling sugar flavoured water for a few dollars with no medicinal purpose whatsoever."

"Oh, I think I'm getting where you are taking me!" the Coroner butted in, and smiling to himself at Chavender's use of such an easy example of quackery, for if any profession had more than its fair share of charlatans and miracle cures, it was or had to do with the medical profession.

It was Pearce who said, "No, not really, but please sir do go on."

Chavender continued, "You may get the gist of it yet, when I explain it a bit more for you Pearce. Now let me see; oh yes, we have just had the miraculous cure, so to bring this into our context, next we must make some assumptions. First, the murderer has timed the dose so he knows how long before the victim becomes compliant to his wishes. Second, he somehow tricks the victim into administering the dose himself by faking a cure for some imagined ailment. Third, this leaves no trace of a struggle because the victim allows himself to be Chloroformed, after seeing how or what wonderful a pain relief drug it is! Now I imagine, how he manages to persuade the victim, would probably go something like this." Stopping and asking, "Now can you see what I mean Pearce? I think the Coroner is way ahead of you here!"

The Coroner nodded and Pearce replied, "I think so Sir, yes?"

So Chavender went on to say, "The murderer fakes a sudden very painful medical problem - oh, say something like a trapped nerve of some sort, would that be good enough doctor?"

"Yes I think so, or more probably it could be sciatica; yes that is better, everyone knows or has heard of how painful that is," said the Coroner.

Chavender returned to his theory, "Now he excuses himself, by asking if he could take a new wonder drug prescribed by his doctor; he gets an okay from the victim. He takes out a small glass bottle and places some of the contents, which is a clear liquid, most probably harmless water on a bandage and inhales deeply for a minute or two, whilst doing so, he closes his eyes as if he was asleep and suddenly he awakes, gets up and cavorts round the room, cured of all his pain, he dances with apparent joy and exclaiming what a marvellous pain relief drug it is. This gets the attention of the now very curious victim, who then asks, 'What is it?'"

"Our murderer now goes into his spiel by saying it's a new experimental drug that he has been given to trail or test, for he which he gets paid fifty pounds a week, and all he has to do is to take the new wonder drug, plus give feedback on any possible side effects, which at the moment, stand at none, and he gets paid all that money for doing absolutely nothing and being pain free into the bargain. This gets the attention of the victim, who by now is positively downright curious, and inquisitively asks more questions and is given grossly exaggerated claims, as to its effectiveness as a pain killer."

"Oh, I get it now, Sir" said Pearce.

The coroner then said, "Yes, that could very well work; yes, work very well indeed. Most people are quite gullible concerning modern medicine, and offering instant pain relief and a cash incentive at the same time. Umm, yes I can see that working very much to the murderer's advantage! Curiosity killed the cat, is the saying that springs to my mind," said the Coroner, and they all chuckled at the little joke.

"Now," continued Chavender, "having got the victim's attention and to some degree, both his confidence and greed, as to the immediate effectiveness of the medicine as a painkiller. The murderer then casually asks if he would like to try it. He goes on to say that he should not do this really, but seeing as they have something in common, that is the burning question which we have yet to find out! He would let him try it, but he mustn't tell anyone about the new experimental wonder drug or he will never get asked again - or much worse still taken off the experimental drugs trials list, never to be trusted to trial any drug again, but on the other hand, if it works for him, he could recommend that he, the victim, gets to test the drug; they are always looking for volunteers and maybe at the same time, he would get paid for testing it. So he must keep quiet about it, for he could not do without the pain relief this drug gives him."

"Ah, greed as well as cure; it is certainly true that the drug pharmaceutical companies are always looking out for guinea pigs to test new drugs on, and they do pay, which I think is common knowledge, but not fifty pounds a week!" the Coroner retorted, and Chavender continued.

"The murderer then goes on to explain how to take the new drug; now the recommended way to administer the drug is to use a mask, saying maybe, 'I carry a mask, but because I'm am now so used to the effect of sleepiness, which by the way is the only side affect it has that I have experienced, I can use a quicker method like a bandage, but you will need to administer the drug with a mask for the first go; this is important, you need to get the airflow and drug mixed correctly, the mask provides this ratio for you, just in case your worried I will leave it up to you to put the mask on'. Okay, here, the victim probably would say yes, as the murderer continues, 'but it needs to go over both your nose and mouth, and you need to take really deep breaths, chest-heaving deep breaths, which is why you need the mask; it maximises the vapour as you breathe in, see its a wonderful non-contact drug. When you breathe it in, you need to get the pain relieving vapour right into your lungs, wherein it gets transferred to the red blood cells, and then the blood carries it around your body, giving you instant pain relief everywhere at once; well, in about six minutes actually to be precise, which means no nasty side effects, but it will make you sleepy - very sleepy at first, but don't worry about that, that's the drug working, and as you saw, the drowsiness wears off very quickly indeed'."

"Ah," said Pearce, "it's an old confidence trick in reality then Sir?"

"Yes it is, Pearce" and Chavender went on to say.

"The murderer will go on to say, if you want, you can administer the first dose yourself, but when the victim gets sleepy enough he, the murderer takes over. Now seeing that its your first go, I suggest I preload the mask for you with the correct amount of painkilling liquid and you can put it on ok! It will make you feel much more comfortable if you put the mask on yourself. It is at this point he takes out a real bottle of Chloroform, with some flashy made up label, shows it to the victim and the victim is now hooked, as a fishermen says, and thinking nothing is amiss; after all, he has just witnessed first-hand at how quick it works to relieve pain and to come round again, he takes the mask, and he puts the mask on; he is advised once again, that because its his first time, that after placing the mask on, he should sit on his hands, palms down - this will help prevent him from pulling the mask off before the drug as had a chance to do its work, for it will take about three or more minutes to be really effective on this first use occasion, and it will definitely make you feel sleepy, okay?"

Chavender paused for effect, letting the story unfold or sink in, as is in the case of Pearce, as he continued, "Now, you see why we have no signs of a struggle; he allows the murderer or better still, he, the victim Chloroforms himself. Once two, maybe three minutes have passed, the victim is or as becomes easier to handle and soon passes into a sleepy state - or should I say has a laissez-faire attitude to life and after three to five minutes lapses into unconsciousness, all without the aid of an adjuvant, as you so wisely put it doctor! Whereupon our murderer administers the fatal injection and the grisly deed is done!"

The Coroner then asked Chavender if he could be sure about this?, but it did seem the most likely explanation that fits all the facts! - the skimpiest of facts in fact! Indeed, even he as a trained medical professional person would be hard pressed to actually, state with certainty in a court of law, that this was the case under any sort of pressure, from any good barrister, worth his weight in salt, would be able to drive not one but two double decker buses side by side through the gaps in your case or should I say theory, as it stands!

Then Chavender replied, "I'm as certain as I can be for now; would you let any one inject *you* in the mouth, if that person was not a dentist? No!"

The two others shook their heads to signify a negative response to Chavender's question.

"Then I'm sure that it was the most probably or most highly likely to have been done this way! Nothing else fits the facts, and I'm certainly not having little green men doing the killing or for that fact Lucrezia Borgia doing the poisoning! Well thanks doctor, for being a sounding board for my theory. Thanks again. Bye."

Saying that, the two detectives left to go back to headquarters. If only Chavender knew how close to the truth he was, he would have blushed with embarrassment!

Chapter 35

On their way back, Pearce asked, or rather stated, "That seems a bit far fetched as a theory goes, Sir! I mean, yes it does fit all our known facts, but you're not making the facts fit by leaving some out are you Sir?"

"No Pearce, we have far too few facts to go on that any idea we may have might well have changed by the time we get back to headquarters. As I already said, its not little green men or Lucrezia Borgia - it is someone living on planet earth, in Middleshire, in Plympton or Bryantsand and it just so happens, as in most cases like these, that the police do everything correct, but they need that little spark of magic from Lady Luck to get the bloodhounds onto the right scent. Unless we actually walk in on the perpetrator doing the grisly deed, or even catch him shortly afterwards by some fluke, or even find all the paraphernalia of murder on him, we need actual hard evidence to put him at the scene of the crime! I have found in the past that there is no amount of experience or manpower that we can throw at any investigation that will actually equal to or compare with any perpetrator we are looking for, until they actually do something really incredibly stupid in the end!"

"Yes Sir, I suppose you're right but I hope it doesn't change Sir; the facts I mean, although it wasn't until near the end that I actually got the full drift of what you were saying! Now I'm not that thick, in fact, I've got papers that say I'm not, but what you said about how our man got the victim to self-medicate, that's got to be a classic Sir, of at least Homeric proportions and you're only going on, now let me see, umm.... Yes... I think I can remember them all; three cups on a drainer, one set of smudged fingerprints, possibly a deadly injection, a very, very small, in fact I would go as far as to say microscopic bit of fibre possibly from a white bandage type gauze, and some denim strands of different colour density, and you have had us in the past, present and future all at the same time - that's stretching it a bit far don't you think so? Are you sure you're not a Timelord sir?"

"No Pearce, I'm not; it was something that I spoke to Wootton about on my second or third day, about how, if you were to use Conan Doyle's Sherlock Holmes mantra of 'if you eliminate the impossible, and whatever is left, no matter how improbable, will be the truth you are seeking'. Taking that, and a great many leaps of faith, or instinct, now that is all I have done in this case so far, those facts as I see it, and by way of lateral thinking, have led me to certain conclusion, that in all the cases so far, I'm led to believe that we have a murderer on the loose! And I think you agree with me on that conclusion, don't you, Pearce?"

"Yes Sir, I do."

The rest of that week passed very slowly; in fact, it would take several hundred pages of repetitious sentences to get the feel of how mind numbingly boring it was for Chavender. He took solace in the fact that the investigations into the phantom burglary call list had reached its conclusion. His report for the senior officers' meeting on Monday was short and to the point. It had been a hard week on him, staying late, starting early, reading file after file of some of the most tedious, deadening, and tiresome reading he had ever read in his life, full of political phrases, for which he, even with his excellent grasp of the English language, had to look up. The long winded socioeconomic-enviropolitical speeches taken almost verbatim, but nothing that pointed to any nefarious activities, and that was only the first three boxes, he still had the pleasure of the last two; he stopped for a moment, his brain suitably numb, as was his bum; he looked up for a quick glance at the whiteboards. Something pricked his subconscious, and for a fleeting moment an idea flashed across it. Just at the same time his mobile phone rang and the idea vanished in a flash back into the box it had flown from; he knew once again he would have to fight his own mind's powers to get it out of that box, but he also knew it would be futile to try and force it.

Seeing on the display it was his wife, he snapped open his phone. "Hi Tiff, what can I do for you love?"

His wife replied, "I hope you are coming home at a reasonable time today Josh? You've hardly been here all week and it is the weekend; you still have a room to redecorate, and perhaps the girls can help you this time seeing as it's their room you're doing. Ma says hello, and she asked if you could possibly pick up some of those butcher's sausages she liked, she said she would do you a fried breakfast Saturday morning as a treat - that's if you get home soon?"

"Okay Tiff love, will do; I have been overdoing this week, but it is a case of needs must, you know, see you soon, bye love you."

Josh's mind, distracted as it was, ended the call early before Tiff's reply of "bye, love you too", which was said into the dead phone. It was probably one of Josh's most annoying habits that he had, apart from the obvious male problem with the toilet seat; she would have to start correcting him on that. Just as she turned to walk away the phone rang, she picked it up.

It was Josh, most apologetically saying, "Sorry, Tiff, I am really sorry, but I wasn't thinking, perhaps I can end the call properly this time, I don't fancy an earbashing when I get home. Bye love, love you."

He waited for the reply but Tiff, getting her own back on him, put the phone down before he had a chance to hear her reply, leaving Josh in a state of agitated apprehension as to the fate that would meet him at home.

Chavender turned for a last quick glance at the boards, but that thought he had was buried deep and nothing sprang to mind, apart from trying to appease his wife's ire at him, for his apparent indifference to her! Whilst he was leaving headquarters, he bumped into Inspector Carr.

"Hello Carr, could you pass on my thanks for uniforms' help this last week at your daily briefs for me?"

"Yes Sir, will do," replied Carr.

As they both walked out of the building, Chavender stopped and asked if there was a florist in town.

"Why, yes Sir, it is on the High Street." Smiling he added, "Had a run in with the missus then?"

Chavender thanked Carr and said, "I know it is a popular usage word Carr, but I would prefer it if you called her my wife or Tiffany. I hate that word, really hate it like using kids for children; my girls are not the offspring of a goat!"

"Sorry Sir, no offence meant, I'll remember that in future."

Chavender went to walk away, but then turned and said to Carr. "Oh blast it, I'm sorry Carr, had a bit of a run in with my wife on the phone just now for working late, and I'm going to get a warm ear tonight for sure, and what's worse I can't cop a deaf 'un this time; if I do it will make it ten times more unbearable for me." After a pause, he added, "Not for me how to tell you to speak properly is it? Thanks anyway for the information about the florist; I hope it will help ease the pain I'm sure to get tonight. Bye Carr, have a good weekend."

"You too, Sir," Carr said almost smirking, but also feeling sorry for him, at the thought of the Detective Chief Inspector getting a warm ear; boy, what he wouldn't give to be a fly on the wall when that happened.

Chapter 36

Chavender found the butchers was just about to close; five minutes more and he would be in it big time, he thought, right up the creek and no paddle! The butchers was an old established family firm founded in 1914 and the present Master Butcher was a third generation daughter. As Chavender walked in, his heart sank, the shelves were all empty, there was no meat anywhere to be seen; in fact, it looked like an advert for a vegetarian shop. Sat at an old butcher's block, scored and stained by many years of service sat an oldish man, looking up and recognising the Detective Chief Inspector at once, and wiping his hands on his immaculate white butcher's coat, he offered his hand.

Chavender accepted the rather firm handshake as the old man called out, "Christina, come here girl, you have an important customer waiting."

"Coming Papa," she shouted from out of the back somewhere, smiling at the thought that the young daughter still answered with a "Papa".

Chavender replied, "I'm not really that much of an important customer you know; this is the first time I've been in this shop!"

The old man retorted, "All my customers are important to me, even first time customers; that is why I survive whilst others go to the wall; my father was an Russian emigre, who left his homeland and found sanctuary in this great country of ours."

"Please don't let me stop you from your work," said Chavender as he looked at the sheet of paper with names and addresses on. To his amazement, by this time, a rather strikingly tall blonde woman appeared, in her late thirties Josh hazarded a guess; she was also dressed in a white coat although this one was not so pristine, for it had a definite pink hue to the lower half. Her handshake was, however, just as firm as her father's.

"Now what can I do for you Sir?" she said.

"Oh, I'm sorry when you answered "Papa" just now, I imagined you would be much younger, about twenty."

"Why, thank you Sir, for such a compliment," she said, acting all coy like. "Actually I'm married with two teenage children and my actual age is twenty-one, as is the case for all girls; we don't get any older in years, we just lose our desirable and shapely female form! Why is it so strange that I love my parents, especially my Papa?" she said looking at her father. "As an only child and brought up amongst butchers and being a daughter, I'd heard all those jokes about 'she was only the butcher's daughter' before I was ten! So naturally I learnt the trade from my grandfather and father and I married a butcher to boot; my son will follow after me and hopefully his offspring after him. My husband owns his family's shop in Plympton, and Alexander, our other son, helps him, we are fortunate in that way, two family shops still competing and doing rather well against the big boys!"

Chavender said, "Well, that's an interesting family history, but I need eight sausages and two dozen rashers of best smoked back bacon please? But I fear I've come too late in the day!"

"Oh don't worry 'bout that," she said and then called out, "George! come here please."

A young boy of eleven came scurrying out from a freezer, his school uniform, Chavender recognised as the same school his girls went too, was covered by a white coat.

"Have we any sausages and bacon left son?"

His reply was negative, but they were making a fresh batch of sausages tonight, and the bacon would be coming with the rest of the meat delivery later on tonight. Chavender's face dropped on hearing this and he said, "I'm sorry for wasting your time, I suppose I'd best go to the supermarket!"

The father put on a dramatic act of staggering backwards and clutching his left chest and sat down on his stool imploring Chavender not do such a grisly deed, "Ooh, my heart! What? Why go and buy a massed produced emulsified offal tube from a supermarket - no, no, only the best home made sausages from our secret sausage formula for such an important customer would do, especially in such a famous butcher's shop."

"Oh father!" Christina said laughingly, "Stop that, stop being so dramatic, he doesn't know you like we do!" and smiled broadly as the grandson rushed in mock horror to ease his grandfather onto his stool!

Christina then turned to Chavender and apologised and then said, "Perhaps we can deliver them in the morning for you? Now, where do you live?"

"How much will that cost?" he said.

"Nothing" came the reply from George. "We have a daily meat delivery route which I help out on."

Chavender paid them and gave his address which the father put on the list.

"Oh that's lucky for you, you should get your meat around seven thirty Saturday morning."

Thanking them profusely, and saying goodbye, Chavender left to get some flowers.

If buying the breakfast meat was an ordeal for him, getting the flowers was traumatic; the only florist that was open was one called A Blaise of Colour; his heart sank, as his mind connected Wendy Blaise with the florist, hoping, but it was not to be! As his run of recent misfortune continued, the florist was just putting the delicate flowers into a lightly heated room, leaving those cut flowers that could survive in the vases with water in. As he entered, the doorbell began tinkle, tinkling, echoing loudly in the near-empty shop to announce his arrival, he stood awkwardly waiting for someone to appear.

"Won't be a moment," came a female voice from the back of the shop; he looked around and saw that the selection of flowers was not great, but at least he could get a dozen pink roses for now and organise a bouquet for Monday. Interrupting his deliberations came a well-known voice, as Wendy Blaise stepped into the shop from a door near the back.

"Hello Josh, what brings you here to my parent's shop? Had a bit of a tiff with your wife then? Need some flowers to make up? You've left it a bit late though, we don't have much left!"

Just then the owner of the shop came out.

"Hello Wendy, so this is that hunk that you have been going on about for the last few weeks! Nice! You lucky thing, I'm so, so jealous and green with envy, you certainly know how to pick them, sister dear."

As she rubbed her hand up and down Josh's left arm, Josh became embarrassed and tried to say something but Wendy got in first.

"No sister dear, this is Woodley's boss, Joshua Chavender, Josh meet my sister Helen"

"I'm so sorry Josh, I thought that you were her boyfriend coming to see Wendy, but she is right you are a fine catch of a man!"

Chavender's embarrassment made him stutter the first few words as he replied, "Hello, Helen, nice to meet you." As his faced darkened to a nice deep beetroot red, pointedly he said, "Look, all I want is a dozen pink roses and could you deliver a nice flowery bouquet to my home for Monday around noon please?"

Helen still trying to apologise replied, "Sorry… yes… I think we can do that for you; all told that will be forty pounds please, and would you like any sentiment with the bouquet?"

He replied, "Yes, just put 'sorry' and 'I love you. Josh xx', on it please." Writing his address down in the delivery ticket book, along with all the other orders for Monday, he said, "Thank you," to which Helen replied, "No problem; around midday Monday, I shall add that to my delivery list, Thanks." Leaving the shop with the flowers he thought he could hear some giggling, as he hurried to his car for the journey home.

Josh was dreading the reception he was going to get at home; he remembered the first time he had annoyed his then girlfriend, now his wife, over something really petty - oh what was it… ah yes!... The inability to pull the tinfoil from its tube properly, without wasting half the roll in the process; he had showed her several times but she persisted in doing it her way. They had ordered in a supposedly meat feast pizza, which actually looked like it was on a meat free diet, so, as he was accustomed to do in his bachelor days, he added extra cheese and meat and put in the oven to cook; this was his fatal mistake. The extra cooking made the crust rather crispy to chew, but it kept its shape as Tiff, in her annoyed state threw it at him; he ducked and the pizza acting much like a frisbee would, flew and dropped its contents over the cream living room carpet before flying out the open window in a wide arch onto the pavement below, leaving them only cheesy garlic bread for tea and a ruined carpet!

Tiff was in the kitchen when Josh came home; his girls' greeting was rather more subdued than normal, his two oldest girls after getting kisses and hugs from him said, "Mummy's been crying since we came home from school." His two youngest girls chipped in, "Yes Daddy, what have you done?" Josh asked if the girls could go and play with Gran for a while whilst he talked with Mummy, and shooing them away, meekly went into the kitchen to meet his fate like a condemned man! Meanwhile Tiff had wiped and dried her tear-streaked face and had just made a cup of tea, when a dozen pink roses appeared round the door jamb followed a little later by Josh.

"For you my love; I am truly sorry about not saying I love you and hanging up on you this afternoon, no, I really am," he said, whilst quickly scanning the kitchen for things that might possibly or could be used as ballistic missiles!

"Oh! You're ok Josh love, thanks for the flowers, they look really nice." Her clearly tear-streaked face smiled as Josh sat down and begun drinking his tea, thinking that he had got of lightly, when Tiff said, "Sue is bringing her girls over tomorrow to help you and the girls decorate their room. I will take my mum and our youngest girls out for they day along with Sue, I need to buy some new clothes. I'm getting fat and I don't want to lose my looks now, do I love, not with the competition I now seem to have, in a newer younger model that seems intent on..." Tiff left the rest unsaid as a sort of threat, Josh trying to extricate himself from the deep hole he appeared to be in, only made it worse by spluttering excuses. Tiff stood up and grabbing the water filter jug, emptied the contents over his head, then turned and asked. "Does my bum look fat in this skirt?" Josh shook the excess water from his hair and coughed out the water that he had involuntarily swallowed. Before he could react or even answer that question, Tiff came and sat on his wet lap, putting her arms round his wet neck and gave him a big full on French kiss. By this time gran and the girls had come in, seeing her daughter on her husband's lap and kissing him passionately, she tapped Josh on the shoulder and said, "My daughter deserves a room you know!" At that they both burst out laughing.

"That's better love, you know you must get out of that nasty habit you have with the phone, you know, hanging up before I have had a chance to say 'Love you and bye'. That's at least twice now that you've done that!" Tiff then went on to explain that Bert was going to spend the day on his new allotment getting it ready, so she thought it would be nice if the Jenkins' girls helped him, with the decorating, whilst she, Sue and the youngest twins went out. Josh groaned at the thought, but he knew that it would be a cheap price to pay, although he knew that Tiff would max out her credit card and he would have to pay it! It was Ma, bringing the proceedings down to earth, who asked, "I thought you were bringing home the sausages and bacon? Well, where is it?" Pointing at the roses on the table and carrying on with, "I can't fry roses for breakfast you know!"

Josh replied rather sheepishly, knowing full well what Ma would make of it, "The butchers will deliver them at seven thirty tomorrow morning for us, they are making a fresh batch tonight."

"Oh, I see… Tut… Tut… Getting your meat delivered now! Uh um, whatever next, toilets that wash your bums!" - at which the four girls sniggered - "As if, why can't you just go out and buy them like normal people do, tisch, tisch, too good for you now is it, tisch pa-fore tut, to buy normal sausages from a supermarket, tut, tut. Oh no, you just have to have them delivered." She was tutting away and shaking her head as she said it! Josh then had to explain how it was late and the shop was empty and so on, but he left out the bit about the florist and Monday delivery of flowers though.

Chapter 37

Saturday, seven thirty, true to his word, George helped delivered the bacon and sausages, by eight thirty, Ma's big Saturday morning breakfast fry up was over. Josh heartily enjoyed his breakfast eating more than he should have and as he helped to wash up and put away, he was on his second mug of tea, when Sue arrived with her girls. After excited greetings between, Sue, Tiff, all the twins and Ma, Tiff said it was time to go. Kissing Josh she left him holding two lists, the one for Josh was quite short, whilst the girls' list was a bit longer. Josh's list was simple "decorate the girls' room". The girls' list contained a long list of things, mainly at what time to let dad have a rest and a cup of tea, which Tiff was sure that Kimberly and Victoria could manage to do without a problem. They would be back by three and Tiff would like to see some great progress being made. Josh, under the due diligence of his girls and the Jenkins' twins, rolled his sleeves up, but first he taught them how to use a roller, then a brush and finally a paint pad, using quick drying acrylic paint they soon had a base coat of matt white on all the walls, this would help the fuchsia pink give the correct sheen. One of the longer walls would be divided into two with a wavy line half way, the bottom half a pale green and the top a sky blue, with white fluffy clouds. It was here that the girls would paste the large cut out mural of the Princess and the Frog. Whilst Josh got on with painting the walls fuchsia pink, the four girls carefully painted the wall and pasted on the background items of pond, trees and sun. Josh looked over every now again and gave his advice on how to prick out the small air bubbles in the paper. By midday two coats of pink and the background were done, the skirting board and windows being a gloss white already, just needed a sugar soap clean, which all the girls did, whilst the large pink up lighter lampshade did its best to throw light all over the ceiling and from there down onto the walls.

Stopping for biscuits and a cup of tea, Josh read both lists again. His list was simple, decorate the room as the girls would like it done, please don't upset them by saying anything out of order, they have chosen everything, even the mural, do as you're told! The 'Told' bit was in capitals and underlined, ending in kiss kiss 'Love Tiff'. Reading the girls' list, it stated that dad would do as he was told, but would need plenty of tea, Kimberly you can make the tea, and Daddy likes it strong remember; Victoria you can be in charge overall and can tell dad what to do, whilst Carol and Anne would help you both - much love from both mums. Kiss. Kiss. Oh Boy was he ever in trouble thought Josh! Victoria could be just like her mum when given half a chance, but being his daughter he could deal with her a little better than his wife.

Soon it was 3pm; Tiff, Sue, Ma and the younger twins, (young) Tiffany and Stephanie were home, carrying in bag after bag of mainly food shopping, but Josh saw at least four large boutique bags go straight up to their bedroom, Josh looked on shocked and felt the wallet in his pocket physically shrink, as the money from it vanished into thin air, in the full knowledge that a large credit card bill would soon be coming his way. Tiff took Josh's arm and went with him to see the progress in the girls' room, "You've done well love, I was right to put Vicky in charge, you have just the mural to go, then we can move all the girls in here and you can do the last room." Giving him a hug and a kiss and taking him back downstairs she told him, "Come on, let's unpack, I haven't spent that much, so don't look so frightened dear."

Sue and her girls said their goodbyes and Josh thanked Carol and Anne for helping him and said, "The cheque's in the post," which the two young girls did not quite catch the drift of, as he waved them off. Going back indoors, Josh could hear his daughters as they talked eagerly about what they had done as the older twins showed off their handiwork in the empty room. Tiff and Ma put away a ton of groceries, before sitting down and drinking the tea that Josh had made. Tiff picked up her lists and said, "Perhaps I should do this more often with you, it seems to have worked."

"What's that then Tiffany?" said her mother. "Leaving notes and lists," replied Tiff and before she could continue to explain, her mother went on, "you know I used to do that all the time with your father, he was so forgetful sometimes, he used to forget he had such a short memory, one time he actually forgot his own birthday, and when he remembered he swore he was a year older than he was! I had to sit him down and write out a list with all the years from his birthdate, to make him believe he was a year younger." Something stirred in Josh's subconscious at Ma's rendition of her story, and the notes that Tiff had written that fleeting idea that he was just beginning to develop when Tiff called him Friday evening, which the butchers and florist were working on when he called on them, now, that idea suddenly pricked into his conscious mind and stayed, as he hammered it in to his consciousness like a railroad spike, so he would not forget.

Sunday saw Josh paste the mural on the wall, the Princess was beautiful as all Princesses should be - well those in fairy tales at any rate. A pale blue sparkly ball gown, golden tresses heaped high, ringlets dangling round her delicately made up face, a small fragile diamond tiara sat firmly on top of her head, slender arms in white elbow length gloves, one foot in a golden slipper, showing from under her gown. The larger than life frog sat on a lily leaf, frog lips pursed awaiting the kiss, small bubbles from both of them leading to a large bubble. Inset was a picture of the rather godlike looking Prince, blonde Elvis Presley style hair, with deep blue eyes and a fine chiselled jaw, his head sat atop square masculine shoulders, strong manly looking arms covered by a white loose shirt as loved by pirates in the B-movies, red trousers and black boots with a flashing sabre, all of which added interest to the overall picture, which Josh could just about deal with, especially all the flora and fauna inaccuracies, but what troubled him most was the Prince's codpiece, accentuated as it was by the tight red trousers! It would not look out of place on a pornstar! It actually shocked him, he was no prude, but this was too much, for it reminded him that one day he would have to have that most dreaded talk of all parents with his daughters and judging by the choice of the mural, it might well be sooner than he thought.

Still, he thought he could lessen the impact a little by using the girls' vanity units to hide the lower half of the Princess and Prince's bodies, whilst the two chest of drawers could frame below the frog, the beds placed either side of the bedside cabinets and the wardrobes placed in the corner by the door helped fill the room, curtains, blinds and lights finished it all off. He was pleased with his efforts; he just hoped Tiff and his girls would be as well. Tiff and the girls came excitedly into the room and took over and very soon changed the rooms completely. He got several hugs from Kimberly and Victoria and received a big kiss from Tiff who, breathing in deep the fresh paint smell, said, "You have to do just as good a job on Tiffany and Stephanie's room now, don't you Josh. Oh by the way, Sue called me today, to thank you for looking after her girls; she said Bert had a lovely time playing in the dirt!"

Chapter 38

At Monday's senior officers' meeting it seemed, as it had for the past few weeks, that Chavender was the only one with something to report, but again he just had to stress that enquiries were ongoing, and certain leads were being followed. They had spent over two hundred man hours on the follow up investigation into the calls, but had actually netted very little in the way of evidence. It was a distinct possibility that the murderer had just started his run of terror. The fraud investigation was now coming to a close, and again they had not been able to link anyone to anything. All concerned knew each other, and they all had stakes or shares in the new construction consortium, called Eco-developments. Whilst the two councillors who were recently on the planning committee could be linked to the recent new estate, but only tenuously, in that they were on the planning committee that approved the sale of the land and the final plans after the council consulted an American company called, Land Use and Consultancy Inc., and paid them a hefty fee of £52,000 for the privilege! They again used this company when they had agreed to the merger and looked at what of the council's land could be sold off. This took the better part of a year and the councils were charged sixty thousand pounds each, it was on their recommendation that they would be basing the sale of council owned land to be developed. Chavender explained that as far as he could make out with the investigations, it looked like Eco-Developments is the foremost or favoured local company to get the biggest share of land and building rights. If the deal went through, it could net many millions of pounds in profit for all the directors, but it's the link between them all that is missing. The councillors, having done their little bit to help, would likely be resigning from office at the merger and would hope that everyone would concentrate on the land purchases in the first few years to notice their involvement. They would skedaddle with the money, and be long gone before someone could investigate possible wrong doings.

"Um...Yes I see," said Featherstonehaugh, "Well it's been a trying few weeks for you Chavender, but I think best thrown in at the deep end, sink or swim, what you know, yes sink or swim."

The Chief Constable was speaking as if he was still in the army, one of his many peculiar traits! Andersonn asked Chavender some operational questions about the temporary deployments and ended in saying "that they seemed to be doing the trick!"

Sword nodded in agreement, whilst Jacobs ended by asking if Chavender was going to do a press release, before the press got anxious and started to make things up. Chavender's reply was that he would arrange a press release for Tuesday morning.

"Thanks for nothing," he muttered under his breath - just what he needed at this moment in time, another meeting with Miss Blaise. Chavender made his way back to his office. Sitting down he picked up the phone and called the CID room, asking for detective sergeants Wootton and Wilson (TAD from Bryantsand) to come to his office in twenty minutes, he then called Detective Inspectors Pearce (TAD from Plympton) and Lister (TAD from Bryantsand) and asked them to come and see him right away.

As the DIs entered, he beckoned them to sit and placing a finger vertically across his lips, intimated that they should sit silently; a knock on the door, a "come in", and the two detective sergeants entered, he beckoned them to sit and using the same gesture to sit silently. Some moments passed before Chavender got up and walked to the boards. Looking at the expectant faces on his detectives, he asked if they had ever had a moment that they could use the word "Serendipity" or better still a "Eureka!" on? Looking at the blank faces he thought not, but they are young, they have time, or was it just his good fortune to see things differently than others? Did events conspire to make him a good detective, certainly his brain worked against him sometimes, like the fact he saw music as colours and not primarily as sound. He knew that sometimes Lady Luck would nudge you along a certain road, until you came to a sudden stop with a billboard a mile high, lit up with neon lights and a big arrow pointing too and saying 'Murderer Here'. Oh for sure Lady Luck had dropped hints, some not so subtle, and some so obscure that even they passed you by, unnoticed by the conscious mind but registering in your subconscious deep, only to fester and gnaw away at you, eating up the thinking power that was required for other more pressing engagements. He went on to explain to them all.

"Now my Eureka moment or, as popularised by comics, the shining lightbulb over one's head, was on Saturday, I'd spent the day painting my oldest daughters' room, with two of my daughters and their two friends, to me it was an NTR job (no thought required), a pleasant change from thinking all sorts of nasty things to do with my job. My eldest daughter, Victoria, was put in charge of me by her mum. Kimberly, the younger, was in charge of tea breaks and biscuits." Here a few sniggers and some wide smiles flashed across the four men sat in his office, as they intimated by gesture that he was under the thumb! Clearing his throat he went on, "My wife, in her infinite wisdom, went shopping to get some new clothes. Why, I don't know, to me the old ones look fine, but she did, thus I was left, surrounded by four nine-year-old girls all intent on talking at once, at the same time, and in unison. I paid no attention to the growing noise, intent as I was in fulfilling the jobs on my list, before my wife came back." Again the sniggers but longer this time and Wootton nearly lost it!

"Sorry Sir," he said, putting his hand over his mouth as if to stifle a yawn, but he continued to snigger.

"Alright, let's have a ruddy good belly laugh now, let's get it out of our system. I know that gesture, and sniggering doesn't help us at all!"

As if on command they could not keep it in, they all lost their composure, imagining Old Beaky being emasculated, and great peels of laughter echoed round the room. Even Chavender laughed with them, till at last they stopped.

"Now can we get on?" he said. "Where was I? Oh yes, that's it, I was just saying I was being, as you would realise, and have so succinctly demonstrated to put it, henpecked by my eldest daughter, who my wife left with strict instructions. I would point out that those of you not married or do not have children will not know that feeling, but I pity you, when, eventually, it does happen, as it surely will!"

Leaving the rest unsaid he went on, pointing at the boards. "Returning to the subject in hand, now what do you see here? Any guesses? No? Yes Lister, what do you see?"

"Well Sir, not to put too fine a point on it, it's a load of names and addresses of those that have died Sir!"

"Yes. Yes, I can see that, but that is the content, it's not what you actually see now is it?"

This time it was Wilson who fell into Chavender's little trap, "Sir, but it is, we have several names, addresses and other bits of information on the boards, what else could it be? I know you've been under it at home Sir, and looking at these boards for days on end, but it is just a list, or several lists to be precise."

It was at this point that Chavender did the old charades trick of touching his nose and pointing at them all. They looked on clearly puzzled by his antics, until he said, "You said it, you said the magic word then, come on do I have to spell it out for you?" Exasperated he then went on to say, "Oh good grief! Okay, well then, I spy with my…"

The four grown men in the room thought he had flipped his lid and startled by his display of childishness, looked on puzzled, until, "Little eye, something beginning with "L"?" finished Chavender. The four men sort of got into the spirit of things and came back with silly replies such as, lights, light switch, lamp and lunacy, and laughter as they chuckled at Chavender, who shook his head a little and sighed deeply in despair.

Giving up the ghost with the detectives, he just let them prattle on, until he almost screamed out in despair, "No, no, and thrice no; what we have here as plain as the nose on my face." Here he tapped the side of his fine nose in a gesture much similar to tapping the temple on one's head, continuing with, "It is a series of lists! These lists form the outer component part to the content we have been staring at the content for so long we forgot about the substantive part that these lists play in our investigation. Now I have one box left from the council to look through." At this point he bent down and pulled the last box from its hiding place and placed it firmly on his desk. On the outside of the box clearly stencilled for all to see was a label marked 'ALL COUNCIL WAITING LISTS'. As the penny began to drop and they saw what he had meant, it was Lister who spoke first. "Well, well, as a detective force to be reckoned with, we must all have been dumber than a sack full of wet mice!"

"Nicely put, Lister" said Pearce. "But Sir," Pearce interjected, "I'm still going to ask the dumbest of questions now."

"What do you mean?"

"Right," said Chavender, pointing to the boards, "we have names, we have addresses and we have deaths, but nothing connects them to each other than the way they died! Okay? In fact the only thing they have in common at the moment is that they are on my white boards and in a list! Now take this one stage further, forget the content, but concentrate on the one fact that joins them all, even though it may well be an artificial one, which is our lists. Now you're going to say lists exist everywhere, and at every level of society; the doctors, hospitals, dentist and national and local government as well as police records, all forms of lists, yes, everywhere, yes, right?" They all nodded and answering his own rhetorical question, he went on to say. "That's correct, they do, so taking this as a starting point and one giant leap of faith again, and trusting my gut feelings, whilst ruling out those lists that I think we have no need for, out of the five I have just named, and for now the Bryantsand-on-Sea council lists, it will leave us to have to only look through the Plympton lists. Now I think if we look through these lists we may just find what we are looking for that connection! We will all pick a list at random and to make it easier, we will look for only one road name and that will be Carew Road, okay? A nice easy name to look for." He then went on to explain after stopping for a moment to let his idea sink in. "Now how you do it is like this; I want you to scan the lists for only addresses that begin with a C, and very soon you will get your eye in, and it will become very easy to pick out that one letter, get the letter read the line." Chavender saw doubt scurry across their faces and continued, "I assure you it will become automatic."

"Okay Sir" came back a chorus of replies, as he handed out files from the box.

Chapter 39

Lister, Pearce, Wootton and Wilson all received a file each: Social Housing, Allotments, Warden Assisted Housing and Car Park Permits, whilst Chavender looked through Council Staff list past and present. He left out the Council Tax list and a few other generic type lists, that he thought would complicate things, but he knew if the lists he had pulled out proved to be a blank, he would have to sift through the rest of them, and chances are all the addresses would be on one of those list he had omitted, which would be of no help to him because they were way by far all-encompassing. As the five men began to skim the lists, turning page after page, eyes moving sideways, occasionally kneading the balls of their thumbs into the eye sockets to relieve the strain, until after half an hour of semi silence, Pearce let out a "Whoop" of joy.

"Got it Sir!" he exclaimed, making them all jump, as he stood up and did a little jig for joy, exclaiming "Yes Sir, YES! Right here on page twenty Carew Road."

Chavender looked on saying, "Grand job, excellent, could you mark it on the board please... Umm... err... What list have you got Pearce?" knowing full well what one it was, for his hunch had included that it would most likely be on this list, than on any of the other lists to include Carew Road, but he kept that information to himself. "Right, keep on looking will you please... Ah Pearce, could you now start over again and look for say 221B Long Acre Road? Thanks."

What threw a minor spanner in the works was Flat 9, 141 London Road, for it was Lister who came up with the next connection in a list, and just like Pearce, Chavender made him write it on the board. This began to set Chavender's mind to wander a little and confirm his suspicions, this was the smoker who died, and if his hunch was right, yes, yes, he thought he would appear on two lists. He stopped Lister and asked him if he could find the breakdown of what the type of social housing was, for instance, flats, houses, bungalows, hostels and maisonettes. A sideways detour into this list could hold things up and muddy the water, which was why he set Lister that task, it at least would leave him free to concentrate on the matter in hand. Lister none the wiser attacked his new task with a keenness that belayed the futility of his search and was soon searching his way through the reams of statistics, making copious notes as he went.

Soon other addresses began to show up on Pearce's list and were written on the boards. *Yes, yes*, Chavender thought, *all becoming clearer now*, at the end of two hours, apart from some crossovers onto other list, all the murder victims' home addresses were on one of the lists. Just to make sure, he had Lister check the Bryantsand-on-Sea list, but once again nothing came to light.

"Right, listen up please," Chavender said, in a commanding sort of voice, but the please was his downfall, always taught to be polite, even his orders had a sort of request value to their nature. "I think we have something to go on now, and I bet if we looked closely at the burglaries list, they may just tie in? Wilson could you help Wootton and Pearce do that for me now please?" Leaving Lister to his work he got up and walked over to the window, looking out over the industrial estate. He looked, but this time he took the time to take the unfolding scene in, in his mind he was preparing the statement he would have to give the press. First of all though he had better clear it with his bosses. Not wanting to give too much away, he phoned the Chief Constable and asked if he could see him and his deputy, in about ten minutes. He told the others to keep looking for correlations in the lists. Walking down the hall, Chavender met Jacobs coming out of his office. Knocking on the Chief Constable's office door, they heard "come in" and both entered. Some twenty minutes later Chavender returned to his office, having explained to the senior officers what would be in the press release, and received their approval.

Back in his office the other detectives were feeling elated, at last they had something to go on other than three cups on a drainer! They wondered how he had managed to figure it out, but it was Wootton who got the closest, after all he did receive some inside information some weeks ago. Sitting down in his chair, it was Lister who spoke first, "Well Sir, I still can't get how you got the idea of the lists, unless of course you are telling us to be henpecked or much worse still, nagged at home!"

"No I'm not, as I already said sometimes you're driving along happily, brain in neutral, just going with the flow, when, booomb! All of a sudden it hits you, like a bug hits a windscreen, splaaat, and you're jolted back to the real world. I have had nothing, and have seen nothing, but lists since last Friday. True the contents of the list varied from meat deliveries, flower deliveries and notes with instructions from my wife."

Here a polite titter came from the assembled officers as Chavender got up and walked to the boards, only this time he went to the board with the fraud investigation on and placed the map that showed the new estate over it and bulldog clipped it in place. The four men looked on, quizzically, and wondered what this meant to the murder investigation.

"Now for part two of my Eureka moment, you, Lister, nearly derailed us, what with finding that address in the housing list, but it just added and confirmed another link in my theoretical chain of events. Here you see the map of the new estate."

Pointing to it and asking Pearce to call Sergeant Jenkins at Plympton for him and to put the phone on speaker.

"Jenkins here Sir."

"Hello Sergeant Jenkins, Chavender speaking - just a couple of questions for you? One, how many years were you on the allotment waiting list, and two the new estate behind you, was that earmarkcd for use as allotments?"

Jenkins replied, "I was first on the list about five years ago, which is about the average waiting time, the land built on behind me was originally designated to be allotments until some Yankee firm told the council that it was very poor land for growing anything on, and it would best serve as building land, that's why the new estate was built."

This was an unsuspected modification for Chavender who immediately recalled that the council used an American firm called Land Use and Consultancy Inc. Well this was a surprise, what a coincidence or was it that the crooks were being incredibly stupid, surely not, but... surely... They would have put some distance between themselves and an outside firm. If they didn't, then this was a really, really dumb thing for them to do." He was just about to say something when Lister piped up, "Sir, that's the name of the firm that was doing the consultancy for the two boroughs!"

Pearce looked on and made the next connection, by saying, "You don't think they would use a firm that had links to any of those suspects in the fraud case, do you Sir?"

"I don't know Pearce, but so far, it is the best lead we have had for a long while, Lister see if you can dig out the reports made by that company, let's see if we can tie them all to something that will float!"

Chavender nearly always chose his words carefully, so as to make the other person think a little, here he used float instead of sink, as would normally be the case, we need something that will not disappear into the depths of the ocean, to be lost forever, but some bit of flotsam or jetsam, that will collect any other tiny titbits of information and drag it along in its wake.

"Right gentlemen, this press report, lets compose it shall we and then call it a day?" Unbeknownst to them all, time had steadily been marching on all afternoon, and now it was close to 7pm. The afternoon had taken its full toll of man hours to look through those lists, but, according to Chavender, it was well worth it. Now instead of going on three cups on a drainer, it had some substantive, hard physical evidence of names and addresses on several lists, all of which pointed to murder!

Twenty more minutes and by 7.30 it was done. Saying "goodnight" to them all he left for home, he had been too busy all day to think about the flower delivery, but he now thought, "Tiff hasn't called to thank me for the flowers, boy I must be in the deep do-do now!" The drive home for him was pleasant and gave him a chance to unwind. By the time he got in, he was mentally ready for the profuse and happy welcome his girls nearly always gave him. Opening the door, he saw the girls' scrum of an octopi as it barrelled its way up the hall into his arms, jabbering away, as usual all at once, about this and that, homework, could he help, friends, and what was said at school, It was Gran who came out and corralled his brood into the front room saying, "Come girls, Daddy needs to talk to Mummy; let's watch a film, shall we?" leaving Josh and his rapidly sinking heart to his fate. Opening the kitchen door the flowers sat on the table, neatly arranged by the florist and Tiff.

Josh rather sheepishly said "Sorry love", as once again he looked for any objects that might fly, although he was a bit worried at the heavy cast iron griddle that Tiff was just putting away.

"Oh Josh you silly old thing you, the flowers are nice, but you didn't have to you, you know," getting up and giving him a kiss, "Here, come, sit down, have a cup of tea." There came a staccato of orders as Tiff poured him a cup of tea.

Taking a sip he said, "You didn't call, I thought I was still in the doghouse!"

"No, not the doghouse any more, but you're out loose in the garden now, on a leash so to speak," she said laughingly and went on to say, as she put on the table in front of him a big plate of bangers and mash for his tea, "Enjoy!"

The press release the next day was a statement given to both local and national press. It basically stated that original enquiries in both cases were ongoing and coming to a satisfactory conclusion. New evidence had come to light in both cases, which were being pursued at this moment in time. This evidence, it was hoped, would lead them closer to the perpetrator in both cases. They were, at the moment, following up the leads in both cases, and looked to arrests being imminent. It then went on to thank the public for all the help they had given the police in trying out the new system and that the system, appeared to have done its job by cutting down the number of wasted trips to the back end of nowhere. It helped to concentrate police activity in the right area and as such it reduced the number of wasted hours to a minimum. Chavender chose to use the word imminent because it gave him a greater degree of time span, it may make some hacks look the word up, in which case they would be the wiser for it. It really was a master piece of obfuscation, it said everything yet meant nothing, it did not state what evidence, or in which case it might be involved with, which to Chavender's mind was just fine. Let them flesh it out, after all if they want to sensationalise it let them, that's what they get paid for. Miss Blaise's paper ran the full statement that evening and her editorial really went to town on it, saying that it was understated, uninformative, confusing and down right baffling to say the least, she went on by saying if one tried to read between the lines, that the police are nowhere near to any sort of conclusion, that would satisfy the public in either case. This statement, even after she had the papers lawyers read it, made no sense what so ever and to try and explain it to the readers would take up several pages. The only word in the statement that raised any sort of cryptic comment and which she had to look up the proper meaning of was "imminent"; this was not the usual police type word, its original connotation, meant or implied a leaning tree that was just about to fall over, but no-one knew when; it also meant in a broad sense, impending or soon, but how soon?, it went on to ask.

Chapter 40

Calling the detective inspectors together later that day, so they could go over what they'd discovered late yesterday, and to formulate plans of enquiries, took Chavender's mind of his domestic strife. He wasn't sure, but something was wrong with his wife. She had been asking those questions lately that required an answer, but either answer was wrong and was likely to get you a four-penny one round the ear. Chavender asked if any of the DIs read any fictional detective stories. Getting no positive response, he told them they should and that there was nothing new, so to speak, under the sun!

"Why, we've even had a body in the library, death by poison marmalade and death of a pipe smoker; we have been weaving in and out of fictional crime stories all the way through our investigations, but none of us knew it! If you think that, like them, you will get a sensational reveal, or, as if by magic, you will be sorely mistaken. To catch our poisoner, will require luck and lots of it, and the same goes for our fraud case. Now Molly-Fergus I want you to go up to Somerset House on Friday and check out the births, deaths and marriages for me for, let me see, Councillors Walker, Melbourne and Ireland?" he said.

She replied, "Are you playing a hunch now Sir, or are we dipping in to this fantasy of yours that we are in a detective novel now?"

"Yes and no. I believe that there is some family connection somewhere and the only way is to look for it - what better place than Somerset House? Now you can travel up

Thursday morning, come back for work Monday, no need to phone through any results, they can wait till Monday, okay? Now the rest of you, and for the rest of this week, we will concentrate on the poisoner?" Chavender set them mundane tasks for a few days, checking and cross checking various files, times and places. He was as certain as he could be that the poisoner would hold off for awhile until he saw which way the wind blew, and to make sure of it he spoke to Miss Blaise.

In a way he was doing a bit of one-upmanship on something she said but, and having got Featherstonehaugh's permission to try it, it warranted her full cooperation. She was summoned, for want of a better word, to see him which she readily agreed to. Chavender made sure Wootton and Carr were also on hand to put the point across. As he explained the plan to her, and how she was going to be complicit in a police tactic that might draw the poisoner out, but would certainly keep him at bay for a week or so. It was a big gamble to take; he knew if he got it wrong someone might die, and it would be no-one's fault but his own, for reading it wrong! Miss Blaise was told she must not reveal any part of the scheme to anyone outside these four walls, not even to her boss. He would take the digs he was allowing her to take at him, and she had to use the phrase "sources close to the investigation", for she had revealed in an editorial article that she had written about the perils of dating a police detective sergeant, so her readership would know how close to the source this information was more than likely to be coming from, hopefully. She knew the risk he was taking, but agreed to do it. He handed her a sheet of paper with the stages of the plan written down and told her she could flesh it out a bit, but not much, it had to be believable, but not sensational. She was to start the story in Thursday's paper and keep it running up to about the middle of next week, or stop when told to. Nodding her agreement, he thanked her and let Wootton escort her home.

Chavender sat down with Carr in the canteen and had a coffee with him, he had been tasked by the Chief Constable to sound Carr out to head up a special tactical squad for when the "navvie invasion" would happen. They would need training in the use of non lethal force and stronger special vehicles, he was to put some ideas down on paper and he was to attend the next Monday meeting.

That night Josh had, what one could only describe as a nightmare of epic proportions. He dreamt he was driving home as usual on the road half way up the valley side, the River Ouster was gently meandering its way across the wide valley floor and downstream to exit into the sea at Bryantsand when, all of a sudden, the river dried up, it stopped flowing completely and the whole of the opposite valley side, took on the characteristics of a river in full flood. Trees, soil and large boulders flowed down the gently sloping valley side, into the empty river bed and swept along the entire valley floor, pushing everything in front of it. It was like looking at what one saw in news reports about rivers in flood, a dark grey green moving mass of debris mixed and swirling up and down. The opposite hill was stripped of soil and vegetation, thus leaving several large bare terraces some one hundred feet high, of dark, sharp rock. The next moment his car vanished and he was atop the other valley side, dropping down the several terraces like steps, landing and dropping instantaneously. He reached the foot of the terraces in an instant, meeting some other people he began climbing over large boulders to the other side into a small unknown town, walking along the street, it suddenly started to shake as the earthquake struck, buildings wobbled and swayed madly, but strangely enough they did not disintegrate, but acted as a jelly would, wobbling on a plate. Strangely none of the people were affected by the shaking, he and they walked quite normally, on a road that was stable and firm. The next moment, somehow, a TV news report was blaring away, about how although the countryside had suffered severe damage, no reports of deaths, injuries or even, for that fact, damage to property had occurred. Walking up the street he saw he was heading for a seventeenth century gated coach house, through which he saw Chavender Mansion, it was at this point that his nightmare was rudely interrupted by two sharp elbow blows in the side from Tiff, as his constant rolling proved too much for her. Awaking, it took him several heart stopping minutes to regain his composure and bearings before drifting off into a deep trouble free sleep.

Miss Blaise certainly went to town on the police, Chavender and the poisons case, accusing the police of complicity, foolishness and being disinclined to prosecute enquires with gusto, in fact, that they were hiding information, or not pursuing certain lines of questioning, and that sources close to the investigation implied that an arrest would be made this weekend. Once again it was all too contradictory in essence, but she was sure of her source, at least about the arrest and that it would be sooner rather than later. The public loved it, the local paper had to increase its print run to keep up with the demand, but most importantly of all it had the desired effect of keeping the killer from pursuing his agenda.

Once again, Josh's weekend at home was spent painting the youngest girls' room, but at least their mural was less overtly sexual than his oldest girls' was! They had picked a theme on the Yellow Brick Road. It was late on Sunday when he noticed that Ma's plaster cast had been replaced with a plastic and bandage type of support, which could come off when she needed to wash or take a shower. Josh asked several question about the support which Ma answered but Tiff was puzzled by, for it looked like any ordinary bit of surgical support and she said "it could be bought at any chemist!" Josh thought long and hard on the implications it could have on his case, for here he was most certain of, was one method of applying the chloroform to the victim's mouth, without causing or being at all suspicious of the true intent of the cast on the suspect's hand.

That Monday's senior officers' brief, whilst still overshadowed by Chavender's cases and general overview of the CID caseload, was, in part, taken over by Inspector Carr's suggestions on how to deal with the 'navvie' invasion if and when it came. The Chief Constable thanked Carr for his input and said he would see what he could do for him. Thanking them all, they left his office to head back to Chavender's office. He invited Carr to come along and before long they were seated.

It was Sword who asked the first question, "Well Josh, scuttlebutt," using the old navy term his father taught him, "are you really henpecked at home? Please tell me that's not so? Come on man own up! Do you wear the trousers or does your wife?"

He winked conspiratorially at Andersonn, who chipped in with a, "Yes Josh, are you?" Chavender answered, "No... I am not really henpecked or even nagged at home. I was just hitting a bit of a rough patch at home, you know, new job, new friends, new house to decorate and so forth, and two high level cases to investigate did not help smooth the transition from life in the capital city to life in the country."

After they listened for several minutes whilst Chavender explained what was happening, the two Chief Inspectors wished him luck and left him to talk with Inspector Carr.

Chapter 41

Chavender sat silently for a moment whilst Carr looked over the list. Shaking his head, he marvelled at how Chavender had reached such a conclusion as he had. It still had not quite sunk in when Chavender spoke, "Well Inspector, too far fetched or entirely believable, what do you think, uh? Quite a good story so far, and of course the papers' editorials are doing my ego the power of good, so to speak! The public have turned right against me at the moment, just look at this morning's edition and the letters page, quick to criticise us aren't they?"

"Yes Sir" Carr said.

Chavender continued, "Anyway, that's not what I want from you, your plan seems great on paper, but if you need more bodies when the time comes just say the word and I'll try to arrange some help for you. I like that idea of using the trucks that transport defendants to the courts idea too, save our vans getting beat in, so did the Chief Constable. Now I want your opinion on something." As he went on to explain his theory to Carr on how the murderer might chloroform his victims. Carr nodded and told Chavender that it seemed a plausible way or theory, but how did he propose catching him. Here Chavender explained further, that here was that incredibly stupid thing that would crack the case, and what would be required of the Duty Sergeant here at headquarters to do on the hour and to make sure that that information was passed on to the beat constables, all patrol cars and all CID staff. Carr nodded his approval and said he would make sure it was done as he wished.

That evening's paper, according to the plan, led with 'Police Baffled' and 'Inspector's Clueless again'. It went on to say that the police have totally lost the plot and according to sources close to the investigation, 'The Police are dumber than a sack full of wet mice', carrying on with 'police backtrack on arrest, persisting with her theme Miss Blaise, continued her personal attack on the new crime boss, as being a policeman of the old school, and that he was blind to any ideas or suggestions from the lower ranks and file. She went on to say that although it was great having a hero for a crime boss, someone with brains would not go amiss. Or that he wasn't smart enough to admit that he was clueless as to the identity of the poisoner. Of course the national dailies picked up on it as well as the national news media, who added their tuppence-worth to the story, and to some extent the Middleshire CID became, or was looked upon by the bigger police forces CID, as poor simple straw sucking country bumpkins who did not know their "arse from their elbow!" Scotland Yard even called with the offer of several of Chavender's old colleagues to come to the "aid and succour" of the Middleshire CID, all of which were politely turned down by Featherstonehaugh.

Throughout that day the Duty Sergeant called the hospitals on the hour every hour for an update which mostly came back negative, which is what Chavender wanted. Then the entire force was alerted to this fact and were warned to be on the look out for someone with a plaster cast on either hand. Whilst discreet enquiries were going on at the chemist to see if any one would remember selling a medical type wrist support in the past few months. He also had a detective trawl through the A and E log for similar accidents prior to November, just in case a real accident had happened and he thought it was a good disguise so continued with it. It was then that Chavender remembered he had sent Molly-Fergus on a mission, so he called her to come and see him at once.

"So sorry, Molly-Fergus, I am so sorry, I forgot about you, but did you have a good time in the ol' smoke?" using a natural born Londoner's term for his city. "I hope you stayed north of the water? See any decent shows? Now what did you find out for me?"

"Well," she said, "my boyfriend proposed and I accepted", as she waved the ring under his nose, and before he could say congratulations, she went on. "It was most romantic, we went out for a meal on the River Thames, and around midnight when the moon was up, he went down on one knee and popped the question. As you can see I said yes."

"Well congratulations Molly, when is the happy day?"

"Oh not till next year, but thanks Sir."

Calming down a bit she went on to say, "Now what you really want to hear about is what I found out for you at Somerset House." At this he suddenly fixed his attention on her as she explained what she had discovered. "Well Sir, it seems that Councillor Ireland's mother remarried when he was seven and just starting boarding school here in England. She married an American citizen, who took her off to the States, where she had two children, two half brothers for Ireland. One of these half brothers set up a business in the states called, Land Use and Consultancy Inc. This firm, at his bidding, got the consultancy contract ahead of its rivals, due to a last minute push by Councillor Walker; no one on the council knew about the family connection apart from these two. It all looked legitimate on paper, due to the name of the CEO of the American company being different to either Walker or Ireland, sir. Thus showing no real family ties to any one on the Council, this was supposedly an independent company, free from all undue influence, Sir"

"Grand job Molly, but I don't really think we can recommend a prosecution to the CPS on our flimsy evidence, although at a push we may get them on insider trading, but it may well be a case for the council to take civil action to reclaim the monies spent on two bogus land use reports. This seems to be the end of this trail for now; I will have a word with the Chief Constable and see what he says, but I fear that our investigations have so far been wasted and have borne no good evidence."

"Yes sir, but we can't give up yet, I mean, if wrongdoing has been done surely we should prosecute?" she said in all earnest.

"I agree, Molly, but it will be seen as a waste of public money, and the courts are getting enough stick at being too lenient as it is! If we have a case, all I can do is present it, but I fear we would be laughed out of court, as it stands." With that he congratulated her again and wished her well for the future. Chavender turned to his whiteboards and own feeling of despair.

As the week progressed the usual everyday crimes began to make their presence felt again, as manhours were slowly used up in their investigations; the regular calls to all hospitals began to grind a bit, but Chavender insisted that they happen and saw that the information was passed down to all in the force. Miss Blaise, according to plan, started to ease up on the poison case and went hell for leather at the Council, when the Leader of the Council went on record to announce that all future building plans for the joint councils would go through another revue, but a civil action was being taken out against the directors of Eco-Developments and Land Use and Consultancy Inc., to reclaim all monies, lost or otherwise, and to seek compensation over the sale of council owned land at under the market value. The council went on to say that an independent revue would take place over the future sale of any council land before being submitted to planning. In some ways Miss Blaise was happier taking pot shots at such public figures rather than the police, not because of her crush on Josh, but she had learnt a lot more about how the police were being swamped by incessant reams of paperwork over any arrest and the fact that somehow central government had emasculated their powers in some way, shape or form.

Chapter 42

Meanwhile the murderer was planning to strike again. It had been a few weeks since he had last struck, and judging by what the papers said about the ineffective police investigation, he felt it was safe to go out and kill again. He carefully prepared his killing kit, whilst looking at the different list of names he had, and selected one. Having done a doorstep visit already, he knew what kind of clothes were required, and having been to several charity shops out of town to get them, he felt that these would leave little or no clues whatsoever for the police to pick up on, and link him to the murder scene or the murder.

Chavender sat in his office looking at the same list, thinking where and when will you strike next? He had already worked out that the murder victims' names had been roughly in the middle of the list, but this still left well over two hundred households to cover; he could not afford to station a man in each house permanently, and it was too great a risk to let these people know, for fear of the only identifying mark being disclosed, which would lose them the only real possible chance of catching him, or even to assign or station a constable on every street. No, now it was a waiting game, a potluck waiting game, he had to hope that one of the police cars or a constable on his beat, would be in the right place at the right time! He was really troubled, he could not stop the killer from killing once more, as he could not protect everyone who was at peril - he had to narrow the odds down a bit, but how could he?

It was whilst pondering this question, and reading through all the rehashed forensics reports that the first of two ideas struck him. The first idea was to do with the fibres, okay, they were of the same type of cloth but the dye density was slightly different, as if coming from two sets of trousers; if this was the case, the question sprang to his mind was it potluck or did he know roughly what type of clothes to wear? If it was pot luck, he should do the lottery! For nearly every type of fibre they looked at, proved that they were a very close match, almost undetectable! Now how could he do that? Unless, of course he prearranged a visit, probably only a short visit, just to have a look-see at the house, and the type of clothes being worn by the householder. Yes, that would do it he thought, quickly scribbling it down on paper, fearing to trust his memory. His second and probably best thought came when he picked up the joint allotment list, looking at it he suddenly realised that although all the names were on the list, only people living in Plympton had so far been targeted, what he needed was the list for the allocation of allotments for Plympton only, quickly scouring the box the list came in, he found a separate folder with all the lists in, as if before a joining of the councils, just what he needed, but then, dismay, the Plympton allotment list was spread over six sites - now how could this help?

This, Chavender now felt, was the crux of the case, make or break! Finding a highlighter pen he read through the lists, highlighting names as they appeared; once all were highlighted, he then went through and dated them, soon a distinct pattern was emerging. It appeared if you read across the lists of the murder victims, although at various positions either high or low on the list, they followed or read across each list, leaving one list shorter than the rest by one name. Was this the incredibly stupid thing he was looking for, he summoned all the help he could muster and began phoning names on the list, asking just one question, "Did they have someone coming round soon to talk to them about allotments?"

After a full hour of calling names on the list, Chavender had narrowed the possible target list down to ten names. He then called them once again, for although he asked the right question, he did not ask the correct question, as was pointed out by one of his detective constables, once he sat back to take stock of the situation. He thanked the young constable for reminding him of his shortcomings in the question asking department, and set about the task of asking the correct question. After asking if they had an appointment with someone soon, for example, within the next day or so, three names off the list were revealed, those had arranged a verbally agreed appointment for the next day at 3pm, whilst the names left on the list had appointments for a week's time.

This flummoxed Chavender for a while. Why arrange for three appointments at the same time? Perhaps as cover in case one was out? Surely not? If you arrange to meet someone, you meet them. Perhaps it was the murderer's back up plan in case one of the victims had visitors, or something compromised a clean getaway? Yes, yes that would do it, but just to be on the safe side he would cover all the names on the list. He asked Molly-Fergus to call Smith, Pearce, and Lister in for an immediate meeting. "No" was not an option, he stressed, even if the four horsemen of the apocalypse was coming down the road they must attend, they must literally drop whatever they are on and get to headquarters ASAP, no arguments accepted! Afterwards she was to muster all available other ranks in the duty room. He was going to see the Chief Constable. Before he left he called Carr to see if what he required was available, and asking him to bring four fire armed trained officers along to the general meeting, but prior to that, could he attend a meeting in half an hour in his office? Chavender was more nervous of this meeting with the Chief Constable than any before, for here he had to outline his plan to catch the murderer in the act. However, it still left some small, very slim chance that the murderer could or would change his mind, and that they would all be in the wrong place, he asked for, and received the authority to use lethal and non lethal force, it was to be a mix of armed uniform officers and plain clothes detectives.

Chapter 43

Carr met Chavender coming out of the Chief Constable's office, and as they entered Chavender's office, he could feel the tension amongst those assembled officers; something was going to happen, and soon. He was offered a seat, on Chavender's side of the desk, along with Molly-Fergus. Chavender waited for the rest of his DIs to show up. Pearce was the last one to enter the office.

"What's the to-do then? Why the sudden rush? Why the drop everything instruction Molly?"

Chavender raised his hand to silence the room. "Alright you lot listen up, please, I've called this meeting and an other one in the duty room in about ten minutes time, to appraise you of the situation, no questions now please, that will be later, okay? I - I mean we - have managed to decipher, or get a foot in the door of the murderer. Now, I would like you to leave and go to the duty room, collecting all available DSs and DCs along the way. Inspector Carr and I will be along shortly, say five minutes. Molly-Fergus can you, at Inspector Carr's behest, arrange for the following uniform constables to attend please?" He handed her a hastily scribbled list of names. He then phoned Donaldson to see if he could supply any fast response crews and asked if he could come to the meeting.

Needless to say, the officers tasked with coming to the meeting, were all abuzz with the anticipation of action at last. As they filled the duty room to capacity, Chavender, Donaldson and Carr, delayed their arrival to sort out some last minute details, but eventually arrived some twenty or so minutes later than everyone else. By this time the tension in the room was electric, and the mood among the Police officers was intense. As Chavender entered the room they all rose and being told to take their seats, he mounted the podium.

"Now listen up, please!" he started to say, "This is important! You must know what will be required of you." He then went on to say, "Four addresses have been selected as the prime targets, and others on the same list will have officers in attendance. I will be in overall command of the entire situation, from CID, uniform, traffic and the armed response teams." At the mention of armed response teams, the armed officers entered the room, this Chavender calculated, would at least settle the nerves a little; he then went on to say, "This is a joint effort, no one-upmanship will be tolerated. Okay?" the assembled officers all nodded in agreement. He went on to explain that the four prime victims, would have four officers, one of which will be Taser trained; he had already gained the authority to use force, if need be. At the other addresses, he would station those officers trained in the use of fire arms, along with one DS and two uniform officers. "You must," looking at the armed policemen, "Shoot to kill, not to wound, if you do loose off your weapon, you must immediately, A, make it safe, B, unload unused ammunition and C, hand over your unloaded weapon and ammunition to the person designated as in charge. Have you got that?" Looking at the four men earmarked for such a duty, they just nodded and shuffled uncomfortably, as the attention of the room was focused on them for a few short seconds.

Next he spoke to the prime crews, whose task it would be to make sure that if the murderer turned up. He would only be allowed to go so far before they intervened, it was at the point of administering the chloroform-soaked mask, that they would rush in and incapacitate him, using the Taser gun to prevent his escape or continuing with his foul deed. Traffic cars would seal the ends of the street or road and set up a perimeter of about a half mile, blocking all known exits. Back up would be two armed response vehicles and several squad cars suitably deployed nearby, or being most probably held at the local police stations. Two paramedics teams and the police helicopter will be on alert. In general, once the suspect has entered an area, as yet unknown, the back up teams will quietly seal the area.

"It must be stressed," he went on to say, "This man has killed, so the use of lethal and non lethal Taser force is authorised, use it, please; I don't want anyone getting ideas of bravery and try and knock the needle away, use the weapons to either kill or incapacitate the murderer. Got it?"

The assembled officers looked on as Chavender went on to explain, how the operation was to take place, and who was in which crew. He then asked Donaldson to pick four numbers and give them to the four prime crews; he then chose at random a name to go with the number, but he assigned the other crews to specific houses. He hoped in this way to avoid any feelings of favouritism to his DIs. Needless to say, it was the crew headed by Molly-Fergus, who got the prime suspect's victim, Pearce, Smith and Inspector Carr (armed with the Taser, due to lack of trained officers) were her partners. Lister and Small, plus two others again one armed with a Taser were assigned to the secondary suspect's victim, whilst Wootton and Carruthers, each headed up the other two, four man teams. To these teams suitable call signs and back up units were arranged. Wilson, Jones, Smith A, and Haylocks each headed a five-man containment team with two traffic cars assigned to them, these would seal the area, no sirens or blues were to be used around the prime suspect's victim's homes.

Chavender would be in command central somewhere nearby, along with the paramedics and several motorcycle cops, and two police dog handlers. He would only call up the helicopter if essential, but the arresting crews would be responsible for listening in. For, once in place, he would not give any orders, radio and phone silence would be maintained, he would only let the crew know if they were the one in the firing line, and then only by phone, after that they were to call the shots, either plan A, got him, or plan B, contain the area. If it was successful, he would order all other crews to stand down and make safe. If the suspect managed to evade arrest, he would call all crews to come to his command centre and he would execute a search and arrest procedure. Chavender finally completed his brief, and ordered all crews to their designated positions. He then called both Chief Inspectors and appraised them of the situation, and getting the 'best of British' from them both, left to take command of the forthcoming state of affairs, it was one thirty on a damp grey afternoon when he arrived at his command centre.

Chavender's choice of prime murder victims fell on a Mr and Mrs L. Silver. His command centre was two doors down, in a small block of flats on the opposite side. He chose this place due to its side driveway leading to a rear car park area, that could accommodate three police motorcycles, and two cars without being seen from the road. It was less than what he actually required, and the paramedic cars had to be some distance away. Still it had a good high view of the target house and he had stationed a man in houses at each end of the street. They would all be using mobile phones for contact, just in case the murderer was listening in to the police frequency. The same scenario was played out at the other target addresses, except of course for the command centre. The inside teams would have to hide as best they could, and were to give instructions that all doors must be left open, if the murderer shut them, that would be fine, for Chavender expected only one door to be shut, and that would be the one into the room were the attempted murder would take place; this he covered with a hidden CCTV camera and recorder. It took some twenty-odd minutes to get all teams set and the waiting began.

Chapter 44

Meanwhile on the outskirts of Plympton, in a small parish soon to be swallowed up by the planned expansion of both towns, a man was preparing to murder once again. He calmly went about collecting his murder kit together, as if he was going for a picnic in the park. He filled his syringes, checked that the bottles of Chloroform were clearly marked so he would not gas himself, checked his briefcase for the other impedimenta of his killing kit. Slipped his clip board, comb over wig, fake Borough ID card and wrist support bandage in, checked his attire with his notes and left to get in his car. It would take him some forty minutes to arrive at the victim's address, during which time he would listen in on the police radio frequency.

Chavender's one guess at what he would be doing was spot on, so, just in case, he had headquarters fake a major incident on the half hour, two hours beforehand, complete with police cars rushing willy-nilly, and making lots of noise for some ten minutes around the hour mark, hoping that this would make the murderer feel safer.

Of course it also alerted the press to the fact that something was going on. Reporters were sent out to cover the incident but found nothing had happened to warrant all the fuss! Miss Blaise was sent out to cover the non-existent event, which somewhat annoyed her. She tried to get hold of Woodley, to try and find out what was happening, but he ignored her calls. She even tried Josh's number but he also ignored her calls. Whilst calling Plympton police station was another futile exercise, for she thought she was speaking with the village idiot, who made no sense whatsoever! Her keen sense of smell for a story began to kick in, so she waited, most unlikely for her, patiently, as she sat in the park not realising, that she was a few short streets away from all the action that was shortly going to unfold in that quite corner of Plympton. She could still hear sirens wailing away in the distance, but she paid no head to them.

The murderer, whilst on his way to the Silver's, was listening to the police frequency and heard and saw police cars rushing by in the opposite direction, allegedly to a major incident in the docks at Plympton. What he actually heard was fake radio traffic between three police cars and the station at Plympton, with the occasional aside from a Bryantsand-on-Sea police car and station. The murderer felt quietly confident that the majority of police cars were otherwise occupied or involved, leaving him a free run, perhaps he could kill two people today? He would see how the first one went before calling the next victims to say he would be to them at about 6pm, if that was okay with them. This would give him enough time to go home and change. Driving along, blissfully unaware that he was heading into a trap, he pulled up, about half a mile away from the Silver's house, and waited for a moment, as he waited in his car, he listened once more to the police frequency, satisfying himself that all was okay, he started with practiced ease to don his disguise.

Slowly walking the short distance to the Silver's house, he felt confident that once again he would kill, with all the skill of a surgeon, albeit a deadly one! He took his time getting to the victim's address he had selected, ambling along trying not to look too out of place, which of course he was not, after all he merged in very nicely with the general feel and look of the neighbourhood, dressed as he was quite respectfully and in his mid-fifties, briefcase by his side, hand bandaged, comb over wig, he looked just like an every day sort of person, not even the neighbourhood curtain twitchers spotted, or took any notice of him. As he passed by the house with a constable in, he was still unaware that like a fly in a Venus Fly trap; he was already caught, only he did not know it!

The Constable, who had been given an instruction to look out for someone with a bandaged hand, saw the suspect and called Chavender, who then alerted the team in the Silver's house. He then saw the suspect walk past his hide out, noting with a wry smile that his hypothesis of a bandaged wrist was correct. The suspect walked up the path to the front door of the Silver's house, and, ringing the bell, waited. When the door was opened, he showed his ID badge to Mr Silver, who, expecting him, let him in. Once the suspect was inside, Chavender then called the other teams, requesting that they leave one man to prevent those people from contacting the press. He asked if they could all assemble quietly near his command centre some half mile away, and for traffic to block the roads, no one in or out for the time being. All this police action did not go unaware by the residents, who soon came out and started to wonder what all the police activity was about!

It was just bad luck that DS Wootton, chose to block the roads near the park. His marked police cars, parked side by side blocking the road at the junction as instructed. The police then taped across the pavement to prevent access, whilst constables directed or stopped people from using that road.

Miss Blaise saw all this activity and seeing her boyfriend, she went across to him, stating furiously, rather than asking nicely, "What the hell is going on? Woodley, you haven't answered any of my calls, and then I'm sent on a wild goose chase, and now this, why the blocking of the road?"

DS Wootton's jaw dropped, as if someone had poleaxed him with a sucker punch, when he saw his girlfriend walk up to him, waving her arms wildly and pointing a finger at him, red in the face as if all her current hassles were caused by him. He took her forcibly by the elbow, she squirmed under his firm grasp as he walked her away from the roadblock, she continued to question him. Thinking fast, he sat her in the fast pursuit police car and called Chavender.

"Hello Sir, DS Wootton speaking. Miss Blaise has just turned up, I've put her in a police car, what do you want me to do with her?"

Chavender thought for a moment and in a exacerbated voice replied, "Why don't you *marry* the woman, for crying out loud Wootton!" It was the first thing that came to mind but he had not realised he had said it out loud. Continuing with a quieter but stuttered, "But... no... but seriously, take her mobile phone off her, tell her to be quiet and she can be the first reporter on the scene when were are done okay! Oh, if she doesn't agree with your marriage proposal arrest her!"

"Got it Sir," Wootton replied; a silly grin spread across his face, as he realised how easily his boss was rattled at the mention of Miss Blaise's name, especially when he heard the tone of Chavender's voice, when he said marry the woman! He might just do that, he thought.

As he returned to the police car and an indignant Miss Blaise, and getting in beside her, hiding his face somewhat, he asked for her phone. She hesitated for a second or two before handing over her phone and then asked, "Why? Woodley, why do you want my phone? And why am I in a police car?" Then the penny dropped and Miss Blaise asked pointedly, "You've got orders to arrest me again? Haven't you?" she practically screamed, which caused some of the constables to look into the car, only to see Wootton squirm and retreat into the corner of the rear of the police car, trying to defend himself against the barrage of slaps that he was receiving, in the region of his shoulders and face. She finally stopped hitting him, a spent force. Tears rolling down her pretty face, falling in big droplets from her lower jaws onto her blouse, as her sobbing eased, she said resignedly, "It's that big ass jerk of a boss of yours, isn't it? I'm right aren't I? He has had it in for me ever since I gave him that peck on the cheek a few weeks back! After all I've done for him this last week, in those fake stories I wrote just for him! Really can't trust that man. I bet Josh is laughing his cotton socks off, right now." Wootton collected her into his arms and laid her still crying gently, onto his shoulder, until Wendy said rather wearily, "Sorry Woodley, I am sorry." Wootton thought to himself, weaker sex, my Aunt Fanny, they are! Females are supposed to be the weaker sex? You've got to be kidding me, those slaps really hurt!

As he spoke gently to her, "Chavender says, if you sit here quietly and make no fuss, you will be the first reporter on the scene; that is all I can say for now, other than that, he gave me two ultimatums, the first of which was to arrest you, which I won't do, and the second I will ask you later.Nnow will you sit quietly, Wendy?"

"Yes Woodley I will," she answered and realising what his second question was most likely to be, added "to both questions."

Chapter 45

Inside the Silver's residence, Molly-Fergus and her team chose to wait in the adjoining garage, monitoring the remote CCTV footage. The back door was left open and they had worked out how to get into the front room quickly. The Silvers had instructions to leave the back door open wide and to show the suspect straight into the front room. Mrs Silver, offering him a cup of tea, bade him to sit in the easy chair, in the far corner away from the door. He accepted the cup of tea and waited for Mrs Silver to bring the tea things in; after taking a sip, he started to talk about how the waiting list for an allotment was very long, up to five years in some cases. He mentioned that the Silvers had been on the waiting for at least three years, which he and the council felt was a long time indeed to wait. Carrying on with "the council was trialling a way to shorten the waiting times!" It was at this point that he thought *and I have my own way of shortening the waiting times - and this time I can get two for the price of one!* He continued with an explanation that sounded plausible enough, "It involved those tenants of allotments who were elderly, infirm or not capable any more, of maintaining the standard as laid down in the allotment agreement. It would be a buddy system. They would match up people as best they could and would, for a while, share the allotment, that is until the older tenant decides not to continue with his ownership. The more active or younger tenant is already in place on the allotment so naturally takes it over full time, fees would be shared as well as some of the produce." The Silvers thought it was a wonderful idea, and nodded in general agreement as they asked some questions, writing down any points requiring clarification later.

He now had their full attention, which was what he wanted. All of a sudden he let out a small yell, his faced registered pain as the drawing pin, hidden in his bandage was pressed into the ball of his thumb; he passed it off as sciatica, and a broken wrist to boot. Now, if only he could walk about a bit, if that was okay, it might ease. "It may get irritating for you both if you try to follow me round the room so just keep looking forward, I can write whilst standing still for a bit so it should take no longer than I have already stated. Okay? Thanks." The Silvers agreed, and his walk round the settee lasted only a few minutes when he said, "It's no good, I'm going to have to take my pain relief drug, I hope you don't mind, it will only take a minute or so. It is a new drug on trail that I take, it's a wonderful new drug; it works like magic, last for hours, and do you know the best part about it, I get paid to take it! No, really, I do, fifty pounds a week, just to report back any side effects, which are none!" Here the Silvers were all agog, for they both had suffered from attacks of sciatica, and were both incapacitated by it in the past, so knew how painful it could be. Here he went on to say, "Well. apart from a little sleepiness when I first took it, it really is a wonderful and marvellous drug" he sat down and pulled out a small clear bottle and a mask. Showing them, he even let them smell the bottle top, a faint sweet odour was all they could detect, as he started to splash some of the clear liquid on to the mask and placed it over his nose and mouth, and breathing deeply, he shut his eyes for a few seconds. Then, jumping up, he began walking about without the noticeable limp of before. He then tentatively offered to let the Silvers try it if they liked; they both said, "yes please." The murderer was delighted, he had two masks available and would take full use of the opportunity.

It was at this point that Molly-Fergus and her team went into action; purposely wearing soft shoes, they crept silently and entered the house via the back door. Inspector Carr, leading and Taser in hand, Molly-Fergus behind, remote monitor in hand, Pearce headed for the front door whilst Smith stayed by the back door. The suspect had sat back down in the armchair furthest away from the shut living room door, and was continuing his hard sell of the new wonder drug. The Silvers' attention was firmly fixed on the suspects, as he showed them a new bottle, the mask and letting them read the dosage instructions on how to take it, and the length of time the first dose took to take effect, he even let them try the mask on without the drug, just so they could get a feel of how it felt. Molly-Fergus grabbed the door handle, standing to the left of Carr, behind the wall, so he had free access after the door was open, she nodded and mouthed, 'one, two, three' and threw open the door. It crashed into the wall with a loud thud, and as Carr entered, Taser stretched towards the suspect, he shouted "ARMED POLICE! STAY WHERE YOU ARE! ARMED POLICE! I WILL FIRE MY TAZER IF YOU MOVE!" and once again "ARMED POLICE!" The Silvers jumped at the noise the door had made and turned towards the door, whilst the suspect began to get up, turning and looking for a way out. Carr and now Molly-Fergus filled the doorway, his only real chance of escape was gone, and with Carr still menacingly, fixing his Taser on the suspect and threatening to shoot, he looked at the window and back to Carr. He picked up the small coffee table, which Carr thought he was going to use to protect himself, and threw it at the window. Being single glazed, the window shattered as the table hit it with all the force he could muster exploding outwards into a thousand shards of glass.

Chavender, in his vantage point, was alarmed that his plan was going awry, and started to head downstairs towards the Silvers' house. It was at this point that Carr warned him again that he would shoot if he moved. Taking no heed of the warnings, the suspect started to move towards the window, and with Carr's final warning ringing in his ears, he took his chance to escape, moving quickly, he turned to leap out of the window, it was then that Carr fired his weapon. The two barbs of the Taser hit home, sending a incapacitating shock to the suspect's body, who immediately started to convulse in agony on the floor. Carr kept his eyes on the suspect as Molly-Fergus entered the room, phone in hand assuring Chavender that all was well, and that the suspect had not got further than breaking the window.

Chavender, to his relief, called the four blocking cars to the address and sent instructions for the others to stand down and return to headquarters to meet in the canteen, where he would stand them a coffee before the debrief. His next task was to inform the Chief Constable, followed by Chief Inspectors' Sword and Andersonn, that the operation was a success, and that a suspect was now in police custody. Sword heaved a sigh of relief when he thanked Chavender for letting him know.

The paramedics were sent into the Silvers' house to treat both of them for shock and to see if the suspect had suffered any ill effects from being shocked by the Tazer. As the police cars stopped outside, Chavender calmly walked over to the house, where by now the suspect had been handcuffed and arrested, his comb over wig left lying on the floor, as his entire body was convulsed by the shock of the Taser gun. Walking inside he saw Carr over by the sink being sick, Molly-Fergus shaking a little and the Silvers being attended to by the paramedics.

He went over to Molly-Fergus and gave her a hug and said, "Thanks"; he then went to Carr and patted him on the shoulder, again saying "Thanks." Looking at Pearce and Smith he called them over and thanking them both, he asked if they would escort the suspect back to headquarters; they both nodded in agreement. He surveyed the scene once more before, in a rather fatherly way, ushered the two inspectors into his car for the drive back to headquarters, knowing full well, what the after effects would be from the shooting.

Outside the neighbours began to come out, wondering what all the police fuss was about. They saw the suspect, flanked by two men, being placed in a police car and whisked away to headquarters, without riders of police bikes, blue lights and sirens blaring away, making sure they had a free passage. Wootton and Miss Blaise showed up and she immediately went into reporter mode. Forgetting Wootton she started to ask questions from the neighbours, and even managed to get a statement from Chavender, as she managed to file a copy of sorts before all the other papers. The stop the press headline she wrote, shouted out in big bold letters 'special operation to catch serial killer from your on scene reporter Miss Blaise'. The article then went on to explain how she, thanks to her instinct, was in the right place at the right time, and not that she had a sulk on! But she had to wait for the press conference later to get all the facts. As always with Chavender, the thrill of the capture was an anticlimax for him, the reasoning, abstract thought or deductive part, was his forte, it provoked his brain into thinking, which kept him feeling alive, energetic and young at heart, just like a vampire needs to suck blood, he needed his brain to be thinking, even if, sometimes, it played tricks on him! Driving slowly back to headquarters with the two inspectors in the back of his car, he felt much like his fictional hero, Sherlock Holmes 'for now the ennui sets in', but unlike Holmes, he had a wife and four children to find ease and comfort with and not the needle, Violin or pipe which Holmes found so rewarding. Upon his arrival back at headquarters, he found the rest of the teams waiting for him and all the top brass of Middleshire County Constabulary in the canteen. As he entered they all stood up, and gave him a round of applause, as the Chief Constable shook him by the hand and said "Well done, my laddo!"

As the other senior officers took the opportunity to congratulate him on a job well done, he stood on a chair and said, "Well, thanks to all your hard work, and putting up with my three cups theory, we have the murderer in custody. Coffees on me, please Sue."

The teams filed for coffee, the excited chatter died away, and the Chief Constable spoke to Chavender about the hastily called press conference, for two hours time, at 8pm.

It gave Chavender and Pearce a brief period to hold the initial interview with the suspect, which proved rather illuminating for his other ongoing case! It transpired that he had lost his council seat and position on the planning committee to Councillor Walker in a rather muddy and smeared reelection campaign, which alleged that he was crooked and took backhanders from developers. He even opposed the new housing estate and queried the number of houses being built in such a small area, instead of its intended function, as allotments. the list for which he had been on for years, much to his annoyance!

The suspect also admitted how he'd managed to gas the first couple. He'd arranged an appointment with them, he'd chosen them due to the location of their house being stuck in the corner with no other house backing on to them. After blocking the outlet pipe from their sink with a homemade stopper on the open end by the drain, he then, during their meeting, poured down enough ammonia so that the sink appeared blocked. He even suggested to them to use bleach to unblock the sink. He offered to check and stepped outside for them to let them know if it had worked, so he was safe from the gas.

Once they had gassed themselves, he did not know how long to give them, but it was something like an hour or so, he then unblocked the drain and using the attached cord pulled the cover off and left them to die. He knew the affect that the gas would have after reading about it in a book. Breathing difficulties, and a general incapacity to be coherent, in fact, delirious, so he was not too concerned about being around at the time. He even called the emergency services once he knew they were so incapacitated that he knew he would be safe, thus clearing the blockage and removing the evidence, leaving only an empty bleach bottle and no other bottle. It was this that so baffled the Police which was why they could not find any other such deadly bottles at any of the addresses that they checked, they only thought they did.

At the national press conference Chavender, flanked by Featherstonehaugh and Jacobs, announced, "that after a police operation this afternoon involving over forty officers, they had one suspect in custody, and that investigations were ongoing, but he felt confident that the recent spate of murders was now over. The suspect, a Mr Brian Whiggle, ex-council member for Plympton, was being charged with two counts of attempted murder, and the poisoning of several other persons. Our forensic investigations into the other deaths, have led us to believe that he may well have killed several other people. We have yet to conclude our interview with him, and he will be arraigned in the morning, at the County Magistrates Court, this will allow us the time to conclude our investigations."

The Chief Constable then spoke, and thanked all those who took part and heaped praise on Chavender and the detectives, who'd followed what little clues they had to a satisfactory conclusion.

After an hour it was over, as the press began to disappear, Miss Blaise came up to Chavender, who on his guard, wondered what she was going to do, "Oh you're safe Josh," seeing his look of fear just like a rabbit caught in the headlights of a car. "Woodley asked me to marry him today, and I said yes, thanks to you! Be it on your head if it don't work out," she jokingly threatened with a pointed finger, as she gave him a peck on the cheek. He was still slightly embarrassed by her outward display of affection for him, but that was beginning to wear off.

Watching at home was Tiff, Ma and the girls. It was Ma who broke the spell of silence as she said, "That husband of yours, tisch, pafaw, tut, tut, if his head gets any bigger, it wont fit through the front door! Tisch, pafaw, tut. Its about the only time you girls get to see him lately, when he is on TV! Bah, poppycock, brilliant detective work? More like lucky guess work, he can't detect that you're pregnant, now can he? Pafaw, tut, tut, as if you can hide it any more!" She pointed at the slight bulge in her daughter's tummy. Tiff laughed at her ma and at her worsening manner of speech, as the twins looked excitedly at their mother as they exclaimed, "Are you going to have another baby Mummy? Is it going to be twins again, or a girl or boy, do you know yet? Doesn't daddy know?" In their usual all at once chatty voice, soon the clamour of the twins died down and gave way to silence, as they turned the TV over to watch yet another Disney DVD.

As she got up to cook some sausages for tea, Tiff thought tonight would be a good time to tell Josh about the baby. But, it was in the early hours before Josh finally left headquarters. On his drive home, through the blackened countryside, he saw that familiar, now peaceful, well at least, he thought, murder free, glow on the horizon, as the urban sprawl of the two towns lit the night sky. When Josh finally got home, as was to be expected, the house was in blackness as everyone was in bed. Tired, he sat in the kitchen for awhile, drinking a cup of tea and eating the cold sausage sandwich which Tiff had left for him before going up to bed. It wasn't long before sleep overtook him, and snoring loudly he woke his wife. She, true to form, nudged him in the ribs before cuddling in against him saying gently, "Josh, love, I've got something to tell you, I'm pregnant!" and he, in his somnolent state, replied, "That's nice Tiff, I'll do it in the morning for you."